NOTHING ELSE MATTERS

A Sam Casey Mystery

NOTHING ELSE MATTERS

A Sam Casey Mystery

S.D. TOOLEY

Full Moon Publishing

Published by
Full Moon Publishing
P.O. Box 408
Schererville, IN 46375

This book is a work of fiction. Names, characters, places, and incidents are the product of the author's imagination or are used fictitiously. Any resemblance to actual events, locales, or persons, living or dead, is coincidental. Any slights of people, places, or organizations is purely unintentional.

Library of Congress Catalog Number 99-62926
ISBN 0-9666021-2-9

10 9 8 7 6 5 4 3 2 1

Published April 2000
Printed in the United States of America

ACKNOWLEDGMENTS

George J. Behnle, Jr., retired Chief Investigator for the Cook County medical examiner; **Pam Berda** of Rush Presbyterian St. Luke's Hospital in Chicago; **Dan Gunnell**, Firearms Training Coordinator for the Illinois State Police Forensic Science Center in Chicago; members of the Highland, Indiana Police Department, specifically **Chief Joseph Kwasny**, **Corporal Robert J. Reynolds**, and **Officer John E. Banasiak**, as well as my fellow class members at the Citizens Police Academy; **Mel McNairy** of the Indianapolis Police Department; **Chris Roerden,** my editor; and **William Sherlock**, User Agency Coordinator for the Illinois State Police Forensic Science Center in Chicago.

NOTHING ELSE MATTERS

1

He watched the man leave the back of the church, glance around the empty parking lot, and climb into a silver Cadillac. As part of his typical surveillance, he had been following his target for the past two days, from the modest two-story home to the stark white brick church, to the homes of parishioners who were shut-ins, and the homeless in soup kitchens. How confusing. The preacher was obviously dedicated to his work and a loving husband. A pity he had to die.

Returning to his hotel room, he peeled out of his tattered coat, and with a weary hand, slid the gray wig off and tossed it on the bed. A cascade of white-blonde hair fell past his shirt collar. Standing at the window, he gazed out at the lake, at the fog snaking around the breakwater and curling its cottony fingers around the base of a lighthouse. The fog made Lake Michigan look like a dark, barren land, uninhabited, the remains of some unknown annihilation. A faint light blinked in the distance, probably from a tanker that had dropped anchor during the night.

The fog prevented him from seeing much of Chasen Heights, a suburb south of Chicago. His job had taken him to a variety of interesting cities, but he had never stayed long enough to enjoy the local entertainment. Turning away from the window, he snapped on the table lamp and kicked off his shoes. A suitcase lay open on the king-sized bed.

Facial features were sharply defined, as if carved from a piece of granite, with inset eyes that seemed to pierce through the room darkness like bright blue beacons. His body was taut and muscular, carved out of the same fine piece of granite.

Another suitcase lay on the table. He sat down and worked the combination locks. The lid popped open revealing wigs, eyeglasses, beards, all in different colors. He unzipped a leather pouch and added his drivers license to the rest of the fake I.D.s. As he closed the lid, the light from the lamp cast a glow on his tattoo. It was a self-inflicted work of art on the back of his left hand, a black bird with streaks of red and yellow on the wing tips. Across the bottom of the image was the word *SPARROW.*

2

"Hello? Anybody home?" Sam set her suitcases down and shoved the front door shut. Through the tall windows in the sitting room, she watched the cab circle the drive and head back out to the street. Inhaling deeply, she took in the aromas of her house expecting a hint of coffee and fresh fry bread. But the only odors that invaded her senses were cleaning solutions and burning leaves. Strange combination.

Tilting her head, she gazed up the stairway toward the second floor and called out, "Mom?" Silence answered back. With a shrug she crossed the foyer and down a couple stairs to the connecting living and dining rooms. Even though it was quiet, the house looked the same and home never felt so good.

Standing in front of one of the bay windows in the dining room, Sam admired the painted landscape. Her two-hour cab ride home through Indiana farmlands strewn with large pillows of hay and barren crops, had given the bleak reminder that winter was nudging its way in. But here the acres were bursting in fall colors from brightly colored mums to spirea and maple trees which refused to let the winds tug at their branches. In the distance, she could see the charred remains of what might have been leaves and dead branches. The mulcher the landscaper used supposedly eliminated most of the fallen foliage but Alex liked the smell of burning leaves. Alex insisted on making his own little bonfire, the laws be damned.

Shoving her hands in the pockets of her corduroy shorts, she trudged off to the kitchen to see if Abby had left a note. But then, why would she? Abby didn't know her daughter was going to check herself out early and surprise her.

The mid-morning sun brightened the airy kitchen as it sliced through the windows. Ivy had snaked its way up the greenhouse window in back of the sink as though seeking the sun's attention. The top of the oak cabinets served as a showcase for a variety of baskets and pottery.

But something wasn't right. Sam touched the stove. It was cold, the countertops spotless. Abby always had fresh fruit on the counter and baked goodies lying around. Except for the morning paper folded up on the kitchen counter, the entire house looked ready for a real estate showing.

She opened the refrigerator and was relieved to see it still had food in it, if you considered butter, cream cheese, and bottles of iced tea, food.

"Of course," Sam said. "Abby and Alex are grocery shopping."

Flipping on the small TV sitting on the counter, Sam went about zapping a cup of water in the microwave to make a cup of herbal tea. She half-listened to the news reporter.

> *Bodies found at a burial site in the Iron Triangle are enroute to a Honolulu laboratory for testing. An eighty-four-member, two-nation team, which has spent the last year searching for MIAs in Viet Nam, believes the body count to be sixty-seven. A list of names compiled from the dog tags has been forwarded to the Pentagon.*

"Still, after all these years." Shaking her head, she clicked off the TV, then rummaged around the cabinets for something to eat. "Just one cookie, that's all I ask for," she mumbled, slamming cabinet doors, the bread box lid, and the top drawer where Abby was known to squirrel away Oreo cookies. Nothing. Out of desperation, she opened the freezer door, willing to eat ice cream at nine o'clock in the morning. Nothing. But then several Ziploc® bags beckoned to her and she smiled as she saw homemade chocolate chip cookies through the clear plastic.

Snatching the newspaper off the kitchen table, she hauled the cookies and tea to the dining room and stretched out on one of the window seats. Leaving the unopened paper on her lap, she unfastened her long, thick hair from the banana clip and massaged her scalp.

Feeling the hard cookies, she thought about zapping them in the microwave but was too fatigued from the ride home. Instead, she took a sip of tea, leaned back and closed her eyes against the bright sunlight. She wanted to think only happy thoughts about being home, getting back to work at the precinct. But unpleasant thoughts seemed to dominate. She didn't want to think about the past ten weeks because it would remind her of her last case, which had made a more negative impact than her resultant trip to the loony farm. A suspect had killed a cop using her gun, which got her suspended from the force. No witnesses, only a body and her gun.

The brain was a crazy animal, blocking out traumatic events. It was only natural that the mind of a five-year-old child would want to repress such a horrible scene as watching her father blown to bits in a car bomb. That experience could have stayed repressed as far as Sam was concerned. Unfortunately, in her last case, her father's killer resurfaced, demonstrating new and better methods for blowing up vehicles. Watching her own Jeep blow up brought those childhood memories rushing back and had thrown her into the same catatonic state she had experienced at age five.

If only the doctors at Sara Binyon's had focused on just her father's death, that would have been fine. But they had to delve into Sam's current feelings and that was something she didn't care to share and didn't feel it was anyone's damn business. Doctor Talbot had been insistent, kept encouraging her to talk about it. "Sergeant Casey, how do you feel about the murdered cop?" *I didn't kill him.* "How do you feel about your suspension?" *Wonderful experience. Everyone should go through it once.* "Why so much hostility toward Jake?" *Jake who?*

She opened her eyes and blinked against the light. Her head was pounding from lack of food. Jamming a fingertip into one of the cookies, Sam decided it had thawed enough. Opening the paper, a front page story stopped her cookie in mid-bite. The face glaring back at her made her skin crawl. Captain Dennis Murphy, with his beady eyes and patented smile reserved only for the cameras, was being honored at a dinner tonight. It shouldn't have surprised her after all that had happened, after his questionable connection to the man who had killed her father, that they would reward him with a promotion to chief of police. It was back to politics as usual.

Sam glared at the picture smiling up at her. "You wouldn't catch me giving you the time of day let alone attending your reception."

A two-tone, sienna-colored van pulled up and stopped in front of the detached garage. Sam watched through the bay window as Abby climbed out first and walked around to the back of the vehicle, her long colorful skirt brushing the tops of her moccasins. Alex followed suit. Sam's cup of tea stopped midway and her brows scrunched. Where did they get a van? When Sam left ten weeks ago, Abby had a blue Taurus and Alex had a truck. Why hadn't Abby mentioned it during one of her visits? Something else puzzled her. The van was filled with boxes and hanging clothes.

Alex rummaged around in the back but he wasn't bringing out any bags of groceries. The plot thickened. If Sam didn't know better, she would say the van was packed for a trip, a very long trip.

She crossed the room and entered the kitchen just as Abby slid open the patio door.

"Samantha!" Abby beamed. They embraced in the kitchen. Sam held on tight to her mother. "Why didn't you tell me you were coming home? The doctor didn't say anything." Abby pulled her over to the kitchen table and they sat down next to each other. "Alex and I would have picked you up."

"I wanted to surprise you." Sam admired her mother's flawless skin, her high cheekbones, and the hint of silver in the thick braid of hair. "You look wonderful."

Abby waved a hand adorned in silver and turquoise bracelets and rings. "I look the same as I did when I saw you three days ago."

But Sam marveled at her mother's adherence to tradition. Abby Two Eagles continued her Sioux customs even though she no longer lived on the reservation. From her colorful, sweeping skirts to her ornate turquoise and coral jewelry, Abby did more than look the part of a medicine woman. She lived it.

Abby framed her daughter's face in her hands. "Are you sure you didn't leave too early? Doctor Talbot says you are still having flashbacks."

"I'm fine, really. He said I'd have them for a while. I just have to write everything down when I wake up." She pulled Abby's hands from her face and kissed them. "I just missed you. I need my life back."

"Sam." Alex stood in the doorway, a wide smile spreading across his bronzed face. "When did you get home?"

"About an hour ago." She jumped up and hugged Alex, her fingers brushing against his gray ponytail. She peered around him toward the garage. "Whose van is that?"

"Mine," Abby replied. "We thought it could carry more when we make our trips to the reservation."

Puzzled, Sam stared at the van packed and ready to go. "Is that where you are headed?"

"Sweetheart, we thought we'd be back before you were released," Abby replied. She looked quickly at Alex. "But maybe we shouldn't go."

"Something important happening back at Eagle Ridge?"

"Yes." Abby rose and put on a kettle of water. She still preferred the old-fashioned way of heating up water.

Sam retrieved her cup of tea and cookies from the dining room.

Abby continued. "They are having an important meeting regarding the casino that will be opening soon." Although they no longer lived on the reservation, Abby and Alex visited at least four times a year.

"When were you leaving?" Sam blinked back tears as she gave her cup of tea fifteen seconds in the microwave.

Alex checked his watch. "We were going to drive straight through but I can make motel reservations and break it up into a two-day trip."

Abby nodded. "That would be best. Then I can spend a few hours with Sam." Abby tugged on her daughter's arm. "Come, I want to show you the bedroom."

Sam stood in the center of the master bedroom. It was the last room to be completed in an intense remodeling project. "It's absolutely gorgeous, Mom." She opened the drawers under the king-sized platform bed and surveyed the lighted bridge connecting the two side hutches. "You have such great taste."

She flipped on the light in the remodeled master bath with its added whirlpool and double-sized shower stall. The skylights brightened the room and the mirrors behind the whirlpool added more depth.

Sam made a move toward the walk-in closet but Abby intercepted her and casually turned her toward the door saying, "Why don't we all go out for an early lunch seeing that there isn't any food in the house."

Puzzled seemed to be the word of the day and Sam was beginning to wonder if the cab had left her on a different planet. "They had to cut into the cedar closet to expand the bathroom. I just wanted to see how much closet they left me."

Abby sighed and reluctantly let Sam open the closet doors. The use of closet organizers provided ample shelving and stacked hanging. Sam's clothes had been moved from her old bedroom down the hall to the master bedroom. Shoe cabinets were against the far wall under the rack of shirts, men's shirts. Then she looked at the opposite wall where men's suits and pants hung. A regular his-and-hers closet.

"Mom, what...?" Sam stammered. "You have got to be kidding!"

Abby sighed heavily. "Samantha, you have to face the facts."

"You let Jake move in here?"

"Husbands usually live with their wives."

Whatever strength and positive attitude Sam had mustered when she left Sara Binyon's earlier was disintegrating. Uncontrollable tears welled as she stumbled to the bed and lowered herself onto the edge.

"Mom, how could you? You know Jake is the reason I was suspended."

"We've been over this before, Samantha. You were suspended because of the officer who was shot. Jake had nothing to do with that."

"Well, kudos to Jake," Sam mumbled. "He works with the Bureau behind my back to conceal facts about my father's death and you think that's peachy keen. Has he got you snowed." She laughed, a nervous paranoid laugh of someone who should have spent a little more time at Sara Binyon's. She swiped at the tears funneling down her cheeks, pressed her lips tightly. The past ten weeks had been an emotional roller coaster. The car should have been stopping and letting her off. Instead, it seemed to have coasted on through and was now taking her on another spin.

Abby sat down next to her daughter and wrapped an arm around her shoulder. "I love you. And I would never do anything that wasn't in your best interest."

Sam stared into her mother's eyes. She always had a difficult time seeing herself in her mother. Abby's skin was much more olive-complexioned and her eyes never flashed anger. They were gentle eyes with a voice that was soothing. And although an inch shorter than Sam, Abby had a stature and demeanor that made her appear taller than her five foot six inches.

"Mom, the night I spent with Jake I thought was my last. I thought I was going to be killed; I felt it." Sam searched her mother's face for a hint of understanding. "I wanted to make sure you were taken care of. I thought if Jake and I shared the traditional wedding vows, then, according to our custom, he would have to take care of you after I died. I was thinking of you."

Abby patted Sam's hand. "Then you can think of me now. He was my choice, Samantha." She rose from the bed.

"Then you marry him!" Sam blurted. "The marriage is not legal without my signing the marriage license." She watched Abby walk toward the patio doors. Visions churned in Sam's head, memories of Abby's previous trips to Sara Binyon's, of papers she had Sam sign. "No." Sam shook her head wildly and jumped from the bed. "Don't tell me..." But she didn't need to hear Abby say the words. She could see it in the way Abby straightened her shoulders, tilted her chin, displayed that *my-decision-is-final* stance.

Abby followed many traditions. And one was choosing her daughter's husband. Abby had taken an instant liking to Jake Mitchell, a bond Sam couldn't quite understand. And Sam would sooner walk on glass shavings than spend a lifetime with a man she couldn't trust.

"No court will uphold my signature. I was in a rest home, for godsake." She stormed over to the desk and rummaged through the drawers. "I'll just call Jason and have him start the proceedings for an annulment."

Abby again sighed heavily, pressing a hand against the squash necklace peeking out from beneath her firmly starched collar. "The least you can do is listen to what Jake has to say. He does love you."

"He loves my money," Sam replied, flipping through the pages of her directory.

"It's not like we're multi-millionaires, Samantha. Besides, money means nothing to him. You are being stubborn. You never answered any of his letters, refused to let him visit you during the entire time you were gone."

"Doctor Talbot said to avoid all stressful situations and Jake was at the top of my stress list." Remembering the newspaper article featuring Murphy's smug face, Sam added, "Well, he's near the top." She picked up the receiver and started punching numbers. The headache that had started during the ride home was increasing with each pounding of the keypad. "There isn't anything you can say or do that will make me change my mind."

Hands clasped in front of her, Abby patiently waited while her daughter made a call to the family attorney. As Sam brought the receiver to her mouth, Abby calmly announced, "My grandchild will not be born without its father."

3

Sparrow plugged in his computer and hooked up the modem. While the system loaded, he checked the refrigerator for a bottle of orange juice. He took a long swallow and surveyed his surroundings. His one-bedroom suite at the Ritz Carlton was a little too Victorian, too Queen Anne for his liking, but when you live from hotel to hotel, all that really mattered was a bed, a shower, and good food.

He opened a small envelope taped to a larger brown envelope and again read the specifics on Reverend Everett Smith. He was forty-nine years of age, African American, just under six feet, and one hundred and sixty pounds. Picking up the photo he had received last week, he studied the man he had been tailing. A short-cropped beard hugged his youthful face. Only the receding hairline seemed to give away his age.

Nothing in the report gave Sparrow a hint as to what Reverend Smith had done to warrant extermination. That's why Sparrow liked to survey his target beforehand. Surveillance usually revealed the evil deeds of the person to be killed. But Reverend Smith was being targeted for some reason not yet clear to Sparrow.

Turning to the computer, he accessed his offshore accounts. He had specifically requested his fee be wire-transferred. But none of his accounts reflected receipt of two hundred thousand dollars. He stared at the larger envelope and didn't like what he was thinking. Tearing open the bag, he dumped out the contents. One thing he despised was people not following orders.

Next, he accessed the Internet and sent a message to his contact, who quickly responded that they only deal in cash. Sparrow reminded him that wasn't their agreement. *Sorry* was the response. Sparrow had half a mind to cancel the job. A mercenary for hire, Sparrow always demanded full payment up front and always by wire transfer. Something about this assignment hadn't felt right from the start. He reminded himself that dealing with foreigners had always been a royal pain.

He signed off the Internet and checked his watch. A dull pain was building in his head. The pain intensified quickly. He pulled a bottle from his shirt pocket, shook out a pill and swallowed it dry. With hands pressed to the sides of his head, he inhaled deeply. Slowly the pain subsided. Too many preparations had to be made and he couldn't let anything distract him, not even a migraine.

The two security guards sat next to each other at the employee entrance to the River Queen Casino. He joked and laughed; she smiled, flirted with her eyes. They were positioned at the end of a long hallway, a distance from the employee locker room and time clock. After a brief glance toward the engineer in the dark blue uniform and dark blue hat, they returned to their private conversation.

Sparrow didn't look suspicious. His badge was official, even had his picture on it. Of course, if they had looked closer they would have seen that his fair complexion and blue eyes were in complete contrast to the I.D. picture of a full-faced man with brown hair.

He was proceeding as planned, even though his instincts were telling him to be cautious. But in order to find out what the foreigners were up to, he had to play it out. They were insistent that the hit be made in the casino tonight. It almost felt as though he were being tested, to see if he could follow orders, which he resented. Most of his jobs were on a referral basis. No one needed to be convinced of his capabilities.

Sparrow boarded the boat, turned and walked down the stairs. Two engineers passed him on the stairwell. The maintenance room was around the corner. No one was in it. He opened his gym bag and went to work.

4

The front door was braced open by the cooler, the van parked and running at the curb. Sam leaned against the door jamb and watched as a rust-colored dog came bounding from around the back of the garage in response to Alex's shrill whistle.

"Come on, girl. You don't want to be left behind." Alex held open the van door for Poco. The Irish setter immediately claimed an area behind the driver's seat where Alex had tossed Poco's blanket. Alex peeled out of his jacket and hung it up in the back, then returned to the house.

"Will you call and let me know you made it there all right?" Sam asked.

"Of course."

She gave him a hug. "Do me a favor?"

"Sure." Alex smiled. "Anything for you, Sam."

Sam had known Alex Red Cloud since she was sixteen. A reservation transplant, he had shown up on their doorstep ten years before claiming the spirits told him in a vision to watch over *wicasa waken*, the holy man or medicine woman. He lived in the gate house on the back of the one hundred acres, and in the summer preferred to live in his self-constructed tipi.

"During your drive to Eagle Ridge, could you use your

influence on Abby to talk her out of this marriage thing?" Alex grimaced. Sam quickly added, "I know how you feel about Jake and I trust your instincts. Could you try to convince her that she made a mistake, maybe get her to change her mind?" Sam brushed dog hairs from Alex's shirt and straightened his collar. Batting her baby blues at him when she was younger had worked wonders.

"Abby knows how I feel, knew it before she made her decision. I believe you should marry Lakota. But face it. How easy has it ever been for any of us to change *wicasa waken's* mind?"

"Not easy at all," Abby said as she appeared at the bottom of the staircase, one last suitcase in hand. Alex retrieved the suitcase as Abby unfolded a piece of paper and handed it to Sam. "This is the name of an excellent obstetrician in town."

Alex jerked his head around. "Obstetrician? Isn't that a...?"

"Yes, it's a baby doctor," Abby replied.

Shaking his head, Alex headed for the door muttering, "More diluting of the gene pool."

"Still having morning sickness?" Abby touched the back of her hand to Sam's cheeks. "It will be stopping soon. I had morning and evening sickness when I was pregnant with you."

"That's kind of how it's going." She gave a weak laugh. "How silly of me to think I could keep my pregnancy from you."

"Just keep crackers handy." Abby placed a hand on Sam's shoulder. "Don't wait too long before telling Jake."

Alex made one last appearance in the doorway. "Anything else?"

"Just me. And I'll be out in a minute."

"Do you have to go?" Sam pleaded. "I just got home."

Abby swept her shawl around her shoulders and tied it loosely. "Samantha, if I stick around I'll be nothing but a referee for you and Jake. You two will never solve your own problems."

"But," Sam started, wrapping her arms around herself, and feeling the warmth of the jogging suit she had changed into after their quick lunch. "I don't know what to do."

Abby gave her daughter one last hug and kissed her on the cheek. "You are my daughter. Look within yourself for the answers." She smiled and brushed stray wisps of hair from Sam's face.

As they walked outside, Sam asked, "No parting words of wisdom?" The van door closed and Abby pressed the button to roll the window down. Sam peered into the van, admiring the new car smell.

Abby's dark eyes twinkled, revealing hints of mischief and mystery, and replied simply, "The only way to communicate is not to talk at all." With that, the window closed and the van rolled down the driveway.

"Not to talk at all?" Sam mused. "What one earth does that mean? We aren't talking now!"

She closed the front door and stood in the foyer, listening to the sounds of the house—the gentle humming of the ceiling fans, the subtle creaks and moans of aged wood, the tapping of acorns on the roof. The grandmother's clock in the foyer clanged. Slowly Sam climbed the staircase and stood at the top landing. She started to the right, as though on a parade-of-homes tour. It had only been ten weeks, but she felt she needed to inspect her surroundings again, get a feel for her terrain. At least, that was what Doctor Talbot had suggested. He said the flashbacks would stop, not to fight them. That they really weren't nightmares. Just the mind's way of sorting things out, cleaning house so to speak.

Her old bedroom was across from Abby's. Not nearly as big as the master bedroom but this was her comfort zone. It looked so empty now, remnants of her youth still wedged in the mirror frame, the colorful quilt hand-sewn by one of Abby's friends on the reservation.

She continued down the hall and peered into the next bedroom. What little furniture that had been in there before was now removed, including the curtains off the window. Bright sunlight warmed up the room. One lone dresser pressed against a wall.

"Of course," Sam sighed, noticing several books. Abby already suspected Sam's condition and picked up books on pregnancy and decorating nurseries. She stared at her reflection in the dresser mirror. She had lost a few pounds after entering Sara Binyon's. But then Abby started bringing her food and desserts and she gained it right back.

Pushing her fingers through her hair, she couldn't imagine how springy her hair would be if she didn't keep it long so the weight could tame some of the natural curl. The highlights the summer sun had added to her light brown hair were gone now, as was her tan. The reflection in the mirror was from two different worlds. She sat on the proverbial gene fence. Blue eyes and curly hair from her Caucasian father, prominent cheekbones from her mother. The best of both worlds yet not accepted fully in either one. It had served her well, helped her build a tough shell, sometimes a little too tough.

But impending motherhood was softening her. And she wasn't quite sure she was ready for the change. Peering closer into the mirror, Sam wondered where this new-mother glow was she had heard about. Instead, the eyes staring back looked tired, the otherwise flawless skin was flushed and starting to blemish. Truth was, she look just as she felt-miserable.

She should have begged Abby to take her with to Eagle Ridge. But Sam was glad the subject never came up. She wanted to concentrate on her hearing with the Board of Police and Fire Commissioners and finally getting back to work, keeping her mind occupied.

Turning to leave, several items drew her attention to the window seat. They were bean-stuffed animals, all furry and cuddly. "Oh, Mom," she sighed and curled up on the window seat. "How did I ever get myself in this situation? This happens to sixteen-year-old girls, not a twenty-six-year-old woman."

She picked up a brightly-colored bear and checked a tag attached to its ear. It said Valentina™. It was a Ty Beanie Baby®. She vaguely remembered reading about these. Something to do with a police report about a UPS driver stalked by frantic mothers trying to get a jump on the next new shipment. Holding Valentina™ up by its arms Sam had to admit, it was adorable. And she knew her mother. This was Abby's subtle way of pushing her daughter's maternal instincts button. Sam was doing her best to fight the warm, gooey feelings that were invading her senses.

"Just how long have you been stockpiling these, Mom?" Sam carried Valentina™ downstairs and set her on the edge of the counter while she went through the motions of making another cup of tea. She leaned against the island counter and stared out at the patio. Maybe she would go out and cut some flowers. Maybe she'd take a walk around the acres or take a ride around the property in Alex's cart.

Her gaze dropped down to the counter where an itinerary lay. It was Jake's and he was out of town. Sam read his travel schedule while stroking the leg of the pink bear. He was in San Diego at a conference and wouldn't be home for two more days. She heaved a sigh of relief.

"A reprieve for two days. Thank you, god." The microwave beeped and as she dipped a tea bag in the water, her eyes caught a glimpse of the front page with Murphy's smiling face. Scooting onto the stool, she unfolded the paper and read the article again as she sipped her tea. Slowly, a plan unfolded in her mind and she smiled. "I wonder if I have anything in my closet appropriate for a reception."

5

"Are you sure you're up to this? You don't look too well, Sam." Benny Lau held out his hands for her coat. Sam decided to keep her brown suede cape as Benny's wife, Lea, handed her coat to her husband.

"Are you referring to my mental or physical health?" Sam hadn't bothered to check the garage for available cars. She knew her Jeep was in a rubble heap somewhere and thought Jake's was probably at the airport garage. But she had no intention of touching anything of his. So she had called Benny, her friend and mentor, for a ride to the reception. He was the Chasen Heights medical examiner and one of the few men in the department to patiently answer her many questions when she first started out. He loved enthusiastic students almost as much as he loved his job.

"Both, actually."

"Dear, Sam looks fine," Lea chimed in. She carried her age as well as Benny. Both were close to fifty, not a speck of gray. Lea had a quick smile and large eyes that focused so intensely on whoever was speaking that she drew people to her.

Sam checked her reflection in a mirror around the corner expecting to see dark circles under her eyes and a shallow complexion. She did need some sleep but it didn't show. Sam had taken great pains to prepare for tonight. Her mass of natural curly hair was pulled back in a clip with stray tendrils framing her face. A hunt through Abby's jewelry box had netted her a stunning squash necklace which she promptly borrowed. Suede and fringe were the order of the day and she felt ready to do battle. It would be the first time she had seen Murphy since the incident. Other than stomach flutters, she felt fine.

"Looks like I'm going to be with the two prettiest ladies in the place." Benny beamed through his dark-rimmed glasses.

They entered the banquet room at the Cypress during cocktail hour. The oval-shaped bar was shoulder to shoulder with bodies. Two hundred of Chasen Heights' finest had come to help celebrate Dennis Murphy's promotion. Most had felt obligated to dole out fifty dollars each for the prime rib dinner.

The room was furnished with colorful floral drapes and rattan chairs. The large faux pineapple centerpieces were filled with live gardenias, and faux palm trees dotted the pink marble floor. The room seemed to have jumped off the pages of a Florida Keys decorator's handbook.

Sam recognized several of the people at the bar. Dorsey, who was close to retirement last time she had seen him, Sergeant Ed Scofield, several of the younger recruits, all from Precinct Six. And Sam recognized some fellow workers from The First, also known as Headquarters. Murphy was making his way around the bar.

"Great turnout, Dennis." The man pumping Murphy's hand was Mayor Jenkins. And wherever Jenkins was, the entire slate of aldermen wasn't far behind.

Murphy seemed mechanical. His smile too broad as he turned to face the cameras while shaking hands. Sam wondered how long it would be until Murphy turned on his good friend Jenkins and ran for mayor.

The stench from cigars and cigarettes attacked her senses. Sam watched the smoke rise up toward the lights where it hovered like some giant skull and cross bones. She found herself wondering how safe it was for the baby. Reaching down, she clasped the small leather pouch hanging from her neck. It was a medicine bundle, a gift from Abby on her twenty-first birthday and contained her umbilical cord, sage, and pipestone.

Abby didn't need to nudge maternal thoughts into Sam's psyche. Those thoughts had been flooding her head lately and she now wondered if it was due to hormonal changes. For one thing, she had the itchy boob syndrome. They were swollen, her bra was too tight, and she hadn't had time to do any shopping. For once in her life she was developing a cleavage she could be proud of.

The loud voices in the room were dissipating, reduced to a low drone. Sam was suddenly aware that the room was becoming quiet. Heads were doing double-takes toward the doorway, toward her.

"You really know how to silence a room," Lea whispered.

"Funny," Benny said. "A room full of cops who are supposed to uphold the law that everyone is innocent until proven guilty yet they can't give one of their own that same benefit."

Sam hadn't thought she would be able to sneak in without being recognized. But she had hoped they could at least wait a half hour before the buzzing started. And she knew they weren't staring because of what she was wearing. There were enough feathers on her in the form of earrings and bordering her cape to sew a feather quilt. They were staring because of the reason for her suspension—a fellow cop had died from three bullets to the back, from her gun. It didn't matter to them that the cop had died of a broken neck before he took the three bullets.

"I guess I do," Sam replied.

Polite seemed to be the order of the night. Sergeant Dorsey politely welcomed her back. Janet Gabriello, the department secretary, politely told her she was looking great. Most people avoided her as if she was on a weekend leave and due back to the home by midnight.

A tall, black man, the size of a linebacker, strode up to her and offered a mitt-sized hand. "You must be Sergeant Casey," he said in a deep, Barry White-type voice. The smile on his round face was genuine.

Somewhere between his chin and tie, she knew there had to be a neck. Benny introduced Sam to Captain Lamon Robinson. Her hand was swallowed up by his. The handshake was firm. Sam said, "It's a pity the Homicide Department is in such good hands now and I'm not there to profit from it."

Lamon laughed heartily. "You sure know the right things to say. I've heard a lot about you, Sergeant. Some are a little unbelievable." He leaned closer so only she could hear. "Hang in there. I know a setup when I see one."

Sam liked him, and wished she could spend more time picking his brain. But she was spotted by Murphy who pushed his way through.

"It is so great to see you, Sam." Chief Murphy's plastic smile conveyed the same sincerity as his handshake, a limp grasp by two fingers and a quick release.

"I guess congratulations are in order on your promotion," Sam said dryly. She noticed he hadn't changed much. He wore what was probably the most expensive tuxedo on the rack. A man driven by power and prestige.

"Well, I guess my predecessor's integrity left a lot to be desired." The corners of Murphy's mouth turned up slightly. Chief Don Connelley had been Murphy's adversary. It hadn't helped that Connelley had been Sam's godfather and had been one of the people Sam trusted the most. It hadn't helped that he had been her father's closest friend. Don Connelley was one subject Sam didn't care to broach, but Murphy plodded on. "Sometimes the people you put all your trust in just end up disappointing us, don't they?" His smiling eyes mocked her and Sam was beginning to feel the small bites of her crackers slowly rising. They were standing near the bar and Murphy made no attempt to move their conversation to more private quarters.

In an attempt to change the subject, Sam said, "It will feel great to be back at work. I have my hearing in a couple weeks so..."

"That's what I wanted to talk to you about." His smile broadened, creasing the corners of his eyes. "The Board of Police and Fire Commissioners won't be able to meet for at least four more months on your case. They have such a backlog."

Sam's crackers were now in stage two. Eyeing him suspiciously, she said, "I'm sure it has nothing to do with the fact that in your position as chief you'll be appointing new members to the Board of Police and Fire Commissioners."

Murphy arched his eyebrows in surprise. "My, that does fall under my jurisdiction, doesn't it?" With a shrug he added, "I'm sure you are still struggling with some kind of defense as to how your gun fired those fatal shots." He paused a beat, making sure he had the attention of everyone close by.

Lamon stepped closer. "Chief, I'm sure we don't have to discuss this now."

Murphy dismissed him with the wave of a hand and pushed on. "Of course, you will be submitting a written statement to I.A. I am kind of curious what Connelley had to do with your father's death. And how did he end up in your Jeep that morning?" Murphy cleared his throat and smiled that Cheshire grin.

She could feel her heart pounding and swallowed to keep her crackers from coming up but did think they'd look great right now splattered on Murphy's silk tie.

Fire flashed in her eyes and the words tumbled out before she could reel them back. "One thing about Chief Connelley is that he was the epitome of class. He wouldn't have taken an opportunity like tonight to discuss sensitive personnel issues, class which YOU obviously don't have." Her third earring of beads and feathers whipped against her left shoulder as Benny's hand tugged at her elbow.

"By the way, it will be required at your hearing that you take a lie detector test, Sergeant Casey."

"Maybe we can have you take one, too," Sam countered, feeling Benny's hand a little firmer.

The room was silent. Sam was vaguely aware that camera's were clicking. And she suddenly realized the members of the Board of Police and Fire Commissioners were standing directly behind Murphy.

Murphy tilted his head, a victorious smile on his face the deeper Sam dug her grave. "And I'm sure we will definitely need a report from your psychiatrist on your mental health."

Psychiatrist. He was making her sound like a raving mental case.

"You bastard," Sam whispered. She vaguely remembered being dragged out by Benny. It wasn't until she was in the safety of his car that she broke down in uncontrollable sobs.

6

The faint beat of a rock tune was drowned out by the incessant ringing of slot machines. Over one thousand enthusiastic gamblers filled three floors of the River Queen Casino as it floated back to its dock at the Calumet Marina. It usually sailed eight miles along the lake shore from Chasen Heights to Chicago and back, treating its guests on the observation deck to a spectacular view of the skyline.

Cocktail waitresses in hot pink satin jackets that just barely covered their rears weaved their way between the aisles. They seemed cloned...long blonde hair, long nails, hot pink lipstick, satin and feather hats.

Dealers in tuxedo shirts with hot pink bow ties came in all sizes and nationalities. The felt layouts by the roulette wheels were stacked with chips; the crap tables were three deep in players and spectators.

Black ceilings dotted with tiny white lights gave the feeling of a night sky. Large black domes hung from the ceiling every twenty feet, concealing surveillance cameras. Security guards in white shirts with turquoise epaulets roamed the floors watching for unruly guests and delivering fills of chips to the tables.

A small room at the bow of the boat on the second floor was set aside as a non-smoking room. It was there, near a five-dollar slot machine, that Everett Smith sat watching the players, checking his watch occasionally, patting the brown satchel that hung from his shoulder.

An Asian woman tethered to her slot machine by a coiled blue plastic chain looked curiously at him. She fed silver dollar tokens into the machine three at a time. As though she weren't losing her money fast enough, she started to feed the machine next to her.

Reverend Smith gave her a passing glance, then shook his head. He was dressed conservatively in a dark blue V-neck sweater over a dark blue shirt. His navy blue trench coat was thrown over the back of his chair. Checking his watch again, he gazed nervously at his surroundings.

In fifteen minutes the boat would be docking and he could get off. But he had yet to meet the man who was supposed to take the satchel.

Sparrow watched Everett Smith from the bar in the main casino. He had followed his target to the observation deck and then to the deli on the third floor where the Reverend had a sandwich and cup of coffee. Sparrow thought it odd that Reverend Smith didn't spend any time gambling. Just kept clutching the satchel and watching the gamblers with part disdain and part disinterest.

That feeling crept into Sparrow's gut again. Something wasn't right. His instincts told him to move cautiously. He searched the room, looking for some reason why the alarm bells in his head were ringing.

No one was giving Sparrow a second glance. He had on a gray wig and short graying beard, a white shirt open at the collar, a green sweater, and slightly tattered brown suit. Nothing flashy. He was a master of disguise. Today he was Mustafa Habib, a sixty-year-old businessman from New York City. He walked with a slight limp but was assisted by a sturdy metal cane with ingrained wood at the handle grip.

Square rose-tinted glasses sat snugly on his nose. He took a sip of his vodka and tonic, a drink he had been nursing most of the cruise. He needed all of his faculties tonight.

Sparrow was an expert at martial arts and jungle warfare, and fluent in five languages. Previously Special Forces, which was so many years ago it almost seemed like a different lifetime, he had learned not only how to stalk a victim, but also how to tell when someone was stalking. And he had noticed it an hour ago.

A man approximately five-foot-eight, wearing blue jeans, a blue knit shirt, and blue jean jacket, had been glancing once too often at Reverend Smith, following at a far enough distance, but his eyes never left him. His appearance was seedy at best, with a five o-clock shadow and oil-slick hair. He had sat in the same seat Sparrow now sat in, had ordered a beer, and then wandered off to the non-smoking room to casually play a quarter slot machine, glancing every so often at Reverend Smith.

Sparrow picked up the matchbook the man had left on the bar. *Beverly Hills - Where the Customer Always Comes First.* He stored the information in his memory bank. The remote control in his left pocket would be cutting the power on the boat at approximately five minutes before docking. The night scope in his right pocket would fit easily onto the nickel-plated Beretta 950 JetFire pistol concealed in his cane. The butt of the gun served as the grip for the cane. Also a weapons expert, Sparrow had equipped the gun with a sound suppressor.

He could hear the boat's engines, smell the fuel, as the three-hundred-foot River Queen maneuvered into its dock space. Senior citizens, businessmen, blue jean-clad yuppies, passengers in all shapes and colors were beginning to line up near the doorway opposite the bar leaving Sparrow a clear line to the seat Smith occupied.

The boat shifted slightly as it hit the dock. Sparrow pressed the button on the remote control and threw the room into total darkness. Laughter and comments were bantered around. "Grab the money," someone joked. No panic, no confusion. The generator lights snapped on casting a shadowy glow to the room. Sparrow could see that the dealers had covered their bankrolls with some type of metal and glass lids. He touched the remote control again and killed the generator lights.

Working swiftly, he released the gun from the cane, snapped on the night vision scope with a laser sight, and pointed it at Smith's chest. The alarm bells were ringing again as he instead kept a close eye on the stalker who had just moved in front of the Reverend. Sparrow saw the change in the Reverend's body as it slumped against the slot machine. The stalker slipped the satchel from Reverend Smith's grasp and faded into the crowd.

Something was definitely wrong, Sparrow thought. It was too much of a coincidence that on the night he was to eliminate a target, someone else did. Within ten seconds the lights were back on to the applause of the passengers. Sparrow's gun was safely back in the cane, the night vision scope back in his pocket. He kept his eye on the man in blue jeans, and as the doors opened, followed him.

7

The restaurant on the outskirts of town was dimly lit with high-backed booths, something Sam preferred about now. She didn't think she would have an appetite after her altercation with Murphy and almost had Benny pull over because she thought she was going to be sick. Seated in a booth across from Benny and Lea, Sam felt their sympathetic eyes, which made hers well up again.

"I'm sorry," Sam said as she dabbed her cheeks. "Guess I'm out of practice in dealing with Murphy." Not to mention her hormones which were out of whack and making her bare her normally well-hidden emotions.

Lea reached across and grabbed Sam's hand. "You gave him just what he deserved."

"Yes, I did. I gave him my job on a silver platter."

The waiter came and Sam ordered a glass of wine. *One glass of wine wouldn't hurt, shouldn't hurt*, Sam thought. She leaned back against the cushioned seat and perused the menu.

"Maybe it's best that you don't go back to work just yet," Lea said. "It brings back so many negative feelings."

Sam peered at them over the top of her menu. "You both think I'm pushing it too fast?"

Benny nodded. "Yes. You have been through more in the past

few months than most people I know."

"Enough with this talk of shootings and Murphy. Sam needs to think positive thoughts. Happy thoughts." Lea's face brightened the room. Eyes wide in excitement, a broad smile. When the waiter brought their drinks, she held hers up in a toast. "To a brighter tomorrow."

Sam tried to quell the jitters in her stomach, thinking not of tomorrow but of two tomorrows, when she would have to face Jake.

The conversation turned to Benny and Lea's three children, gymnastics, their families back in Honolulu, and Beanie Babies®.

"Beanie Babies?" Sam blinked. Throughout her meal of filet and baked potato, Sam listened as Lea rattled on about a store called Spoil 'em Silly in Crown Point, Indiana. That was where Lea purchased the stuffed animals for her youngest daughter. But she admitted they were also for her. She was collecting them.

Just as the waiter brought Sam's pumpkin pie and whipped cream, Benny's cellular phone rang. Several minutes later he hung up and announced. "We have a homicide at the River Queen Casino." He looked at his own slice of pie sitting in front of him. "But I can finish my pie first. The body ain't goin' anywhere."

Guests milled around the spacious lobby of the River Queen pavilion waiting to be questioned by police. The press was cordoned off in the VIP lounge just off the entrance to the ramp. Benny had dropped Lea off at home, and against his better judgment, let Sam talk him into letting her tag along.

They were met at the bottom of the ramp by two police officers and six of the casino's security guards. Benny showed his identification. Sam presented her shield and they each signed the log book which documented everyone who was accessing the crime scene. Neither of them bothered to mention that she was officially off duty and had no business being there.

They boarded the boat and Sam paused, surveying her surroundings in awe. Mirrored ceilings reflected the flashing lights; pulsating neons advertised progressive jackpots. The carpeting was a kaleidoscope of color in hues of stained glass. She had never been to Vegas and knew nothing about gambling. Even though the casino boat had been closed after the discovery of the body, she could still feel the excitement in the air.

"This way," the young officer said as he led them to the area roped off by black and yellow tape.

The body was lying on the floor in front of a five-dollar slot machine. Crime Lab technicians moved around the room cautiously. Sam peered over the tape to survey the body. The area would not be accessible until the Crime Lab had completed taking pictures. She could feel the aura pulsating in the room, and wished she could get close to the body. Although Abby's powers were with the living, Sam's were with the dead. She could sense things about the victim and killer just by touching the deceased or an item the killer had touched. Neither of them could predict when it would happen and sometimes they couldn't sense anything. But Sam could feel the aura pulling her from all directions and it was unusually strong.

Several feet behind her and to her left, Sam saw Frank Travis seated at a mini-baccarat table questioning a security officer. Frank was Jake's partner and she assumed the primary on the case since Jake was out of town. Frank looked different but she couldn't put her finger on it.

Standing near the table was a dark-haired man, streaks of blonde at the temple, medium height and build. If he didn't blink every few seconds, one could almost mistaken him for a mannequin.

Others stood around looking just as grim, men in dark suits and ties, official. Sam guessed them to be state police who were part of the Illinois Gaming Board, members who were on the boat at all times. IGB. Sam smiled. She had heard of them referred somewhat affectionately as KGB, by gamblers arrested on suspicion of theft or cheating.

Sam said, "Looks like a gun shot wound, Benny. What do you think?" A dab of blood was visible on the front of the victim's shirt. Eyelids were partially closed and staring toward them.

"Probably a small caliber," Benny agreed.

"Excuse me." A uniformed officer, whose badge read *Reynolds*, appeared at Sam's side. "Ma'am, would you follow me?"

Sam's gaze darted to Benny. "Guess Murphy must have found out already."

She followed Officer Reynolds off the boat and down the ramp to the pavilion. How like Murphy to keep tabs on her whereabouts. He probably even knew where she went for dinner. Sam half-expected to see television crews set up in the pavilion to catch her altercation with Murphy on tape for the ten o'clock news. But instead, Reynolds led her through a door and down another hallway. He held open a door marked *Training Room* and closed the door behind her.

Only one overhead light above a crap table was lit. She could barely make out blackjack tables and a roulette wheel surrounded by stools. Then an eerie feeling crept up her spine. She wasn't alone. In a darkened corner she could see tasseled loafers, legs crossed at the ankles. But the shoes weren't ostrich-skinned so she doubted it was Murphy. The pants were charcoal gray, pleats pressed flat against a firm stomach. One hand was shoved into a pants pocket, the jacket opened revealing a shield clamped on a belt.

A match, lit by the flick of a thumbnail, illuminated an unsmiling face, brows hunkered over deep set eyes with a hardened look that bordered on despise. It was Jake. Sam braced herself for the barrage of rhetoric: *You could have called, could have answered my letters. What happened to all we shared? Did it mean nothing to you?*

Instead Jake said, "I hear you caused a bit of a scene at Murphy's dinner." He inhaled long and deep, letting the smoke drift out slowly.

Sam held her breath. For ten weeks she had hoped all her feelings for him were dead. But damn, he looked good. He wasn't drop dead gorgeous. It took time for him to grow on you. It was his quiet reserve that attracted women. Tall and muscular, rugged looking with a ruddy complexion and furrowed eyebrows. He smiled rarely, as if life hadn't shown him anything worth smiling about.

"Rumor mill is still fast and furious." She fumbled with the stray hairs caught in her earring then stopped. Why care what she looked like? "Thought you were out of town." She moved to one of the blackjack tables, her suede boots scuffing along the carpeting.

"It ended early." He pushed away from the wall, his eyes assessing her in one sweeping gaze.

This time she braced herself for a barrage of apologies: *I'm sorry you had to go through that. I should have been there with you. Why didn't you tell me you were home?*

But again, she couldn't predict his thoughts. Instead, he said, "You should have known better than to go anywhere near him."

Another long drag and a piercing glare that made Sam gather her cape around her tighter.

There was a knock on the door and Reynolds stuck his head in. "Sergeant?"

Sam and Jake both responded, "Yes?"

Sam jerked her head around. That explained the suit. Jake had always preferred to dress casual, sometimes even wearing gym shoes just to piss off Murphy. Now he looked just like what he was...a former FBI agent.

Reynolds told Jake, "They're ready for you, sir."

Sam's icy glare rested on Jake. "How silly of me. Of course you were promoted. That was Murphy's deal with you. And what orders did he give you tonight? Bar me from the crime scene?"

Jake walked over to the blackjack table and stuffed his cigarette into an ashtray. Sam didn't think she had ever seen him this cold or distant. But now another problem surfaced. Jake was a sergeant and so was she. In the same department. And they were married. One of them would have to go. Knowing Murphy, she just knew it would be her.

Finally, Jake said, "I need your shield, Sergeant."

Sam blinked. "It was destroyed in the explosion."

Jake waited, looked at Reynolds and back to Sam. "You used it to gain access to the boat tonight. It should have been confiscated after..." He looked away.

Sam could see his temples pulse. Jake pulled out another cigarette. Two cigarettes in the space of five minutes. She only knew him to limit himself to two a day. She hoped he was also losing sleep.

He gazed at Reynolds again and nodded, those unspoken signals cops used. Reynolds made a move towards Sam's shoulder strap purse.

"What?" She jerked the purse away. "Are you going to strip search me next?" But when she jerked it away from Reynolds, the purse floated in the direction of Jake. He pulled the purse from her grasp and quickly found the shield before Sam had a chance to react. She stared at the I.D. in his hand and willed herself not to be reduced to tears in front of him. Even though she had the suspension hanging over her head, at least she had her shield, that one reminder of who and what she was, of the life she would go back to sooner rather than later. And now that was gone. Murphy would make sure her return was later if at all. Jake handed her purse back. Her breath caught and to keep the tears from spilling over, Sam went through the motions of checking out the contents of her purse as if he might have taken something else.

"Did you come with Benny?" Jake asked.

"What else was I supposed to do? If you recall, the remains of my Jeep could fit in a shoebox."

"Did you check the garage? You have a new one which I'm sure will meet with your approval." He turned away from her, stopping to put out his cigarette, and whispered something to Officer Reynolds.

Sam stood dumbfounded. Why hadn't Abby mentioned she had bought Sam a new Jeep? This wasn't the way she had planned it. She had wanted to release the same kind of venom on Jake as she had on Murphy. She obviously used it all up on the new chief. But Jake was good at disarming. She hadn't expected him to return early from his trip. She hadn't anticipated him being promoted. She hadn't thought that he would be as cold-hearted as he was. That was her specialty.

"Ma'am." Reynolds held the door open.

Jake still held her shield in his hand and she stared at it. A sick feeling started in the pit of her stomach. For some reason she knew she would never see it again. Sam turned slowly and walked out of the room.

Jake slid onto a stool and lit another cigarette. Leaning his arms on the blackjack table he traced a thumbnail across his forehead. Abby had called him earlier to tell him that she and Alex were on their way to Eagle Ridge and that Sam was home.

Tough love. That was the only way he knew how to handle her. But it was tougher on him. Sometimes she was easy to figure out. He knew she wouldn't waste time confronting Murphy. She had looked fragile, her emotions raw. She was trying to put up a good front but he could see right through it. Tonight. Other times, he couldn't figure her out at all.

Sam had a mystery about her that was more than skin deep. To him, the culture of the Lakota Sioux was shrouded in mystery. Jake always dealt in logic so to be in Sam's world was sometimes difficult for him to adjust to, and many times logic seemed to have no place. Like the day Alex did a rain dance and it rained only on the vegetable garden. Or the day Sam instructed two mourning doves to fly through her office window and deposit their last meal on Murphy's desk.

Fortunately for Jake, he preferred a tomboy, because Sam did not spend a lot of time on makeup or nails. That was the second thing that had attracted him...her subtle beauty. She was a chameleon who could go from tomboy to raving beauty with the stroke of an eyebrow pencil.

Frank appeared in the doorway with shirtsleeves rolled up, beads of perspiration on his dark skin, and tired eyes that drooped at the corners. He was sporting a new shaved-head look and kept patting his head as if forgetting he no longer had hair. “Hey, partner. Crime techs are done. Are you coming?”

“In a minute.” Jake poked at Sam’s shield, giving it a quarter turn, then another, until it was facing him again.

“Uh, oh.” Frank slid onto the stool next to Jake and made a cursory examination of his furrowed brow, loosened tie, tight jaw line. Frank’s smile was broad and surrounded by new growth. He was just starting to grow a mustache and partial beard. “You look like you’ve been playing *good cop/bad cop* without me.”

Jake took one last drag and pressed the cigarette butt into the ashtray. “More like bastard cop.” His fingers moved the shield 360 degrees. “Sam’s back.”

Frank’s gaze dropped to the shield. “No shit?”

Jake filled his partner in on Murphy’s reception, at least what gossip he had heard.

“That’s a shame.” Frank eyed the number of cigarette butts in the ashtray. “She looked that good, huh?” He smiled again, a smile as infectious as his laugh.

Jake ran a hand through his thick hair, exposing a deep scar near the hairline. The natural curl to his hair usually covered that reminder from his youth. “I don’t know, Frank. She’s in bad shape. The way some people talk, she sounded psychotic at the reception. And now,” he held up the shield. “Murphy had me confiscate it. You should have seen the look on Sam’s face.”

They were silent for a while. Jake lit another cigarette. Finally, Frank asked, “Still need my spare room for a while?”

Jake shrugged. “Abby had me promise her to give it two weeks, to wait until she returns.” He took a long drag. “It’s going to be a damn long two weeks."

"I take it things didn't go well?"

He swiveled his chair to face Frank. "In the space of five minutes, I took her shield and she found out Murphy promoted me. How well do you think it went?"

"She's got to know it's regulation to turn in her shield in a suspension case such as hers." Frank picked up a few of the casino chips and examined them, placed them on the betting circle. "You think she got out too early?"

"She's an emotional basket case, Frank." Jake stood and checked his watch. "Let's get this over with."

The late model BMW never got more than two blocks ahead of him. Sparrow had followed the man with the satchel since they'd left the River Queen. The driver had hopped onto the Skyway after leaving the casino, followed the Dan Ryan Expressway, and turned onto a residential street just west of White Sox Park in Chicago. The man parked across the street from a twelve-story apartment complex and entered the building. Sparrow checked the inside pocket of his trench coat and left his car.

The man stared straight ahead, hugging the satchel close to his body. Sparrow followed and observed the man entering an apartment on the second floor. After making a mental note of the apartment number, Sparrow walked back down the stairs to the entrance to look for a name on the mailbox. *Amid Gustaf.* Most of the names on the mailbox were Middle Eastern.

He returned to the second floor and knocked on the door. It was pulled open against a sturdy chain. "We have problems," Sparrow said in a thick Middle Eastern accent.

The dark eyes regarded him suspiciously. "Who are you?"

"Kaheeb. Let me in. Or do you want me to discuss in the hallway about the man on the river boat casino who isn't dead and can identify you?"

Without any regard as to who the hell Kaheeb was, Amid opened the door. Once inside, Sparrow grabbed Amid in a headlock and put a knife to his throat.

"You can make this real easy, or real painful," Sparrow whispered, dropping his accent. Amid didn't flinch but Sparrow saw his eyes flash over to the satchel sitting on the worn couch.

All the furniture in the room was worn. But Amid had the latest in stereo equipment, a wide screen television, several VCRs, and boxes of video cameras stacked in a corner. Amid was obviously into a lot of things.

Sparrow gave a firm pinch to the lower right side of Amid's neck and the man dropped to the floor. While Amid was enjoying his siesta, Sparrow inspected the apartment. He turned on the stereo and found a rock station but was careful not to turn the volume so loud that the neighbors might be tempted to call the cops. He picked up the satchel. It was brown leather, about a foot high by a foot wide, heavy, with a locked clasp.

A quick dig through Amid's pockets failed to produce a key. Sparrow moved to the bedroom. The closets were filled with expensive silk shirts, cashmere coats. The dresser top was covered with gold bracelets and necklaces. The top drawer contained stacks of hundred dollar bills and a passport stating Amid was from Iran. But still no key.

He moved Amid to the bed, where he tied his hands and legs to the four corners using rope from the boxes of video cameras that had been tied together. He sat at the foot of the bed and proceeded to pick the lock on the satchel. That was when Amid began to stir.

Without looking up Sparrow said, "I hate it when a nagging voice sounds alarms in my head." He looked over at Amid, who seemed dazed. Amid glared at Sparrow with no fear in his eyes. Sparrow wasn't surprised. After all, Amid came from a country where people welcomed the opportunity to beat themselves to a frenzy all in the name of worshiping some fanatical religious zealot.

"Why," Sparrow continued, "were you following the man? Why do I get the feeling that I was being used to take the fall for killing him when all the while you were going to do it?" Sparrow removed his rose-tinted glasses and shoved them in his pocket. "And why is this satchel so important?"

"You ask too many questions, you capitalist swine," Amid said.

"Tsk, tsk. Name calling isn't going to get us anywhere." Sparrow twisted the pick in the lock and gently rolled the tumblers. "There we go. See?" Sparrow added with a Spanish accent, "I dunt' need no stinkin' key." He picked up the satchel and dumped the contents out on the bed. Numerous layers of green felt were wrapped around two objects. Sparrow unfolded them. Two printing plates fell between Amid's legs.

Amid looked at the plates and smiled mockingly.

Sparrow picked up the plates and studied them. They were for U.S. currency...a fifty-dollar and a one-hundred-dollar bill. It didn't take long for it to register: his two-hundred-thousand-dollar payment was counterfeit.

Amid threw back his head and cackled. "You greedy capitalist pig."

Sparrow pulled out a dresser drawer and found a pair of socks. He shoved the socks in Amid's mouth and wrapped a silk tie around the man's head to keep the socks in place.

Sparrow pulled his gray wig and beard off and threw them across the room. His hair fell down past his shoulders as Amid looked with shock at the transformation. With a knee on Amid's chest, he pressed a thumb to his neck and said, "I'm going to ask you just one time so listen carefully and be ready with your answers. Who hired me? Where do I find him? How did the dead man get these plates? Now, you can reply in any language you want. Nod if you're ready to talk."

Amid remained motionless, moving his eyes to stare up at the ceiling. He didn't even have time to react when Sparrow reached into an inside pocket of his trench coat, pulled out a fifteen-inch combat blade machete and chopped off three of Amid's fingers.

A guttural, muffled scream, drowned out by the rock music, came from behind the socks as Amid grimaced in pain, thrashing his body against the ropes. Sparrow wiped the knife on Amid's shirtsleeve, ripped the tie down to his chin and pulled the sock out of his mouth saying, "Any answers come to that pea brain of yours?"

Amid's dark eyes teared but he still showed no fear. He just pulled back his head and spit in Sparrow's face.

The veins near Sparrow's temple pulsated as he glared at his victim. With the back of one sleeve, he wiped the spittle from his face. Remaining calm, he stood, turned as though walking away, and with one quick movement turned back and slashed out with the machete.

9

Sam sat at the bar and watched as Jake and Frank entered the crime scene area. Now she knew what was different about Frank. He shaved his head and was growing one of those Fu Manchu beards.

While Officer Reynolds searched for someone to give her a ride home, Sam had managed to casually stroll past the security guard at the doorway to the casino boat and ease her way over to the bar where she had a good view of the non-smoking room. The bar was cluttered with half-empty glasses and smelly ashtrays. The bartenders hadn't had time to clean up before security removed everyone from the boat.

Out of boredom, Sam picked up a red matchbook and tapped it on the bar, turned it, tapped it. The chill in the air was immediate. All other sounds in the room ceased, replaced by voices crying out. Suddenly, she saw a vision of a hand with a tattoo of, what? A bird? Then she saw a name under the bird...Sparrow. Voices cried out again. But there was more. She saw bodies too numerous to count, flash in front of her eyes.

A part of her had wondered if her powers had dissipated any during her stay at Sara Binyon's. She had felt out of practice. After all, there weren't any dead bodies at the rest home. Any doubts she had were now safely eliminated.

Her eyes focused on an empty glass next to the matchbook. Just reaching for it she could feel sparks of electricity. She carefully wrapped the glass in a napkin and shoved it in the pocket of her cape. The killer had held this glass. The aura was strong and seemed to be coming from different directions. It was even stronger than what she had felt when she and Benny stood by the taped area. Suddenly, the barstool swiveled and she was face-to-face with Jake.

"I thought I sent you home." Jake slipped out of his sportscoat and tossed it on the bar stool next to her. Then he placed his hands on the padded armrest behind her, barricading her on all sides. His eyes swept the room, the bar area, then rested on her face. He leaned close to her, a little too close for comfort. It reminded her of another time she could feel his warm breath on her.

"I'm waiting for a ride." She glanced toward the crime scene. "What did Benny say?"

He straightened and propped one foot on the rung of her chair. "Don't try to get involved, Sam. You don't want to do anything to jeopardize your hearing."

"I can help." She tried to make it sound like a statement rather than groveling. "I need to help." Now she did border on groveling but she didn't care. She needed to keep busy, keep the nightmares away.

Jake stared at his shoes, jammed a fist onto his hip, and placed a hand on the back of the stool next to hers. She could see him mulling things over in his head. Or he was pausing to calm his anger.

"Sam, if you want to do something, why don't you spend your time off finding proof of your innocence."

"What?" She stared incredulously at him. "Excuse me, but wasn't that the department's job to investigate? What have they been doing for ten weeks? Matter of fact, that would have been your job, unless..." He didn't flinch.

"I don't care to have this discussion now."

"And why not?" Her voice raised several decibels. She crossed her arms and waited, contemplating if she could find a locksmith this late at night to change the locks on all the doors at home.

Jake pulled a small rubber ball out of his jacket pocket and started squeezing it. *A new stress reducer*, Sam thought. Probably sanctioned by Murphy himself. Jake just kept squeezing it and staring at her.

Finally, he said, "Frank and I combed that entire parking lot where Officer Richard's body was found. We came up with nothing, Sam. I personally visited Hilliard in prison but he's still claiming no involvement. His hands are clean."

State Representative Preston Hilliard was an intricate cog in a deception and cover-up dating back to the Korean War, all with ties to Sam's last case and her father's death twenty years ago. Jake paced a short path in front of her, still squeezing that rubber ball. "I wanted to beat the truth out of him, that arrogant bastard."

"Can I read the case report?"

He stopped pacing, jammed the ball into his pants pocket. But before he could respond, a security guard and Officer Reynolds called him over. Sam watched their animated discussion, the security guard pointing at Sam, Jake motioning toward the door. Both men waited while Jake returned to where Sam was sitting.

"What?"

He held out his hand, palm side up. "The glass you took from the bar. I need it back."

Sam sighed. The surveillance cameras. One minor detail she forgot. "Promise me you'll check it for fingerprints."

"It's an open-and-shut case. Everything is on camera." He nodded toward the doorway. "Officer Reynolds has a car ready at the curb. Go home and get some rest. You look like hell." He turned and walked away.

"Damn him." She left the casino in a blur of suede and feathers and cursed Jake during the entire ride home. Once there, she slammed the front door shut and watched the squad car through the blinds as it disappeared down the driveway. She leaned against the door and smiled. Out of her left pocket she slowly pulled out the matchbook that said, *Beverly Hills.*

10

Jake looked up at the clock in Benny's office and rubbed his eyes. The chair was comfortable, his sweater warm. It wouldn't take much for him to nod off.

He and Frank had reviewed endless surveillance tapes until their eyes burned. They even had a condensed version made with just the segments where Reverend Smith appeared. That had taken most of their time. Tapes didn't show anyone suspicious close to the Reverend at the time of his death. But the ten seconds the power went out was the crucial time.

Brent, the starched, Vegas-style shift supervisor, had promised to have his staff contact everyone who had a ticket for last night's eight o'clock cruise. Most of the passengers had left the boat before security discovered the body. Jake hoped to be able to narrow the list down to just those on the second floor during the time of the power outage. The engineers had located a breaker attached to the fuse box. Unfortunately, the Crime Lab was unable to lift any prints.

Jake had gone home at three in the morning to catch a couple of hours' sleep and take a hot shower. He had checked in on Sam, pulled the covers up, and then spent five minutes watching her sleep. Even beneath the sheet and flannel blanket he could see every curve of her body. He had slept in her old bedroom down the hall. But it didn't make it any easier.

After meeting Frank for a quick breakfast, they now sat in Benny's lab waiting for the autopsy on Reverend Everett Smith to begin.

"You two give new meaning to the phrase, 'crack of dawn'," Benny joked as he slipped a lab coat on over his Hawaiian shirt.

"Never a dull moment." Frank poured three cups of coffee from the coffee maker against the wall. The sterile white room held eight examining tables. The walls were brightened with colorful posters of Hawaii.

They sipped their coffee while Benny filled them in on the preliminaries. "Small entrance wound, probably a round-nosed bullet. No powder burns."

"Had to have used a suppressor." Jake said. A silencer at close range would have left minimal if any trace of powder burns.

Benny nodded in agreement. "I'm going to find a real mess when I cut him open. Those round nose bullets jump around like a damn pinball machine." He walked over to a table and brought back a large tray. "Thought you might find this interesting." The tray contained the clothing the Reverend had been wearing. Benny dug around and pulled out a money belt.

"Holy shit." Frank's eyes widened. A large quantity of fifties and one-hundred-dollar bills lined the belt. He removed the banded stacks. "Ten, twenty, jezzus, fifty thousand dollars maybe?" Frank's eyes grew even wider.

"Pass the collection plate, please." Jake fanned through one of the stacks checking serial numbers. He pulled one of the fifty-dollar bills out and held it up to the light.

"I swear, always suspicious, Mitchell."

"Never can be too careful." Jake checked the Federal Reserve Bank seal, the lacy border design to make sure the design wasn't broken, and the denomination on the front and back. He felt the paper on both sides, then walked over to the microscope.

"It's real, Jake. I can smell it," Frank laughed.

"What is a man of the cloth doing walking around with this kind of money? The surveillance film didn't show him gambling during the entire cruise. Isn't that a little strange for someone with fifty thousand dollars?"

"What's strange," Benny said, "is this Reverend is the one who had been picketing the casino boats when they first opened."

Jake looked up from the microscope. "He's THAT Reverend?" Benny nodded. Jake turned his attention back to the fifty-dollar bill under the microscope. Around the president's picture was small micro-printing saying, *The United States of America*. These were printed on Series 1990 and newer large denomination bills. Jake checked the Treasury Seal to make sure the points were sharp and clear. The paper had the tiny red and blue fibers embedded.

"If these are counterfeit, they are the best counterfeits I've ever seen," Jake said as he leaned back in the chair. He pulled out a one-hundred-dollar bill and held it up to the light, then under the microscope. Shaking his head, he told Frank, "Take a look."

"What am I looking for?"

"I could be wrong, but the fibers in the paper don't seem right. The color looks too faded and there seem to be too few threads."

Benny pulled out a one-hundred-dollar bill from his own wallet and handed it to Frank for comparison. "I shoulda' known you'd be rolling in dough," Frank said. He compared the two under the microscope. "The paper feels the same but you're right. There's something funny about those fibers."

Carl Underer stood by his office window holding a five-by-seven framed picture. He chewed on one arm of his horn-rimmed glasses and studied the picture. The woman was an attractive blonde. She was smiling, dressed in a bright yellow dress, her long corn silk hair flowing endlessly across her shoulders.

His fingers traced the outline of her face. He remembered where the picture had been taken...a rented beach house in Maui where they had spent four glorious weeks. That was as much time as he had ever spent with her. Four weeks each year. Always a remote place, out of the public eye.

They had met in college. Carl had never planned to marry. His life was going to be with the FBI, Foreign Intelligence. And being in his line of business would jeopardize anyone close to him. If he were in any other line of work, if he had ever planned to marry, it would have been to Judith Hunt. And she loved him enough to let him go.

They were separated for only two years. Judith had left college in her final year explaining that she would finish at a local college near her home in Dallas. And she had married Eric Logan, a CPA. But the marriage ended after two years and one child, a son, Charles.

Like a stroke of fate, Judith and Carl had run into each other when Carl was in Dallas on business. That was when they started their annual trysts, spending four weeks a year in an isolated place, sometimes Alaska, sometimes the desert, mostly one of the islands. And Carl never objected to her bringing Charlie. He was suspicious of Charlie every time he looked at him but he never asked and Judith never offered. Somehow he knew Charlie was his son.

Carl examined each of the award plaques as he pulled them off the wall and packed them into moving boxes. He couldn't help wondering if it had all been worth it. He had been on assignment in Europe when Judith died of breast cancer at the age of thirty-seven. No one knew of their relationship, so he found out too late to even attend the funeral.

Charlie remained with the man presumed to be his father. However, Eric Logan died in a private plane crash four months later. It was only through extensive research that Carl found out

Charlie was living with a foster family. With his FBI connections, Carl was able to keep tabs on the eighteen-year-old Charlie, who was so advanced that he already had two years of college under his belt when he joined the Marines.

A man appeared in the doorway. "You wouldn't be cleaning out your office on a Sunday to avoid saying goodbye to your staff, would you?"

Carl smiled wearily. "You know me too well, Lloyd."

"I've got the car running downstairs as we speak." Lloyd Chandler was Carl's closest friend and the only one who knew about Judith and Charlie. Lloyd, a forensic pathologist with a Ph.D. in psychology, had been with the FBI for the past twenty-four years. A balding spot was ringed with salt-and-pepper hair. He pulled his pipe out of his mouth as he approached.

Carl smiled at Judith's picture. "Can't believe I'm finally retiring."

"You must have heard something," Lloyd said.

Carl nodded slowly and placed the picture in the box. "You heard about the burial site in the Iron Triangle?" Lloyd nodded. "They found Charlie's dog tags."

Lloyd placed a hand on Carl's shoulder. "Almost seems like fate. On the anniversary of Judith's death, Charlie's body is found."

Carl turned and looked at his friend. "When they ship the bodies back here, I want you to do the examination."

"Of course." Lloyd helped him load the boxes onto a dolly. "Hopefully, I can get a few days of fishing in with you before the call comes in."

Carl did one last survey of the office. "I did schedule one quick layover in Chicago before heading down to the Gulf."

The dolly moaned as Lloyd backed it through the doorway. "Chicago?"

"Yes, there are some people at our Chicago office I'd like to see one last time, not to mention Jake and his bride."

11

The man rolled over and looked at the young body next to him. She had long, jet-black hair and high cheekbones. A combination of Filipino and Puerto Rican, Yung was a petite nineteen-year-old with small breasts but a mouth with enough tongue action to keep his old body active.

He gave her a slap on the butt and said, "Go get my paper." She murmured slightly then buried herself deeper in the covers.

"Damn," he muttered as he threw back the covers and climbed out of bed.

Davud Menut had arrived in the States fifteen years before from Tehran, Iran. Davud, a fiftyish man with thinning hair and a slight build, pulled on his jogging suit and slipped into his house slippers.

His eyebrows were darker than his hair and rested evenly over eyes that didn't seem to cooperate with each other. The left eye had had extensive surgery from shrapnel and lazily moved with little control from what was left of the eye muscle.

His two-bedroom suite was located on the second floor over his business. It was expensively decorated with European lines, red and black masculine colors, and a lot of chrome and mirrors. The master bedroom led to a sunroom with a hot tub and wet bar. And the spacious sunken living room held a huge, wide screen TV and plush

U-shaped sectional couch.

Davud took the elevator down to the first floor. He yawned and shook his head to get the cobwebs out. The elevator emptied out to a private foyer with four doors—one that led to his office, a private entrance to each of his businesses, and a door to the back lot.

He opened the back door and inhaled deeply. The dark haze of early morning was just settling, leaving everything wet from dew. Davud bent down to get the morning paper. That was when he saw the brown satchel. Slowly he stood and checked the empty lot. This was not how the exchange had been scheduled. Amid wasn't supposed to arrive until ten o'clock, and certainly not leave the satchel in the bushes.

"Damn help. Can't find anyone any more." Davud gingerly picked up the satchel, closed and locked the back door, and walked into his office. The weight of the satchel didn't surprise him. He smiled at how smoothly everything had gone, and now he would have good news to report to his superiors.

He unfastened the catch, slid the strap up, and let out a scream as Amid's head rolled across his desk.

Sparrow pushed the tray away, having finished his two eggs scrambled, French toast, and bacon, compliments of room service. He sat at the table in his hotel room overlooking the lake and its picturesque view of the sunrise as it burned its way through the haze.

Amid didn't have to talk. Sparrow had found out everything he wanted to know by searching his apartment. A business card in Amid's wallet from Menut Enterprises, another matchbook from Beverly Hills with a handwritten phone number; and by pressing the redial on Amid's phone, he had heard a recording of a man's voice saying "This is five-five-five, two-nine-hundred. You have reached Menut Enterprises." The same number handwritten on the matchbook. He then dialed the number for the weather to erase

Menut's number so the police couldn't trace it when they pressed the redial.

"Yep, stupid capitalist pigs," Sparrow said. The night before, when he had driven to the address on the business card, it just happened to be behind Beverly Hills, a Victoria's Secret-type lingerie shop. Sparrow figured if he was wrong and it wasn't Menut Enterprises, then someone was going to be in for the shock of his or her life when they found his little present.

The first thing he had done when he returned to his hotel room was to check his money. He had seen enough counterfeit bills in his days and knew just about every technique being implemented.

He took a sip of coffee and checked his watch. How long he would let Menut stew, he wasn't sure. Maybe a day, maybe two. A lot of organizations would be interested in the plates. Just about every organized crime family, the Japanese, Russians, Koreans...the list was endless. He had already called the airlines last night and cancelled his flight. He knew his business here was not quite finished.

12

Sam stood in an abandoned parking lot at 1600 Cornell. If anything, the weeds had grown taller though turning brown and losing their sturdiness. She wandered the cracked sidewalks toward the darkened area on the asphalt. She had wanted to stop by the precinct to read the case file, but Records wasn't open on a Sunday.

The morning headlines were filled with the news about the homicide at the casino boat and Sam could only guess that Jake would be kept busy all day just getting statements from passengers and reviewing surveillance tapes. There had been no sign that he had even come home last night...no note on the table, no message on the answering machine. *Just as well*, she thought. And first thing tomorrow she would stop by the precinct and see if she could take a look at the file on her alleged shooting of Stu Richards.

The large warehouse stood vacant, gaping holes for windows where pigeons perched. That night had come back vividly to her at Sara Binyon's and she had often wondered if she ever returned here if she would be able to sense something, some revelation to prove her innocence. She edged closer to the area where the squad car had been, closer to the area where, in the dark, she had tripped over Stu Richards' body.

Sam wrapped her blanket coat around her and squatted down.

Stu Richards died on a damp asphalt parking lot. Even though Benny confirmed the broken neck was the cause of death, the bullets from her gun were still the main focus. And what good would it do now for her to feel any aura. She already knew Cain Valenzio had killed the rookie cop. Unfortunately, soon after, Cain had been conveniently killed by Representative Hilliard's security guards. Sam knew Valenzio was Hilliard's hired hand. But she couldn't prove it. Suspension won't be her only worry. She could actually end up having this baby in prison.

Standing, she turned to look at the vacant buildings across the street. Her memory of that night was clear enough for her to recall hearing sirens as she sped away. This entire industrial park had been abandoned for some time. So who called the police? Who called the fire department? The buildings had been known to hide the addicts and homeless but they would have all run for cover at the first sound of a siren.

Sam walked over to the entrance to the warehouse and sat down at a bench weathered with age, weeds snaking around the concrete legs. Cain had stood near this bench, that was his position when he was shooting at her, shooting at the squad car until he had ignited the fuel tank. She pulled out her cellular phone then hesitated. But she had no other choice. She had to call Jake.

"Jake?" No small talk. She didn't ask him how the investigation at the casino was going. He answered short and sweet with no hint that she was interrupting him. "Where are the remains of the squad car?"

"If you are thinking that Cain blew up the car to eliminate any fingerprints he might have left, we already thought of that."

"Yes, but did you do anything about it? How do you know there wasn't some fragment left with a fingerprint? Maybe Murphy had someone destroy every scrap of steel and falsify the report?"

"You mean someone like me working on Murphy's orders?"

Sam dropped the phone to her chest, his voice muffled between her sweater coat and the mouthpiece. She brought the phone back to her ear.

"I didn't say that." The silence stretched and if it weren't for the voices in the background on Jake's end, she would have thought he had hung up. "I don't put anything past Murphy." Still nothing but breathing from his end. Sam asked, "Who called it in? I remember the sirens as I was leaving. Someone had to have witnessed the fire."

"A fire alarm a few blocks away had been pulled."

"Any fingerprints? Didn't anyone search for some damn witnesses?"

He sighed heavily and this time Sam could detect impatience, could imagine his jaw cemented, the temples throbbing. Probably had that damn ball in his hand squeezing the life out of it.

Finally, Jake said, "I don't know what else I can tell you, Sam. The report is on file. You can stop by and read it."

"In the *closed* or *open* case file, Jake?" She bounded off the bench and headed for her Jeep. "This is my damn life we're talking about. Obviously, I'm the only one concerned about it." She jammed her thumb against the POWER button so he couldn't try to call her back. Placing her phone into one pocket, she pulled a plastic bag of crackers from the other. Talking to Jake had knotted her stomach.

The library wasn't open so she wouldn't be able to read back issues of the local papers but she could access them over the Internet.

"You're going to flatten that puppy." Frank stared at the ball in Jake's hand. "Was that Sam?" He turned back to the plexi-board where he was taping pictures from the surveillance cameras.

"How could you tell?" Jake dropped the ball on his desk and it rested against a paperclip holder. He stared at the stack of typed statements and leaned back in the chair, fingers steepled. "I could just tell she was calling me from the warehouse, probably pacing the parking lot, desperately looking for something, finding exactly what we had found."

"Nothing."

"Right."

Frank tossed the rest of the pictures on the desk and sat down. "So why don't you tell her?"

Jake shrugged. "Would seem like damage control now. Besides, she should trust me. She should know Murphy would be the last person who would get my cooperation. But she's going to think what she wants." He picked up one of the suspected counterfeit bills. "When is the guy from the Treasury Department stopping by?"

"Not until later." Frank sifted through Jake's unanswered phone messages and tossed one in front of him. "And this guy is stopping by later, too."

Jake picked up the phone message from Carl Underer.

Sam stared at the computer screen in her study. Before accessing the Internet to check the back issues of the *Chasen Heights Post Tribune*, she thought she would try to get the case report on Stu Richards. Her computer was tied to the precinct mainframe and with Jake living here, she was sure it was still connected. She typed in her password and pressed ENTER. But the computer said she was an invalid user. The password had been changed.

"Damn!" She tried several passwords, words Jake may have selected. She tried Abby's name, Abby's birth date, Abby's last name. She tried again using Alex's last name and birth date. Then she thought of using Jake's birth date but realized she didn't even know it. So she tried hers. But nothing would let her access the CHPD computer.

She abandoned that idea and accessed the *Chasen Heights Post Tribune* web site, searching through the archives. Seeing the first headline killed her interest of reading any of the rest.

DETECTIVE PRIME SUSPECT IN ROOKIE'S DEATH

13

Sam wasted no time Monday morning getting to Headquarters to submit her statement. Just submit her report, that's all. No one had said anything about being interrogated. But here she was in a plush room that looked more like a waiting room in a bank. Carpeting was thick, tables solid mahogany, chairs cushioned and comfy. There was even a floral arrangement on the credenza. They had spared no expense. But it still had the two-way mirror and Sam cringed at the thought of who was on the other side.

It hadn't taken Sam long to type up her statement last night. There were a few things she didn't include...like where she had spent the evening after Richards died. The last thing she wanted to admit was that she spent the night with Jake. I.A. didn't need to know everything. It wasn't any of their business.

The clock on the wall said eight-fifteen. Sam tried not to compare the wall clock to her watch, not to fidget with the crackers in her pocket or twine her hair around her fingers. She sat calmly, legs crossed at the knee, and it took every ounce of restraint to keep her leg from swinging, a telltale nervous habit.

Across the table from her two men whispered, heads pressed together. There was a chill in the room and Sam gathered her blanket coat around her and shoved her hands in the pockets. Mackenzie and Cerello. It sounded like a law firm. Sam couldn't understand what it was about a position in Internal Affairs that turned a cop into something that more resembled an IRS agent. They scrutinized fellow cops like an IRS agent ripping through the last five years worth of tax returns, looking for that one move of a decimal point, that one forgotten entry, that one little fib.

"Sergeant Casey," Mackenzie started, pushing the button on a tape recorder in the middle of the table, "please state your name for the record." As if testing the system, he gave the date and his and Cerrelo's full names, in a flat monotone voice. He wore narrow square glasses, bifocals, and peered at her over the tops. Thin black straps circling his neck seemed to anchor the glasses to his head.

Already she was stumped. First question and she didn't know whether she should say Samantha Casey or Samantha Mitchell. Slowly, her right leg started to swing.

"Sergeant Samantha Casey," she replied. *So maybe there should be a hyphen in there somewhere*, Sam thought. She just hadn't decided yet.

Jake slipped in through the side door of the adjoining room. It was dark and he could barely make out three other figures. One was Bryant, the Director of Internal Affairs. Another was a woman who Jake guessed to be the department psychologist. And then there was Murphy, face pressed close to the glass.

There were two rows of chairs, as if an execution were taking place on the other side of the room. Sometimes this room was used as training and officers from other departments sat in during interrogations.

Jake leaned against the wall and watched. Sam seemed unusually pale or maybe it was the tinted glass. He had read her statement last night after she went to bed, and had planned on pointing out a few glaring holes, maybe help her polish it up.

Jake wished Sam hadn't left her coat on. It made her look as if she couldn't wait to get out of there. She was bundled up in boots, leggings, and a thick cable knit sweater. Only the guilty are unusually warm. Sam was taking it to extremes, trying to appear so cool she needed layers of clothing to raise her temperature.

It was Mary, Connelley's former secretary now the department's Community Liaison, who had called Jake to tell him about Sam's meeting with I.A. If he had his way, he would never have let Sam go in there without an attorney.

Sam had given them too much to digest in one sitting. And she should have protested and not submitted anything until she had one hundred percent of her memory back. And then there were those other little fibs. It was tough to find a professional way to admit to breaking and entering.

Mackenzie tapped his Mont Blanc pen on the pad of paper while Cerello highlighted certain passages in Sam's statement with a yellow marker. Every so often Cerello would press a pudgy finger to his ear.

"Why was Chief Connelley in your Jeep that morning?" Mackenzie's eyes were flat, and he poised his Mont Blanc ready for her response.

"He had been looking for me and didn't find me at home."

"Why didn't he just call you?"

"I didn't have my phone with me."

"Why was he looking for you?"

This wasn't going to be as easy as she thought. A part of her still didn't want to talk about it and she found herself spitting out the words fast just to get it over with. Connelley had received a call that Sam's life was in danger and he wanted her to leave town.

"Did he say who had told him this?"

"No."

"How was Connelley involved in your father's death?"

"He wasn't."

"He told you that?"

"No. I just knew."

"Why did you leave the Jeep?"

The tempo increased and Sam felt her entire body moving with the rhythm of her leg dancing under the table. "I felt that something was going to happen."

Mackenzie blinked slowly, made another note. "Felt it? Or planned it?"

"What?" Sam watched as the corner of Cerello's mouth twitched, his highlighter continued working overtime. And every so often his partner would glance at the highlighted areas.

Jake moved away from the wall. Murphy was turned sideways, lips lined in a satisfied smile. And as he approached, Jake saw Murphy's lips moving. Then he saw Cerello pressing his finger to an ear piece. He was receiving instructions from Murphy.

"What the hell is going on," Jake demanded.

Murphy turned from the window. "HEY," he called out as Jake stormed out and entered the interrogation room.

"What are you doing?" Logan stood when Jake barged into the room.

"Your line of questioning is off base." Jake grabbed Sam's purse and said, "You're getting out of here."

"I have nothing to hide."

He lifted her bodily from the chair. "You don't talk to them without an attorney present."

"Mitchell." Murphy's voice blared over the intercom. "This is no concern of yours. You have no right to be here."

"I have every right," Jake replied as he hustled Sam to the door. "She's my wife."

"I was doing just fine." Sam tried pulling her arm from Jake's grasp but he held on too tightly.

"You were being set up." Jake steered her toward his car. "Get in the car." He opened the car door.

She watched him hustle around to the driver's side. As usual, he was leaving no room for argument. Making no move to get in, she folded her arms and stood her ground.

He glared at her over the top of the car. "Get in the fuckin' car, NOW."

She barely had time to close the door before he gunned the Riviera out of the parking lot. Then she saw why he was in such a hurry. Three media vans from local newspapers and television stations were pulling into the visitors' parking lot.

The V8 engine roared as Jake made his way down Torrence Avenue. Neither one of them spoke. Sam glanced at his profile, the eyebrows practically touching his top eyelashes, his jaw set.

Turning off Torrence, Jake pulled into a nearby forest preserve where he slammed the car into park. He climbed out of the car and Sam charged out after him.

"What on earth do you think you were doing?" Gravel crunched under her boots and she shaded her eyes from the sunlight.

Jake shoved a cigarette in his mouth and scraped the match with his thumbnail. He regarded her briefly through the cloud of smoke.

Sam watched him pace, the leather trench coat flapping open, one fist shoved into his pocket. Back and forth.

"What were you doing back there? Trying to sabotage my interview?"

He jerked his head around to face her. "Cerello was taking his instructions from Murphy."

"Is that where you were, Jake? In the side room watching everything?"

"Crissake." He balled his fist up and she took a step back. Then he flexed his fingers. In and out his right hand clenched. She half expected him to kick one of the cement barricades. "You left enough gaping holes in your typed statement to fly a damn Concord through." He scuffled through the dried leaves, watched as a forest preserve worker van rolled past.

"You read it?" Sam paced along with him and grabbed his arm. "What? Did you and Murphy discuss it over breakfast?"

He stopped, fixed a wooden glare on her. "I read it off your computer last night. Mary called and told me I.A. was dragging you in this morning."

Her fist grabbed more of his leather coat and she yanked harder. "You had no right."

Jake flicked his cigarette away, grabbed her by her shoulders and literally lifted her off her feet and set her on the rear bumper of his Buick. He jammed a foot on the bumper next to her, his left hand adding pressure to her shoulder.

"Hey." A burly man in a brown forest preserve uniform approached. His eyes regarded Jake's hand on Sam's shoulder. "You okay lady?"

"Get the fuck out of here." Jake straightened, jammed a hand in his pocket and pulled out his shield. "Everything's fine."

The man's eyes caught a glimpse of Jake's gun belt, shifted his eyes to Sam.

"It's okay," she assured him.

The man strolled back to his van.

Jake lit another cigarette, leaned an arm on his bent knee, and got up close to her. Sam could see the steel glint in his eyes, smell the tobacco on his breath.

"Do you have the slightest clue what was happening to you in there?" Jake said.

She tried to force her eyes away from him, tried to focus on the sun slicing through the dark shadows in the woods behind him. But her gaze drifted back to his face, the concern behind his cold eyes, and thought back to the ambush at Headquarters.

"I didn't think they would start to ask questions today."

"Sam, they didn't even ask you about the warehouse or Stu Richards. They could care less. Don't you get it?"

She blinked back tears, her mind trying to decipher too many conflicting issues. "If there were holes in my statement it's because I don't have one hundred percent of my memory back. I thought they were going to wait until Doctor Talbot released his report."

"Sam." His hand moved from her shoulder to her neck, the anger was gone from his face. Compassion softened his eyes. "Aren't you even curious why they didn't focus on Stu Richards?" When she couldn't provide an answer, Jake said, "Why bring up the death of a rookie cop when they can implicate you in Chief Connelley's death?"

14

Everything seemed so surreal and Sam felt numb as the elevator doors opened up onto the fourth floor at the Sixth Precinct. Jake no sooner parked her in his office and got her a cup of tea, then Captain Robinson requested a meeting with him regarding the situation with Murphy and Internal Affairs.

Sam closed the door and hung her coat on the hook. Cradling her cup of tea, she studied what had once been her office. The desk had been moved from the wall by the door to the center of the room close to the windows where Jake could turn his back to the door, prop his feet on the sill, and catch a glimpse of the outside world.

The walls were barren of homey pictures or award plaques. Just a peg board on the wall by the door and a plexi-board on the opposite wall. He had moved the three-drawer filing cabinets against the plate glass windows. She stared out of those windows to the outer office. Desks were cluttered with paper and empty coffee cups. It was an area where you knew people were too busy to worry about such mundane things as straightening up. Not like Headquarters, which was constantly primped for the press and politicians. But the office was quiet today. No keyboards clacking or file drawers closing. No voices on urgent phone calls. All eyes were on her. She guessed it wouldn't take long for the episode with I.A. to sift through the ranks. What she wanted to do was go home and have a good cry, an all out crying jag. That was the only thing she felt could relieve the pressure building in her chest. Turning the wands on the blinds, she shut out the curious stares.

Patting the pocket of her tunic sweater, she withdrew a packet of crackers. Three days. That's all it took. Three days since she came home and already she had managed to make an absolute mess of her life.

She fingered the file folders on the desk. None were on the homicide at the casino boat. There weren't any notes or pictures pinned to the plexi-board and she wondered where he was hiding them all. The rubber ball Jake found so therapeutic was lying against the IN box. She half expected to open the desk drawers and see them stuffed with more of the stress relievers.

Turning from the desk, she touched the heart-shaped leaves of the Rosary Vine spilling over the inside sill and the purple petals of the African violet. All the plants were colorful and flourishing. "Traitors," she whispered. When she had this office all they did was curl up and turn brown.

The door opened and Frank Travis poked his head in. "Gotta minute, Sam?"

She nodded and he entered carrying a large mug of coffee.

He smiled broadly, but it seemed forced somehow. His eyes didn't light up or maybe it was in the way he said her name. There was more beef to his frame, as if he had done some major body building. His neck seemed thicker, shoulders broader.

Frank shut the door and sat down behind the desk.

She watched him move file folders aside, then clasp his hands on the desk. She lowered herself into the chair. Her gaze immediately rested on his shaved head and dusting of a mustache and partial beard. "You've lost a little hair."

Frank patted his head. "Like that? I'm going for the Michael Jordan look." His fingers scraped the stubble around his mouth.

"This comes in handy for filing my nails."

The smile was forced again, revealing a mouth full of stark white teeth against his dark skin. Several months ago Frank would have added his patented rolling laugh, the one that starts at the base of his stomach and keeps building, bringing a twinkle to his eyes, and a smile to anyone within earshot. But Sam heard no hint of that today.

Frank said, "I heard about the deal with I.A. Sorry about that."

All business. No *how's your mother? Nice to see you're home.* "What's this about, Frank?"

He glared, his teeth working on the inside of his mouth, chewing, nibbling. Gone was the smiling jokester.

"I'm sure you had your reasons but I sure as hell don't understand how you could have treated Jake the way you did."

Sam leaned forward. "The way I...?"

"Let me finish." He enunciated each word slowly and waited while she settled back in the seat. "Jake is the closest thing to a brother I have. I respect him. He's probably the best cop I've ever worked with."

Sam inhaled long and deep, trying to quiet her stomach. And she wasn't in the mood for a lecture. "This doesn't involve you."

"Oh, yes it does. He doesn't love easily and to shut him out the way you did just tore him apart."

"I see." She ripped into the plastic spraying cracker crumbs on her sweater. "You respect the fact that he was Murphy's spy and that he kept information from me about my father's death."

"Jeez." He pushed away from the desk and stood up. "Jake was right, you are stubborn as hell." He walked around to where she sat and leaned against the desk. "Take it from me, Sam. I've been married long enough to know you have to talk things out. There are a lot of things you don't know and it's not my place to tell you."

She bit into a cracker, her eyes drifting to the rubber ball on the desk. "One thing I don't understand is why Jake has that stupid rubber ball."

Frank reached behind him and picked it up. "This?" He bounced the ball in his hand, squeezed it. "If you took the time to talk, Sam, you would have found out this is therapy." He squeezed the ball several times. "We weren't too far behind you when we got the call that there was an explosion."

Sam knew he was talking about her Jeep, the bomb that exploded sending debris and Chief Connelley's body sailing over a three-square-block area.

Frank continued. "And when Jake realized there was nothing either of us could do to save you," he tossed the ball back on the desk, watched it roll to an empty coffee cup, then lazily settle against the IN box. "Well, Jake pounded his fist into a nearby brick building. Broke seven bones in his hand."

Sam stopped chewing, the crackers tasting a lot like gravel, and she helped them down with a sip of her lukewarm tea. She blinked away tears and wondered why Abby had never mentioned the broken hand to her.

"Jake and I may have been partners for seven years, but I really can't boast knowing everything about the guy. He's very private, drifted from one woman to the next. I think two years, off and on, might have been the longest he was with any one. Never heard the word love cross his lips. But I did see a change come over him after he met you." A warm smile spread across Frank's face and light flickered behind his dark eyes. "You drove him crazy. You two were like oil and water." Then the light went out, his mood darkened. "The last couple months have been hell. He wasn't sure how things would be between you two so he never told anyone 'cept me and Carl that you two were married. He asked to move in with me until he found a place. Jake's pretty portable, you know." Picking up a carafe from the desk, he poured himself a glass of water, took a long swallow. "Yeah, with Jake, it's just clothes and toiletries. He doesn't haul furniture around. That's the FBI indoctrination again.

Be ready to leave at a moment's notice.

"Didn't you ever ask yourself, Sam, why someone as professional and stick-to-the-rules as Jake, would suddenly start slacking off, dress slovenly, have an I-don't-care attitude?"

"He was trying to piss off Murphy."

"Oh?" Frank's eyebrows lifted. "Really?"

"And what was his constant drinking? Trying to get recruited for AA?" Sam countered.

"He likes his beer, maybe a little more than the next guy. But to drink it in the parking lot, where it would get back to Murphy? Gee, wonder what that was about?" His head bobbed, a proverbial professor coaxing responses from the class. "You weren't around to see Jake when he first got into Homicide. And you weren't around when Murphy got here, to witness the subtle change in Jake. Ask yourself." The professor finger went up. Frank walked back around and sat at the desk. "Ask yourself, Sam. Was Jake trying to piss off Murphy? Or attract him? Gain his trust? Let himself be used?"

He was right. Sam hadn't known Jake before her transfer to the Sixth. Murphy wasn't the cleanest cop but was crafty, knew how to cover his tracks. Did someone else suspect Murphy of some shady dealings?

"You're a smart lady, Sam." Frank's finger tapped his temple. "Use your head. Jake is more Carl than Murphy any day. So, who exactly was pulling Jake's strings?"

She felt her chest tightening, the proverbial knife twisting in her heart. Had Jake been trying to help her all along? And if so, under whose orders? Murphy wouldn't garner any interest from the FBI. So the only one who would ask for his help would be the former chief of police...the dead-and-gone, can't-substantiate-the-story Connelley.

Jake appeared in the doorway. His eyes cold, distant.

"Robinson pissed?" Frank asked as he moved past.

"He's cool." Jake handed Frank a set of keys. "Would you get someone to go with you to pick up Sam's Jeep at Headquarters?"

"No problem." To Sam, Frank said, "Take care."

Jake closed the door once Frank left. He had a file folder in his hand and set it on the table.

"I would suggest you find yourself a good lawyer," Jake said as he slipped out of his sportscoat and sat down behind the desk. "You don't talk to the press, you don't issue any other statements. The subject of Richards and Connelley should be off limits to everyone." His glare was stifling and she understood how suspects cowered when he walked in a room.

"I don't need a lawyer." Tears of anger pushed at the corners and Sam pulled another packet of crackers from her pocket.

He leaned back, pulled an ankle across one knee, and opened the file folder. "I have my report here on the Stu Richards case but I'd like to hear your version."

She tried not to be interested, tried to pull her eyes from the folder but she was curious. "You already read my statement." Her gaze darted from his face back to the folder.

"Your own words, Sam," he repeated, leaning back further in his chair.

She wrapped her hands around the cup and took a sip. "Those are my own words. Everything happened just the way I wrote it. Stu Richards was already dead when I got there."

"They will ask where you went afterward. Your statement says you went home."

For some reason, Sam had hoped everything would have been solved, case closed, by the time she returned and she wouldn't have to relive every single second.

"Did you have to give a statement?" she asked.

"No."

"And if you had been asked?"

"I would have told the truth. You were with me."

Of course he would have, Sam thought. He wouldn't bend a rule if it saved his soul. Which was what Abby thought was such a redeeming quality about him. Probably felt he would keep her on the straight and narrow.

"I wasn't sure what you were going to say." It was a weak excuse but the only thing she could come up with. She studied her cup of tea. It was lukewarm now and getting colder by the second.

"You knew exactly what I would say." Jake waited, eyes unblinking. And he was good at the waiting game. "I.A. is going to look at one lie and assume there are more."

Sam expected him to say, "Were you that ashamed? Embarrassed you had spent the night with me?" But he didn't. He just shoved the folder at her.

"You'll have to read it here. I can't let it out of the office. And when you're done, it will go to Frank. He'll be the primary."

"Why?"

"Murphy didn't like the idea that I never informed him we were married. Conflict of interest. I should have never been the primary. Which should suit you just fine since you feel I have derailed the investigation since the beginning."

He was twisting the knife and she didn't like it. She wanted to scream, throw the folder back at him. But she was tired of arguing and didn't feel she had the strength to throw anything.

Slowly, she opened the folder. Everything was detailed with a check list. The Crime Lab report revealed only one set of prints on her gun...hers. Ballistics proved the bullets retrieved from the deceased were fired from the Glock 9mm left at the scene...her gun. Benny's autopsy report stated Officer Richards had been shot three times. He had also suffered a broken neck but it was inconclusive how he had received it. Crime scene photos were graphic and in full color. Portions of the body had burned prior to the Fire Department's arrival.

She closed her eyes against the horror and felt her hands

tremble. The folder slid from her grasp and she opened her eyes to find that Jake had pulled it from her hands.

"Well, that was thorough," she said.

"Considering how little we had to go on. It would have helped if you had talked to us the moment you started to remember." He jammed an elbow on the armrest and a fist under his chin.

"Doctor Talbot thought it best that I wait until I had one-hundred-percent of my memory back."

"Not according to Doctor Talbot. He thought it was a good idea that you talk about it, but you were the one who was refusing visitors. You let your personal feelings interfere with a murder investigation. Now too much time has elapsed which makes I.A. and the press suspicious. As usual, you've boxed yourself into a damn corner."

"I didn't..." She closed her eyes briefly and looked away, picked at stray threads on her sweater. She didn't have a clue how she was going to get out of this one. One thing Chief Connelley had always been good at was damage control. It was an effort for her to keep her voice from cracking as she whispered, "I didn't kill him."

"I believe you, Sam. But they will try to build a case that if you didn't remember events after Richards was killed, how can they be sure you remembered things exactly as they happened?"

He believed her. The words were unexpected and reverberated in her head. And what really scared her is that it sounded sincere and there were no little voices in her head screaming, *LIAR*.

"Did he have...?" She wasn't sure she wanted to know and now wished she hadn't started to ask.

"He had a wife and she's pregnant."

Her gaze dropped to her hands and she prayed the tears wouldn't start funneling down her cheeks. A part of her wanted him to walk around the desk and wrap a strong arm around her. How clever of Abby. Sam was in desperate need of consoling but she had no one to turn to but Jake. And he was keeping his distance. The tears defied what little willpower she had and Jake pushed a box of tissues across the desk. Sam stared at the box and then at Jake who was looking as unconcerned and detached as the two I.A. officers.

Swiping at the tears with the palms of her hands, she stood and walked over to the windows. The room was getting warm and strange spots were bouncing in front of her eyes. Fresh air was streaming in from the window and she inhaled to calm her stomach and dry up the tears. The outside sill was cracked and pitted and Sam suddenly realized something was missing.

"Where are Tonto and Cochise?" When she had the office, she had fed the two mourning doves sunflower seeds daily. She would talk to them in Lakota and they seemed to understand.

He swiveled his chair toward the window. "They never came back after..." He stared at her but dropped his gaze and turned back to his desk. "At least the window sill is clean now."

Another change, too many for her to hope things could ever be back to normal. Returning to the chair, Sam asked, "Did you check the glass for fingerprints?" Retrieving another packet of crackers, she tore into it, adding to the pile of scraps on the desk.

"It's in the lab."

"Any leads on the murder?"

He regarded her with a shrug. "No need to be concerned."

Shut out again. She was an outsider now, just like other spouses who had no choice but to sit by while their husband or wife discussed cases with only other cops.

Jake eyed the crackers. "Are you sure you're feeling all right?"

"Yes. Why?" She followed his gaze to the crumbs and wrappings littering the desk. "You have your cigarettes. I have my crackers." She scraped the debris into the wastebasket on the side of the desk and returned her attention to the report. "What about satellite?"

"Satellite?" His eyes suddenly softened, then twinkled, amusement turning up the corners. "This isn't *Enemy of the State*, Sam."

"Well, that's exactly how I feel." Sam didn't know why she hadn't noticed it before but Jake was wearing a ring on his left hand. It looked like Alex's handiwork. The gold band was inlaid with coral and turquoise. Definitely looked like a wedding band to her. Another small detail Abby and Alex both neglected to tell her.

"Weren't there any deals you could have offered Hilliard? Would it help if I talked to him?" Sam asked. "I would be willing to wear a wire."

All he did was stare and she realized she had reached a dead end. Hilliard wasn't budging from his original story, that he had no part in any of the deaths, and that he never met Valenzio.

"Excuse me." Sam made a hasty retreat to the restroom. Ten minutes later, looking pasty white and relieved of all stomach contents, she returned to Jake's office. He stood at the window, eyebrows hunched together, worry lines creasing his forehead.

"You were gone so long, I sent Janet looking for you. She said you were sick."

"I'll be fine. I just need to go home." She blew her nose and checked her reflection in a mirror behind the door. Dabbing at the black smudges under her eyes, she was glad she had gotten into the habit of carrying toothpaste and a toothbrush.

He held her coat for her. "Did Doctor Talbot give you medication that doesn't agree with you?"

"I refused to take any drugs." Jamming her arms into the sleeves, she repeated, "I'll be fine." *In about six months.*

15

Instead of going home and resting, Sam felt she needed cheering up and decided to search for the store Lea had told her about. Spoil 'em Silly was located on a tree-lined street leading into the town square in nearby Crown Point, Indiana. The directions she had been given were easy enough to follow. She parked in the side lot next to a van with a collection of Beanie Babies® crammed on the dashboard.

"This must be the place." She tried not to decipher why the prospect of shopping in a children's store was exhilarating. Only shopping for a new Sig Sauer or Colt .9mm would ordinarily give her this kind of a rush.

She looked up at the freshly painted two-story house. Stairs creaked as she walked up to the porch. The house resembled a scaled-down version of a Georgia plantation mansion, and Sam half expected to see someone's grandmother whiling the time on a porch swing.

She maneuvered her way around a young woman with packages at the front door. In the foyer she had to make a quick decision between the stairs in front of her or the room to the left. She decided to stay on the main floor and sidestepped several shoppers at the cash register.

Lea was right. The main room led to others, and they were stocked with every imaginable toy a child could want. The rooms were decorated in primary colors and the shelves were neat and tidy. Sam would have almost missed the Beanie Babies® if it weren't for a little voice that said, "Look Mommy. It's Cheeks."

Cheeks™ was a baboon with a colorful bottom and face. Sam picked up a small shopping basket and started to grab what she could. If the little girl had been in front of her, Sam would have bowled her over.

"Sweetheart," the young mother said, "we just bought you two animals yesterday. You know your father said no more than two a week."

"Nooooo." Big brown eyes filled under a crooked line of bangs as the little girl proceeded to cry and throw herself on the floor screaming.

Embarrassed, the young mother picked her daughter up from the floor and gave Sam an apologetic smile. "I swear, if I ever meet *Mr. Beanie* in the flesh, I'm going to tie him to the bumper of my car and drag his hapless body for five miles." She placed her purchases on the counter while trying to hold her kicking daughter with the other arm. She told the sales clerk, "I'm sorry. I'll have to come back another day for these when I can shop by myself."

The screaming and crying could be heard even after the mother slammed the car doors. Sam wondered if she were up to this. Is that what children do when they shop? She couldn't remember ever acting that way.

She saw another Gobbles™ the turkey on the shelf and even though Abby already had one at home, Sam thought it would be cute to have several out for Thanksgiving decorations. Then she heard a small voice next to her.

"Is that the last Gobbles?" A little boy with carrot-orange hair and freckles tugged on her sleeve. "Do you see any more turkeys?" He stood on his tiptoes and tried to see the shelf where Sam had found the turkey.

Sam wanted to say, "Nope, you lose." Instead, she handed him the bean-stuffed animal. "Here, I already have one at home."

The little boy was all smiles as he ran to find his mother.

The basket was a tangle of bean-stuffed animals. Sam wove her way around the displays to the stairs. They creaked under her weight and made an abrupt ninety-degree turn at the top.

Each of the rooms had something different to offer. In one she found a menagerie of crib bedding, bumper pads, lamps, quilts, and mobiles. She spent ten minutes looking at mobiles and selected one with pelicans sporting red bow ties. Lea had said babies are drawn mainly to red and black in the early months.

The next room held christening gowns in flowing chiffon and trimmed in eyelet lace. Even the windows in the room were draped in white eyelet. On top of the dresser were the smallest socks Sam had ever seen. Picking up a pair, she sank down onto a toy chest and set the basket of Beanie Babies® on the floor.

"My god," she whispered. Her fingers traced the tiny stockings, which couldn't have been more than two-and-a-half inches long. "I can't imagine a being this little!" She touched a tiny nightshirt with the fold-over cuffs that kept a baby from scratching itself. As she realized a small creation would be dependent on her, everything became overwhelming. Sam started to cry. She laid the stockings in her lap and let the tears fall.

"Your first?" An attractive woman in a Dorothy Hamill haircut and a name badge that said *PATTI* stood in the doorway. She handed Sam a tissue and took a seat next to her. Her eyes looked even more expressive behind her large-framed glasses. "I remember when I had my first. No matter how small these clothes look, they grow out of them in a blink of an eye. You can't believe how quick."

"Really?" Sam sniffled. She noticed immediately Patti's flawless complexion, and Sam's fingers automatically felt for the bumps on her own face.

"Don't worry," Patti said, seeing the bumps Sam was trying to conceal. "My face was a mess during my pregnancy."

A girl about four years old came running into the room. "Mommy, I want to go now." Her hair was pulled back with kitty cat barrettes and she wore a sweater with cats on the front.

"Okay, sweetie. In a minute." Patti turned back to Sam. "Believe me, by your second or third, everything is old hat."

"Second or third?" Sam mumbled.

A boy about five in blue jeans and a Superman sweatshirt came running in next. "Mommy, Kelly won't share her candy."

"You tell her that everyone gets one piece. And if she can't share, then I'll take all of the candy." The boy scurried out of the room repeating what his mother had said.

"I don't know if I'm ready for this." Sam placed the socks back on the dresser.

"You don't have much of a choice now. So you might as well sit back and enjoy."

"Enjoy? Did you have morning sickness?"

Patti laughed, breaking out in a wide smile, revealing the most perfect set of teeth Sam had ever seen. Peaches and cream complexion, calm and together, a figure that seemed to have snapped back as if it were shrink-wrapped. Sam was beginning to hate her.

"It got to be a game. I knew what time to eat my favorite foods so I wouldn't give them back." Patti smiled at the thought. "But I didn't have morning sickness with my third."

"Third?" Now Sam was really beginning to hate her. And Patti spoke as if she had fond memories of morning sickness.

The girl in the cat sweater climbed onto Patti's lap just as the five-year-old boy returned trailed by an older boy and girl. Sam's eyebrows slowly inched up her forehead. There were now four children surrounding Patti.

"Kelly, did you share the candy?"

"Yes." Kelly jumped up and down, her ponytail slapping against her back.

"Settle down." Patti's voice was low and calm, even with the two boys roughhousing. "Go pick up the toys in the playroom. We're going to leave in ten minutes to meet your father for lunch."

That was met with a "yeah" from all four children and they scurried out of the room. Sam leaned back against the dresser feeling completely exhausted.

"Don't tell me all four of those kids are yours."

"Yes." Patti laughed again. Perfect smile, perfect teeth, perfect body. Sam wanted to scratch her perfect skin.

"How do you remain so in control?" Sam ran the tissue under her eyes, wondering how much of a mess she made of her face while Patti Perfect sat as cool as a cucumber.

"Believe me. There's no way I could handle a full-time job let alone part-time. I only stop in a couple of hours a week. I own the store."

Patti Perfect, the one who controls the Beanie Babies®. Sam loved her, loved everything about her. "Lea Lau told me about this store."

"We're done, Mom," Kelly announced, as she whipped her ponytail around the doorframe."

"Okay. Watch your brothers and sisters down the stairs." Patti stood up. Sam joined her, not wanting her to leave just yet.

"Lea is wonderful, one of my best customers."

Sam nodded toward the crib bedding decorated with coyote cubs. "Who can I see about getting this entire display?"

"The whole thing?"

"I need everything. This is my first and I just don't know exactly what's needed."

"I can have Connie help you. This is going to be so much fun." Patti led the way down the stairs.

"You seem to have a little of everything here." Sam smiled and hoped she didn't sound too eager. "I noticed you carry Beanie Babies."

16

A hulk of a man sat hunched over a microscope studying the bills Benny had found on the deceased. Slow and methodical, Wiley Cantu was the best the Treasury Department had to offer. His thick curly hair fit snugly and he punctuated each discovery with grunts and groans.

Carl and Lloyd had stopped by the precinct for just a brief visit but were immediately intrigued with the counterfeit bills. "These are great," Carl said. "Some of the best I've seen."

Lloyd hovered over Wiley, his unlit pipe clanging against his teeth. "Anything yet?"

Wiley raised his head as if unsure of the sound he just heard. Slowly he swiveled his head and stared at Lloyd until Lloyd backed away. The Treasury agent emitted a "hummp" and returned his attention to the microscope. Wiley had set up his mini-lab in one of the conference rooms on the fourth floor. He had brought with him samples of other counterfeit bills for comparison

"We've worked with Wiley before. He usually doesn't talk until he has something to report," Carl pointed out. "His expertise is finding the little logo artists like to put on their artwork."

"Hummp," Wiley snorted in response.

"Here we go." Frank entered and set the three bags of

hamburgers, fries, and beverages on the conference room table.

The men ripped into the bags and listened as Carl and Lloyd talked about the charter fishing trip they had planned. Lloyd's white denim hat decorated with fishing lures rested on the side credenza. Both men were dressed in khakis and pullover sweaters. It was unusual to see Carl dressed in anything but a suit. The retired FBI agent's gaze immediately drifted to the wall where pictures hung. They were pictures of the non-smoking room minutes before the power went out. Names had been placed under most of the passengers within a fifty-foot radius of the Reverend.

Carl looked through the glass at the outer office and asked, "Where's Sam?"

Jake explained Sam's run in with I.A. and how Murphy was going to delay her hearing for four months.

"Pity. Sounds like a lot of politics going on."

Lloyd asked Carl, "This is the psychic you told me about?"

Wiley's head lifted and he regarded the statement with mild curiosity.

Frank rolled his eyes. "Gentlemen, don't use that word psychic. If you ever saw what she does, it's far from a crystal ball."

"She's managed to let her curiosity get the best of her, as usual." Jake explained Murphy's dinner, how Benny had brought Sam to the boat, and the glass she had stolen.

"Where's the glass now?" Lloyd asked.

"Lab is lifting prints as we speak," Jake replied.

"Maybe there was more than one person on the hit," Lloyd suggested.

Frank agreed. "That's what it's looking like. The chief engineer had a look at the videotapes from the employee entrance. The electronics had been tampered with so someone had gained access to the hold." He removed a tape from the VCR and inserted another. "This is the man the chief engineer didn't recognize."

The tape showed a tall man, hair tucked under a cap, wearing sunglasses. Frank hit the PAUSE button, then ZOOM. "As you can tell by the picture on his name tag, this is not Hector Lopez. According to Personnel records, Lopez is about five-and-a-half-feet tall and Hispanic."

"What about the casino owners?" Carl asked.

"Out of town and due back sometime today," Jake replied.

"What about the widow?" Lloyd asked between chews of French fries.

"She's been under sedation. Her doctor said I might be able to talk to her a little later," Frank said. He exchanged tapes again. The screen popped into focus. Audio was not used in surveillance cameras.

"How many monitors do they have in the surveillance room?" Carl asked.

Jake pushed his fries toward the center of the table and unwrapped his second burger, suddenly missing Abby's homemade meals. "There are thirty monitors in the surveillance room, ninety cameras on the boat. So we had two-and-a-half hours of tapes from the main cameras to inspect. Their surveillance team made one tape of just the portions Smith was in. The one we're looking at now is the condensed version."

Frank said, "Usually casinos only use black and white film so the fact that these riverboats are using color is a good indication what kind of profits these guys are hauling in." He pointed toward the screen. "These cameras pan and tilt so he's in and out of our view a number of times. Reverend Smith spent a good hour on this floor so that's what we're focusing on now. Jake and I were just starting to give these babies another goin' over. We can always use two more sets of eyes."

They watched in silence as they ate. On the screen Reverend Smith walked with complete disinterest, sometimes shaking his head at the money being passed across the tables. They focused on the few minutes before and after the lights went out.

"Keep your eyes on the Reverend," Jake said.

Frank played it a second time. "Catch that?"

"Yes, his position changed when the lights came back on," Lloyd said. "No one's going to pull a trigger when the lights are on. He obviously used a suppressor, too."

"That's not all. Watch again." Frank pressed PLAY and then PAUSE.

Jake said, "Look at that purse or satchel he's carrying. Now fast forward." Frank forwarded to the points where the lights came back on and pressed the pause button again. "Now he isn't holding that satchel."

"Did you find one on the floor?" Carl asked.

"No," Jake replied.

Pointing his unlit pipe at the screen, Lloyd said, "So what we need to do now is find someone carrying the satchel after the lights went back on."

The figures on the screen crept along in slow motion as gamblers moved toward the exit door. "There," Lloyd said. The man on the screen had the satchel hanging from his shoulder, both hands around it. He had dark features and a quirky smile like someone who just got away with something. And he was shoving ahead, eager to get off the boat.

"Give that man a ceeegar," Frank said. He walked over to the board and tapped on a picture. "This is our man."

"I was going to take the picture with me when I speak to the owners. Care to come with?" Jake asked Carl and Lloyd. "Frank will take another copy to show the widow."

"Oh no," Lloyd moaned. "Don't go dragging Carl anywhere. Once you get him started, there's no way we are going to make it to Florida."

Carl walked over to one of the pictures on the wall and pointed to the same man seated at a slot machine twenty-five feet from the Reverend just before the lights went out. There was a certain animation that seemed to transform Carl's features, the fever of the hunt. His eyes were intense, totally absorbed. "Our man had his eye on the Reverend for some time."

Jake looked at Lloyd and said, "Too late."

17

The office door flew open and a smiling man with a white shirt, suit pants, red suspenders and a bad haircut said, "There's my girl." Sam smiled and stood up. Jason Coleridge, the family attorney, always brought warm, fuzzy feelings to whomever he came in contact with. "Della," Jason said to the woman behind the desk. "Doesn't our girl look just gorgeous?"

"Absolutely." Della nodded in agreement. Her real name was Dorothy but Jason had affectionately called his secretary of twenty years Della to his Perry Mason.

Jason wasn't quite as rotund as Perry, but his hair was as white as Paul Drake's. With a little padding, he made a great Santa at Christmas.

Sam didn't feel that gorgeous. Not even three months pregnant and her body was already starting to redefine her waistline. She was on her way to do some major clothes shopping when Jason called and asked if she could stop by. Then a call to Directory Assistance had given her the address of Beverly Hills, which was her next destination.

"When do I get to meet this new husband of yours?" Jason asked with a twinkle in his eyes.

Sam hesitated, wondering just how many people her mother had told and how many of them knew she was pregnant. "Soon," she replied as her attorney led her into his office and closed the door.

Three men rose from their seats at the conference table when they saw her.

"I hope you don't mind, Sam," Jason said. "These are clients of mine who had asked me earlier this morning if I knew of a private detective, and I thought of you."

She wanted to say she wasn't a private detective, but then again, she wasn't a cop either.

Jason pulled out a chair for her as he introduced the men. "Harold McFadden, William Borden Sr., and William Borden Jr. The owners of the River Queen Casino."

Efrieda Smith sat on the floral brocade couch next to her daughter, Myla, who held her mother's hand and patted it every so often. Both women were dressed in conservative dark suits. Efrieda's hair was short, stylishly straightened, and speckled with a hint of gray. Her daughter was college-age, or older, Frank thought, with a multitude of beaded corn rows falling past her shoulders and clanging like a wind chime whenever she moved her head. The house was modestly furnished and located in a low-income section of Chasen Heights, near their church.

"I'll try to be as brief as possible," Frank said as he turned a page on his notebook. He pulled a picture out of his suit pocket. "Do either one of you recognize this man?"

The two women studied the picture and shook their heads.

"Your husband was carrying this satchel when he boarded the boat. Have you seen it before?"

The women took another look and shook their heads.

"Has your husband had any threats on his life? Any mysterious phone calls?"

Mrs. Smith wiped her tears with a handkerchief. "Everybody

loved my husband. That's the kind of man he was."

"He must have made some enemies during the demonstrations he organized against river boat gambling," Frank pointed out.

Myla seemed to sit up straighter, a defiant look in her eyes. "He stood behind everything he believed in, Detective. He may have ruffled a few feathers but sometimes that's what WE have to do to be heard."

Frank looked at the expensive watch on Myla's arm, the gold necklaces circling her neck, the gold bangle bracelet on her wrist.

"Does Reverend Smith always carry a lot of money on him?"

Myla and Efreida looked at each other. "What do you mean?" Efreida asked.

"He was carrying fifty thousand dollars."

"Fifty thou ...." Efreida couldn't finish the sentence.

"Where would my father get that kind of money?" Myla challenged.

"That's what I'm asking." Frank studied each of their faces, then asked, "What about the scuffle he had with one of the owners a while back?"

"Mr. Borden shoved my father into a crowd of demonstrators, threatened him, it's all on videotape. Check with any news station, Detective." Myla spit out his title as if it were snake venom. Frank got the distinct impression his occupation was low on her list of respectable jobs.

"That didn't answer my question, Ms. Smith," Frank said in his deep, soft-spoken voice. His gaze was penetrating, never wavering from hers. "Has your father recently received threats? I don't care what happened a year ago."

"We are all living under some threat every day of our lives," she replied, her voice dripping with arrogance.

Frank turned to Mrs. Smith. Dealing with the daughter seemed useless at this point. "I would like permission to see your husband's office. I can get a search warrant if need be, but the less time we waste with needless paperwork, the sooner we'll find your husband's killer."

Myla opened her mouth to obviously protest, but her mother held up her hand and whispered, "Enough. Your father hasn't even had a proper burial yet." She stood up and said, "Follow me, Detective Travis."

William Borden Jr. was a younger version of his father. Sam guessed his age at around thirty-five. He was a mirror image of Robert Redford, which had Sam wondering what she would say if he offered her one million dollars for one night, as Redford had done in the movie *Indecent Proposal.*

William Borden Sr., affectionately referred to as Billy Bob by Jason, owned a string of banks, with his son as CEO. They had used every drop of money and then some to invest in the three-hundred-foot River Queen and its safari-style motif pavilion. Both were family men, although Sam got the distinct impression they shared a roving eye.

Harold McFadden owned the largest trucking company in the Midwest, twelve race horses, and a number of luxury homes in various locations. His cheeks hung past his jawbone as if he had had a recent weight loss. His lips were so thin it looked as though Mother Nature omitted lips from his DNA blueprint, and the hair on his arms and head were a sun bleached strawberry blonde. Freckles were too numerous to count.

"Have you spoken to the police yet?" Sam asked.

"Just got back into town an hour ago," Billy Bob replied. "We talked to our senior shift supervisor late last night and took the first flight home."

"Where were you, if I might ask?"

"My home in Key West," Harold replied. "I invited my partners and their families down for the week. It's the first time either one of them has been away from the casino."

"Listen, Detective." Junior paused for a moment, his voice as smooth as butter. "May I call you Sam?" He smiled that Robert Redford smile again. "We don't need this negative publicity. Someone has died on our boat and we're afraid the police are going to drag their feet."

"We're losing a million dollars every day the police keep our boat closed," Billy Bob explained.

"A million dollars?" Sam echoed.

"But this isn't about money," Mister Smooth Voice piped up. "We are number one in the state, with competition breathing down our necks from over the border in Indiana. We want to eliminate any possibility that our competition is behind this. The press has already speculated that it was a mob hit, thereby insinuating mob connections. They are also replaying the shoving match Reverend Smith had with me on our opening day. And we don't need the Illinois Gaming Board breathing down our necks ready to pull our license."

"What about the threat you supposedly made toward Reverend Smith?" Sam asked.

"He said he would see us rot in hell. I told him we would meet him there. The demonstrators interpreted that as my telling him I was going to kill him."

"When's the last time you saw or spoke to Reverend Smith?"

"On opening day, a year ago," William replied, his eyes twinkling, seeming to follow the outline of her face.

Is he flirting with me? Sam wondered. "What about organized crime? Been contacted by anyone? Do you even break bread with any of them?"

The three men shook their heads.

Sam looked at her list of notes and said, "I guess I have all that I need, other than permission to board the boat and view the crime scene."

"Sure, I'll take you personally," Junior said, smiling.

He IS flirting with me, Sam thought, feeling flattered but uncomfortable. She wondered if it was obvious to the others. Maybe they were used to him. Maybe it was his normal demeanor and she was reading into it. Were her hormones running rampant again?

"In case you need them," William Jr. said, handing her a packet of papers, "I made a list of any employees who have been fired in the last thirty days, companies who have cut business ties with us, and high rollers who have had their credit cut off. Oh, and also the names of the owners of the other boats."

"Thank you," Sam said, taking the papers from him but avoiding those sexy eyes, "although I doubt I will need them." She stood up and placed her notepad in her purse. "Someone arranged for Reverend Smith to be on your boat for some reason unknown at this time. But it didn't have anything to do with your business, your competition, or organized crime." She looked into William's baby blues and said, "I have my own car. I'll meet you at the boat."

Sam started on the observation deck and worked her way down. There had been close to twelve thousand people on the boat during the course of the day and night. Too many for her to isolate any aura from the various floors Reverend Smith had visited.

She rode the elevator down from the third floor. On the elevator's wall was a blueprint of the boat showing escape hatches, the location of the bridge, wheel house, and pilot house, and other words she wasn't familiar with. The diagram also listed what looked like occupations—*1st Mate, Boatswain, Deck Hand.*

Once the door opened onto the second floor, she stepped off and walked directly to the non-smoking room. She sat in the chair Reverend Smith had sat in. He had been nervous that night and definitely did not know his killer. Sam could sense that much. But she also had the distinct impression there was more than one person with his eye on Everett Smith.

Jake, Carl, and Lloyd entered the boat and were met by William Borden Jr.

"I left a message at your office that my father and I were back, Sergeant," William said, thrusting his hand to the three men as Jake made the introductions.

"Did you want to talk here or downtown?" Jake asked.

"My office, if you don't mind," William said smiling. "My father and Mr. McFadden are up there now."

"You can have your lawyer present," Carl said.

"We'll see how it goes, Mr. Underer. We already have a private investigator on the case. She's looking over the crime scene now."

William stayed at the entrance. As they approached the crime scene area, Sam rose from the chair. She asked Jake, "Did you get the fingerprints off the glass yet?"

"What are you doing here?" Jake asked.

"Working," Sam replied. She looked at Carl and said, "Looks like you had to call your old boss for backup already."

"I thought you were keeping her on a short leash," Carl whispered, a twinkle lighting up his eyes.

Jake's brows hunched down. "She obviously gnawed through it." He asked Sam, "Since when do you have a P.I. license?"

Sam gave a curt shrug. "I don't." Although the thought was appealing. "I'm just doing a favor for my attorney. Besides, who said I'm charging a fee?"

Jake watched William's eyes scrutinize Sam's body as she exited the boat.

18

After Jake and his team left for William's office, Sam drove to Beverly Hills and was surprised to discover that it was a lingerie shop. Just what she needed, bras. The store was located in an isolated section of town, not in a major shopping center. It was a large building set back from the main street where strip malls and fast food restaurants flourished. The first thing that struck Sam as odd was that the back parking lot was filled, yet only about five customers were in the store.

The front of the store contained racks of tasteful two-piece silk pajamas, boxer shorts sets, and nightgowns. The back of the store had one wall filled with aromatic potpourri, body lotion, scented bath soaps, and the sexier lingerie—body suits, bras, lace underpants, garter belts, satin briefs, and bustiers. She doubted she would find nursing bras here.

She grabbed five differently styled and sized bras and took them into the dressing room. A voice filled the air, laughter, raucous laughter from one of the other dressing rooms. Sam's ears perked. She recognized that voice. It belonged to Jackie Delaney, a one-time call girl who taught Sam how to dress for her undercover work during her first year on the force.

Jackie had found her sassy neck in a wringer one too many

times, the result of Sam having managed to talk her into being wired for sound in hopes that rich oil sheiks and syndicate bosses would talk in their sleep.

Sam made a quick decision on three bras and exited the dressing room. She selected a couple of two-piece stretch-knit lounging suits and three silk pajama sets. After her purchases were paid and bagged, an attractive black woman walked out of a dressing room. Jackie hadn't changed. A full head of long, black curly hair, smooth caramel-colored skin, makeup picture perfect, and two-inch art deco painted nails that looked more like talons.

Jackie was holding up a one-piece lace teddy with holes where the breasts would be. She was laughing and shaking her head. She wore a short red leather skirt, black boots, and a tight black and red sweater stretched over her massive chest. Sam gazed down at her own black leggings and cable knit top and wondered if fashions had really changed that much since she had been gone. Jackie returned the teddy to the rack, turned, and saw Sam standing six feet away, smiling.

"Oh, no," Jackie said as her eyes widened. "Is that you, Sam?" Whenever Sam was around, Jackie had a tendency to want to turn and run the other way because, inevitably, she got pulled into something life-threatening.

"In the flesh. How have you been?" Sam looked at the rack of teddies. "Buying something for Randolph?"

Jackie's smile vanished. "That two-timing dog? Let's not talk about him. I want to hear about you. I haven't talked to you since that awful news about your father."

Sam forced a smile. The tears came quickly and she looked around the room as she clutched several shopping bags.

"Uh, oh. We need to talk, girlfriend."

They found a restaurant down the street and Sam sank into an isolated booth in a corner of the sparsely occupied room.

"Tell Jackie all about it."

A sob escaped as Sam used a napkin to wipe her eyes and blow her nose. Jackie told the waitress to give them a few minutes. Looking around the room quickly, Sam slid an object out of one of her shopping bags and held it up by one scrawny leg. A fluff of white feathers circled the neck of the bird and beady eyes rested shyly over a tan beak.

"Look," Sam cried.

Jackie held the ostrich up by its wings and studied its features. She set the stuffed animal on the table, its spindly legs dangling limply over the edge. One wing had a heart-shaped tag tied around it that said Beanie Babies®. Inside, the tag identified the animal as Stretch™.

"Aw," Jackie cooed, "is he cute!"

Sam leveled an icy stare at her best friend and growled, "I DON'T DO CUTE!"

Jackie stirred her coffee slowly. "Let me see if I have this straight. Your mother arranged a marriage between you and that gorgeous hunk..."

"NEANDERTHAL."

"Okay, that gorgeous Neanderthal. You just spent over two months in a nut house..."

"REST HOME." Sam spit the words out behind clenched teeth.

"Rest home getting your memory back. You are two-and-a-half months pregnant, the hormones of which are forcing you to buy..." she ran a red-lacquered nail under the ostrich's beak, "...items which you normally would not think of buying. You can't have a hearing to be reinstated in your job for at least four months. Your mother went to the reservation..."

"Abandoned me," Sam corrected as she took another swipe at her nose.

Jackie's eyebrows inched their way up her forehead as she emitted another long sigh. "All right, your mother abandoned you, leaving you with the gorgeous Neanderthal..."

Sam leaned across the table, almost lifting herself off the seat. "Will you quit saying that?"

Jackie pressed her lips together, stifling a laugh. "And now," she tapped the ostrich playfully under the chin, "you are upset because you bought a little stuffed animal."

"Little?" Sam squared her shoulders, reached into her shopping bag and tugged more bean-filled animals from her bag. A brightly colored parrot, bears in a variety of colors, a snail, two rabbits, an owl, and a pink flamingo came flying across the table at Jackie. "Now, what do you call this?"

Jackie held one of the bears in her hand and propped the parrot next to the ostrich. With a sympathetic gaze at her friend, she said, "Smart shopping?"

Jackie sat back, eyes sizing up Sam, nails clicking on the table surface.

Sam finally had her crying fit, sobbing into the napkin, eyes puffy and red. But she must have carried on for too long because Jackie's eyes were narrow slits and the tempo of the tap-tapping was increasing.

"What?" Sam demanded.

"What happened to your backbone, girlfriend? Leave it at that funny farm?"

"I told you..."

"Yeah, yeah. It was a posh retreat." Jackie's hands were waving, fingers rippling. To an onlooker it would seem as though they were engaged in some strange sign language. "What happened to my Sam Casey? They reprogram you over there and send back some limp dishrag?" She motioned to their waitress who was only a few feet away. "'Scuse me, Hon. You seen my friend, Sam? About five-seven, big blue eyes, and a set of balls the size of ...?"

"Okay," Sam sniffled. "I get the picture." She apologized to the waitress with a weak smile.

"You know your problem, Sweetie?" Jackie reached across the table and grabbed Sam's hand. "You are in love." She thrust her hands toward the ceiling in a hallelujah gesture. "You are in love and you hate yourself because it is so much easier to hate, despise, reject, you name it."

Sam chewed on those comments while the waitress set their drinks and lunch in front of them. She stared at the chicken salad stuffed pita, trying to come up with some retaliation.

"You know I'm right, girlfriend." Jackie sipped on her Bloody Mary. "You are just scared. This is all new territory for you." She chased the olive around the inside of her drink and finally stabbed it with the straw. "And that man of yours feels the same way. I've seen the way he looks at you."

"You haven't seen him the past few days."

"Don't matter," Jackie said, another wave of her hands. "He's just got his guard up. Believe me. I know men. You just have to meet him halfway."

Sam checked her reflection in Jackie's compact and dabbed at the smudges under her eyes. She reminded her friend about Jake's betrayal and how she couldn't trust him.

"Old news. Don't go living in the past." Jackie picked up one of the Beanies™ and held it under the arms, danced it on the table. "You concentrate on the future."

Sam still wasn't convinced but she promised to take to heart her friend's comments and they spent the rest of their lunch time talking about babies, decorating, and Jackie's plans for the future.

"What are you doing now?" Sam asked.

"Just hangin' around. I have enough money stashed away so I'm just biding my time til something interesting comes along. I don't need my old line of work any more. Besides, I'm over thirty. These guys want the young babes. They don't have an interest in anyone that don't look like jail bait."

Sam showed Jackie the matchbook saying, "I didn't notice these matchbooks in the store. Why would they advertise this way?"

Jackie threw back her head and laughed. "This isn't for the boutique, Sweetie. This is for the big business in the back of the building."

19

It was close to four o'clock when the call from the Chicago Police Department came in. A gravelly voiced Sergeant Cooper reported that they had a homicide in an apartment near White Sox Park. The victim had a ticket from last night's cruise on the River Queen Casino. Carl and Lloyd asked to tag along and they met up with Frank in the parking lot.

During the ride to Chicago, Frank described his visit with Mrs. Smith and her daughter. "Reverend Smith has made several trips this year to South Africa, and most recently returned from Somalia. They have all been goodwill trips delivering food and clothing donated by parishioners."

Jake explained for Frank's benefit their meeting with the owners of the River Queen.

"They hired Sam?" Frank asked.

"They are just doing damage control," Carl explained. "Everything seems to be pointing to organized crime and they are trying to hang onto their gaming license."

"Did you mention the counterfeit money to the Bordens?" Frank asked.

"No," Jake replied, "but they were a little nervous when Carl asked for some sample fifties and one-hundred-dollar bills to check out. With the IGB sitting right next to their office, they were sweating just a little under the collar."

"So, where are we going and why are we going there?" Frank asked.

Jake explained the phone call from Sergeant Cooper. "The name on the lease is Amid Gustaf."

"How did he die?" Frank heard Lloyd and Carl chuckle from the back seat. Frank jerked his gaze back to Jake. "Am I going to want to know this?"

Jake smiled. "According to Cooper, it seems Amid lost his head."

Frank's body shuddered. "Damn. I knew I didn't want to know."

One of Sam's father's pet projects had been his 1957 Chevy BelAir, apple red with red-and-white interior, 283-cubic-inch, V-8 engine, with wide white walls, baby moon hub caps, and fender skirts. It had only twelve thousand miles on it and had been kept on blocks in their five-car garage.

Needless to say, Sam was surprised to see it parked across the street from the crime scene in Chicago. Abby must have given Jake permission to use it. A classic car worth, what, twenty-five thousand dollars? It took all of Sam's restraint to keep her cool.

Sam's new Jeep was equipped with a police scanner, which is how she heard about the body in the apartment building and its possible connection to the River Queen homicide.

The street was littered with police cars, onlookers, residents, and reporters. She didn't see anyone she recognized to help her gain access to the crime scene.

Painted leaves were dropping quickly in the brisk wind. Although thankful that her cable knit top was long-sleeved, Sam wished she had brought along her blanket coat.

As she slowly weaved her way through the crowd, she caught

sight of Benny's car. She hurried her steps and reached him just before he crossed the street.

"Benny, are you taking over jurisdiction?"

"No, Jake just wanted me to take a peek."

The uniformed officer stopped to look at Benny's identification. Benny read the look in Sam's eyes, shook his head and told the officer, "This is Sergeant Casey with CHPD. She's with me." He mumbled as they signed the crime scene log, "I trust you will save me from your husband's wrath,"

"Don't worry. I can handle Jake."

The only clutter in the apartment was in the form of human bodies. Crime Lab technicians, cops, and detectives moved around the living room while Frank and a Chicago detective interviewed a man in the kitchen.

Other than the sweet, metallic smell of blood in the air, there was no visible evidence in the living room that a crime had been committed.

Several men came out of a room to Sam's right. One motioned for Benny to come into the room. The tingling started at the base of her spine and worked its way up. Every part of the room she walked to, she could sense that he had been here. And it wasn't Amid's aura. It was the man with the tattoo. She shivered at the chill and gathered her arms around her. The telephone and recorder on the coffee table had remnants of fingerprint powder. Prints were visible but Sam wondered if he was clever enough to wear gloves or brazen enough not to wear them. One thing she was certain of...the chill she felt was the cold, detached instincts of a killer.

For the first time a vision of a briefcase popped into her head, or a large purse made of brown leather, something the Reverend had at one time but the man in the bedroom stole. Sparrow had touched it. Was that what Sparrow had been after all along?

She moved over to the doorway but then felt a hand on her arm.

"You don't want to go in there," Jake said.

Carl stood behind him with his hands on his hips. "Jake's right. You don't want to go in there."

Sam gave a laugh, shrugged them off, and entered the room. Benny was standing over the body inspecting the wounds.

"We're getting a photo from the Department of Motor Vehicles," Cal Cooper told Carl and Jake. Jake had expected a large man, slovenly dressed, probably with a wad of tobacco in his cheek. Instead, Cal was barely five-eight, slim, three-piece pin-stripe suit, with an unlit cigar as big as his hand jutting out of the corner of his mouth. "Your partner, Frank, is talking to a neighbor who has tentatively identified the victim as the man in that picture from the casino."

"Good. It could be a big break if we can tie him to the Reverend's death," Carl said, "but then we have the problem as to who killed this yokel."

"Sergeant Mitchell?" A member of the Chicago Crime Lab with *Basila* printed above the left pocket of his jump suit, held two clear plastic bags toward Jake. "These were found on the floor."

Carl looked at the bag. "A wig and beard." He turned to Basila and said, "We'll take this with us."

"Haven't found the victim's head yet?" Jake asked.

"Not in the building," Basila replied. "Our men are checking the dumpsters around the area."

Sam tried to pull her gaze from the victim. But Sparrow's aura was overpowering. This wasn't the first time he had killed and she could feel terror. Sparrow dosed it out in large quantities. Fear had been in the sweat of his victim and Sparrow had shown him no mercy.

The bloodstained walls, sheets drenched in blood, just the horror and gore of it all brought back too many memories of her father's body blown to bits. She tried to focus on the foot of the bed rather than on the headless corpse. Her hands touched the bed between the man's legs. She again glimpsed images of a leather bag. Also something heavy, metal.

Her gaze curiously returned to the body. The victim's left hand was missing three fingers, clearly removed with what she assumed to be a very sharp weapon. Without any warning, she felt her last meal on the rise. And there was Jake, hovering like a mother hen, anticipating that this would be more than she could handle.

She wouldn't be able to use the bathroom. The entire apartment was a crime scene area. Jake ushered her down the back stairs to the alley.

"All I need is air." She pushed opened the door and filled her lungs with air and her head with more pleasant thoughts. Her head was spinning and she felt a strong arm around her waist. Scenes like this had never bothered her in the past, although this was her first decapitation. More than likely, her pregnancy was the culprit. She closed her eyes to the alley littered with broken liquor bottles, used condoms, and urine.

"Maybe next time you'll listen to me."

"Don't lecture me, okay? I have to go back in there."

Jake's strong arm steered her down the sidewalk to the front of the building. "I want you to go home."

"I have a case."

"I don't want you involved and I don't want to have to repeat myself."

His voice was as firm as his grip and in the dim alley light Sam could see he had that damn stern FBI look again. A hot cup of tea and a roaring fire sounded tempting about now so she let him win, this time.

Sam said, "If it helps any, Reverend Smith was carrying a brief-case or bag of some type."

"We already know that from the surveillance tapes. It was a satchel."

Some air just escaped from Sam's balloon. She plodded on. "The guy in the bedroom stole the satchel."

With a grin a little too smug to her liking, Jake replied, "We already know that, too."

She felt her teeth clamp down on the sides of her tongue. She didn't have too many cards left in her deck.

"All right," she conceded. "But sooner or later you're going to need me, Sergeant Mitchell."

20

Davud sat in the whirlpool trying to sober up. He was in deep shit with no where to turn. A call to his bosses in Tehran would mean admitting failure and his sure death. But he had stalled them for two days already. It was close to midnight and he could no longer avoid them. He had sent subtle feelers out during the day but received no word on the whereabouts of the printing plates. It had been almost thirty-six hours since he had found the package at his back door and still no contact from his benefactor.

Yung, his nineteen-year-old bed mate, walked in with a plate of fruit.

"You have a long distance call, Davud."

The call he dreaded. They were looking for an update. He would have to wing it. His strength was that he could lie very convincingly.

"Sorry, I'm late. I have had trouble with my courier. He held out for more money," Davud explained. He listened to the rantings and verbal thrashing he had expected. "I took care of it," Davud said. "He won't be a problem any more." That seemed to please his contact. "I have feelers out now. I'm sure we'll have a buyer, soon. Yes, I'll let you know the offers. I'm sure we can get at least five million for them."

Davud hung up, his face ashen. Yung made him another drink, stripped out of her robe and stepped into the whirlpool. He had to buy himself some time. The thief would contact him first, he was sure. Why not? He was able to find him to leave Amid's head. All he had to do now was wait to see how much the thief wanted.

Yung's head dove for Davud's lap as he leaned back. He reached for his remote control and started channel surfing. He loved Americans. They complain about too much sex on television but think nothing of flooding the air waves with commercials about hemorrhoids, feminine protection products, pills for flatulence, and medicine for loose bowels. He always thought Americans needed a healthy dose of more sex. He watched as Yung's head bobbed up and down in the water. She could hold her breath for two minutes. And that's all the time she would need.

Carl was studying a framed picture on the bookcase in Sam's study when Jake walked in with the box of videotapes. Frank had gone home to catch some much-needed sleep.

"Who's this woman with Samuel Casey?" Carl asked.

Jake set the box on the coffee table and walked over to the bookshelf. Lloyd tossed his fishing hat on the bar, then peered over Carl's shoulder.

"She's Melinda Casey, Samuel's wife."

"Wife?" Lloyd scratched his chin with his pipe. "I thought Abby was Sam's mother."

"Long story," Jake said. "Melinda couldn't have children so Abby became a surrogate mother."

Lloyd meandered down the hall to the exercise room, stepped into the kitchen and looked at the huge dining room. Outdoor lights gave him a hint of the patio outside the kitchen.

"This is one helluva house," Lloyd said as he returned to the study. "Never knew being a newspaper writer was so financially rewarding."

"It's not," Jake replied. "It was Melinda's father who built the house as a wedding gift. It's her side of the family that was loaded. Sam inherited everything when they died."

Carl started to pull videos from the box. "They should call this the Casey Hotel it's so damn big."

Jake sat down on the couch, saying, "Hey, no one told you to stay at that fancy Presidential Towers at two hundred bucks a night."

"At your expense," Lloyd winked, "as a taxpayer."

Jake disappeared into the kitchen and put on a pot of coffee. He set out the cups and returned to the study.

"What have you got?" Carl placed his laptop on the coffee table and switched it on.

Jake flipped open his notepad. "We have two crime syndicate families who were at one time involved in counterfeit bills. Yang Chu is a Korean family widespread in California and the Midwest. They are more into smuggling artwork and sometimes drugs. They might be worth looking into," Jake said. "The other one is the Bartucci family. They closed up shop three years ago and moved their operation to the East Coast. Geno Bartucci, the youngest son, was arrested last year for trying to pass counterfeit bills, but he claimed he got them from the cash station. Bartucci is usually into smuggling diamonds out of Africa, but one never knows these days."

"I know. Everyone is diversifying." Carl looked over at Lloyd. "Do you mind if we delay our trip a little?"

Lloyd pulled a sweatshirt on and patted down the wisps of graying hair. "Already cancelled the flight."

"See, he's better than a secretary."

Jake could feel Carl's intense scrutiny and he met his gaze with a "What?"

"I got the distinct impression things aren't quite in honeymoon mode between you and Sam."

Jake shrugged. "She's been through a lot. There are a few things she can't remember after her ordeal and a few too many things she did remember about me."

"Regrets?"

"Never," Jake replied without hesitation.

"That's all that matters. Don't pass up your chance for happiness. It comes around only once." Carl typed instructions into his laptop computer. "I'm going to see what info we have on the Chu and Bartucci families."

Sam stirred her tea with deliberation, half listening to the conversation taking place in the study. They were focusing only on Amid and the counterfeit money. But she knew there was more to the case. Her man at the bar, the one with the tattoo. He was the key. She could feel it.

Teacup in hand, she glanced down to make sure her leggings and wrinkled, oversized sweatshirt she had napped in were presentable, and made an appearance in the study. The three men sat on the couch, papers strewn out on the coffee table. Jake looked up from the debris.

Sam found it strange to see Carl dressed in casual clothes. He had been an excellent mentor to Jake. Taught him how to hold back, keep everything classified and everyone at a distance. No one was asking about Sparrow. Not even Lloyd, who seemed the most congenial of the three, though maybe it was his unlit pipe that gave him the friendly professor appearance.

Sam gaze darted from Jake to Carl. "It takes a little time but I'm getting it back."

Carl stared. "It?"

"My touch." She smiled. "Thought two-and-a-half-months would make me a little rusty. I'm a little slow on the uptake, but I'm getting it back. If you let me help, you'll be on your flight to Florida in no time."

Carl's smile was fatherly. "Thanks, Sam. We appreciate the offer but it's pretty much wrapped up. Amid was probably killed by a neighbor who thought he had real money on him or his superiors who felt he was no longer needed. Once we have a line on the counterfeiters, Lloyd and I will be out of here."

Sam curled up on the high-backed chair and sipped her tea. "So you did nothing with the glass from the bar?"

"No, Sam." Jake massaged his right hand, clenched and unclenched his fist. "The video tape shows Amid sitting at the bar so that's who you probably picked up on."

Carl said, "I was sorry to hear about your hearing being held up."

"Ummm." Sam sipped her tea. "It's just as well. It gives me time to check things out myself. I had to go to the office to read the case file. Unfortunately," she turned to Jake, "when I tried to access the file here at home on my computer, my password had been changed."

"That's standard procedure, Sam," Jake said.

"Sure." Silence again. Sam drained her tea. "I tried to read the newspaper articles from the shooting and Chief Connelley..." she paused, restrained a nervous laugh, "but I couldn't get past the headlines." She stared into her empty cup and realized she was rambling. Carl's fatherly eyes showed concern. Jake's showed worry. Lloyd wasn't sure how to react. "Well, I guess I'll get another cup of tea."

She no sooner reached the sink then Jake was behind her, placing his hand on hers, pulling the cup away.

"Sit. I'll get it."

She scooted onto the counter stool and watched him place a cup of water in the microwave and fill the coffee carafe from the coffeemaker. He did busy work, filling cups, setting them on a serving tray, his eyes straying every so often to her face.

"It IS standard procedure, Sam."

His voice was low, soft, sounding a little like Doctor Talbot. *Don't agitate the patient* was probably the first lesson Talbot learned in school.

"It's my damn computer and it's in my damn house." Her voice wavered and she clasped her hands to keep them from trembling. "Will you tell me your access code?"

The microwave beeped. He studied her as he placed a tea bag in the cup and set the cup in front of her. Leaning on his elbows, he seemed to scrutinize her face and Sam nervously raked a hand through her unruly hair.

"I'm really worried about you, Sam. You're trying to get back into the swing of things and I don't think you're ready."

"Was that a yes or a no?"

No reply. He dipped the tea bag several times then set the used bag on a saucer. "Do you know you have nightmares?"

Changing the subject, one of his specialties. She took a sip of tea. Yes, she knew she had vivid dreams, but didn't know they bordered on screaming nightmares.

"Sorry. I didn't mean to wake you. I didn't know they were..."

"Do they ever wake you?"

He was making this about her now, clever tactic. He got off the password and the Smith case. "Thanks," she said curtly, "but I already have a shrink."

He stared intently, unblinking. "I don't think he's doing a good job."

Her breath caught. She didn't like the little game of one-upsman-ship they were playing, especially when she was on the receiving end. His words stung, but what hurt most was that she knew he was right. What started out as a quick return home, quiet time with Abby, and a return to work, ended up being a total nightmare with Abby gone, an extended suspension, and murder charges looming over her head. And that didn't even touch on her current condition and marital status. Too much? Jake didn't know the half of it.

She blinked away the tears and left, crossed the dining room to the staircase. It didn't matter that Jake wouldn't give her the new access code. She had another source who could hack into the mainframe anytime she wanted. And as long as Jake and his pals were going to be tight-lipped, she wouldn't share her information about the man with the tattoo or Beverly Hills.

Jackie had told her the business in back of Beverly Hills was a body shop of sorts owned by a man named Davud Menut. For forty dollars per half-hour, a young sexy lady would dance on a table and strip. Clients were supplied with enough cream and tissues for their use. However, they were not allowed to touch the girls. The girls paid rent on their space so were more or less considered renting their own business. If the cops busted the place, only the girl and client were arrested, not Davud. So far, he hadn't had any problems with the cops.

Tomorrow, Jackie would take Sam to Beverly Hills on the pretense of job hunting. Sam smiled as she climbed the staircase to her bedroom. The advertisement on the matchbook now made sense... *Beverly Hills - Where the Customer Always Comes First.*

21

Tuesday morning Sam woke famished with no hint of morning sickness. She showered and dressed and stood at the railing listening for signs of life on the first floor. Nothing. Padding down to the kitchen, she felt like a heavy weight had been lifted from her shoulders. She had spent considerable time last night lying on the upholstered chaise in her room staring out at the stars and just thinking. The answers were within her, Abby had said. Sam's decision had been easier than she thought. And her heart-to-heart talk with Jackie had finally sunk in. She had to concentrate on the present, think first of her health and her baby's health and focus only on Sparrow. She owed her first clients her complete attention. And she was getting pretty fond of P.I. work. It would give her something to do until her hearing. Right now, those were the only things she had control over. The rest would take care of itself.

On the island counter sat a vegetable omelet on a plate covered with plastic wrap. Jake was too thoughtful for his own good and Sam was having a hard time staying mad at him. She zapped the omelet in the microwave and carried it into the study. Jake was gone as well as the box of videotapes. Smiling, she retrieved a tape from the bookcase. While Jake was discussing strategies with Carl and Lloyd last night, Sam had called Tim Miesner, the sixteen-year-old town genius with a Mensa I.Q. He had helped Sam occasionally with computer searches, film development, and other side jobs. Too smart for his own peers, he found his computer more alluring than girls and considered himself a junior James Bond. When she had asked him to also check his computer for someone named Sparrow, she could practically feel his enthusiasm over the phone.

She told Tim she would leave a tape outside in the empty cooler Abby kept on the patio. She needed a copy made and both tapes returned to the cooler by six o'clock this morning. All she needed was the condensed version. She had returned the original to Carl's box, and hid hers in the bookcase. Now with her plate in hand, she popped in her copy of the video and pressed the PLAY button.

She focused only on the bar area and zipped through until she found her man, the one sitting on the same barstool she had sat on when she found the matchbook. He was elderly, wore tinted glasses, tattered jacket. Hands, smooth and well-manicured, played with the matchbook. She pressed the PAUSE button, zoomed in on his face. He never bent his head down as though he could care less if his face were caught on camera. His eyes were distorted behind the glasses but looked blue or gray. Could be using contacts though. Then she recognized the beard and hair. They looked identical to what was found at Amid's apartment.

"Did you sleep well?" The rotund woman asked as Abby entered the kitchen of the tidy three-bedroom house.

"Very well, thank you."

Cora Chasing Hawk had lived on the Eagle Ridge Reservation in South Dakota all of her life. She was Abby's closest friend.

"Isn't it time you called Sam?" Cora fastened the left strap on her bib overalls and ran a quick hand through her short hair.

Abby shook her head as she leaned over Cora's pot of corn chowder. "She needs some time alone with her husband. I will give her a few more days."

"Umm, letting her stew." Cora set the pot of coffee on the wooden table and brought out a plate of fry bread.

They sat at a butcher-block table in the middle of the kitchen. Scatter rugs dotted the floors of Cora's pre-fab house. She was hoping to one day buy wall-to-wall carpeting. The home had been part of a new housing development started five years before and cost thirty-thousand dollars, which was a lot of money on a reservation with close to sixty percent unemployment.

"Your new son-in-law sounds like exactly what Sam needs to keep her in line," Cora said.

Abby smiled. "He is a unique individual." She planned on calling Jake later at the office to see how things were going, mainly to find out how Sam was feeling.

"Tell me about the Council."

Cora replied, "Still a bunch of old biddies, nothing's changed. Those men need more women on that Council."

"You should have run."

Cora waved her hand. "Just what I need. To argue with a bunch of old coots about casino profits. Hell, we don't even have the casino open yet and their eyes are already glossing over adding up their share." Cora studied Abby. "What we need is you, back here, back home."

Abby reached across the table and patted her hand. "I am home."

"You know what I mean, Abigail."

"I make four trips a year. That's about all the Council can stomach of me right now. And tonight's meeting should prove to be a reminder for you."

"Only because you give them hell." Cora let out a cheerful laugh.

"I plan on keeping silent at the meeting. They don't care to hear my opinions anyway. And my place is with Sam. And now with a grandchild coming, there's no way I could ever leave."

Cora sighed. "I know the feeling. I just wish my grandkids weren't so far away." She turned the front page of the local paper toward Abby saying, "Remember Ramon, Colette Zell's son who was missing in Viet Nam?"

Abby glanced over the article concerning the sixty-seven MIAs found. "Oh, no, not Ramon."

"Yes. His body has already been shipped back. Colette is having a giveaway tomorrow in honor of her son." A giveaway was a tribal custom, a traditional rite of expressing the importance of human relationships over material things by giving away items you treasure most.

"Good. I have brought a number of things with me for just such an occasion." Abby checked her watch. "We should start preparing some of the food for tonight."

"Sit, we have time. Now," Cora said with a sly smile, "exactly where does Alex sleep in that big house of yours?"

22

"I thought we were doing this together," Jackie whispered.

"I'm a married woman, and pregnant. I can't be seen on some table stripping for some guy," Sam replied.

"Oh, sure. Now you hide behind your marital status. Any other day, you're denying Jake even exists."

They sat on a leather couch in a small reception area in back of the Beverly Hills boutique. Expensive artwork decorated the walls. The girl behind the desk peered at her under a fringe of Buster Brown bangs.

The entrance was a door off the back parking lot with a black and gold canopy that said *Bev's*. During the ten minutes the girls had been there, six men had come through, called the receptionist by her first name, Holly, and walked through a side door. They looked like businessmen spending their lunch hour doing something they wouldn't want their wives or girlfriends to find out about.

Sam looked toward the opened door after one of the men walked through. There seemed to be a series of doors along the hallway and she could hear the faint sound of music playing.

"I don't believe the things I do for you," Jackie said.

Sam leaned over and read Jackie's application. "Lying a little about your age?"

"What else is new."

"You danced in a bar in Turkey?"

Jackie shrugged. "Well, for a Turkish businessman in Chicago but who's going to check it out?" She swayed over to the desk and handed the application to Holly.

"How soon can you start?"

Jackie smiled. "Sooner the better."

"Of course, you know you have to audition for our owner."

"No problem." Jackie sat back down as Holly disappeared across the hall.

"You don't have to strip all the way, do you?" Sam asked.

"Wouldn't be my first time, Sweetie."

Holly walked in with a short, gray-haired man wearing an expensive-looking suit and a Rolex watch. She introduced him as Mr. Menut. He was rubbing his hands together in gleeful anticipation. Sam felt like a prime piece of sirloin and imagined that the wobble in his one eye was caused from years of trying to look at dancers who were able to swing their breasts in opposite directions.

"Ladies, who is first?" Mr. Menut asked.

Sam flustered and said, "I'm just here for moral support."

Davud ran his eyes down Sam's legs, which extended well beyond the hem of her black wool shorts, and said, "That's a shame."

Under her black and turquoise crop jacket Sam wore a turquoise turtleneck. The more skin covered, the better, Sam had thought while getting dressed this morning. She had wanted to avoid any confusion as to who was applying for the job.

It was Jackie who wore the skin-tight red knit dress with the scooped neckline that exposed her massive cleavage. She had gone back to the store yesterday to buy the teddy with the cutouts and now wore it under her dress.

Sam paced like a nervous father as she heard the music across the hall in Mr. Menut's office.

* * *

Behind the closed door, Jackie had the old man sweating as she bumped and swayed her way through a routine that ended in her stripping out of her red dress and exposing her fifty dollar teddy. She had dark areolas the size of Mason jar lids and had to hold the old man at bay by saying, "I can make you a lot of money, Honey, but nobody touches the merchandise."

She was hired on the spot.

After Jackie left his office, Davud went upstairs to take out his sexual frustrations on Yung.

When he returned to his office, he received the call he had been waiting for.

"I think I have something you want," the voice said.

"Describe it to me."

"First things first," the voice said. "You gave me the wrong information on this man of the cloth."

"Doesn't matter."

"It matters to me," the voice bellowed.

"Now you find religion? Just tell me what you have."

After several moments of silence, the caller replied, "There are two. One says fifty, the other says one hundred. Amid was an example of what happens when someone is not cooperative."

Davud pulled out his top drawer and checked to see if his .357 Magnum was still there. His fist clenched in anger as he pounded the desk.

"I am not a patient man. What are your terms, Mister...?"

"Sparrow will do just fine."

"Mr. Sparrow, you were paid quite handsomely for your work but taking the satchel was not part of the deal."

"I'm not a stupid man, Mr. Menut. You hired someone else to

kill him and were going to set me up for the fall. Now I find out I was paid in counterfeit money."

Counterfeit? Menut's superiors hadn't told him that. Now they leave him to deal with this madman.

"I want my two hundred thousand in legitimate money, for my efforts. Then I want five million dollars for the plates."

"Five million? Are you out of your fuckin' mind?" Davud's bad eye wobbled as he moved his head. "I can't get my hands on that kind of money."

"You have twenty-four hours."

"I need more time."

There was a pause. Then Sparrow said, "Okay. Forty-eight hours. And, Mr. Menut?" Davud didn't reply. He was sure his caller could hear him panting in the phone. "Check your mailbox in case you don't think I'm serious."

Davud rushed to the back door and opened the mailbox. Inside was a brown coin envelope. His hand shook as he pulled it out. He closed the door, cautiously opened the envelope, then jumped back dropping the envelope and its contents on the floor.

"Are you all right, Mr. Menut?" Sam asked.

"Yes, yes." Davud quickly picked up the envelope and the object and hurried to the safety of his office. Leaning against the door, he opened his hand to reveal one of Amid's bloody fingers.

23

Jake leaned back in his chair and watched with surprise as the mourning doves landed on the windowsill. He wasn't even going to attempt to figure out how they knew Sam was back.

He had agreed to let Carl interview Yang Chu and Geno Bartucci. Carl felt the presence of the FBI might get faster results. Wiley had to attend a meeting at his Chicago office but would be back later in the afternoon to continue his inspection of the counterfeit bills.

Jake checked the computer again to see if it had dug up anything on Amid Gustaf other than that he was an Iranian citizen, had a green card, had no known place of employment, and had never filed a tax return. It was anyone's guess what he had done with his time here in the States. The Iranian Embassy even claimed ignorance of Amid's existence.

Jake answered the phone on the first ring and was pleasantly surprised to hear from Abby.

"A friendly voice."

"Oh, Jacob. Is it that bad?"

"Could be better."

"I'm sorry. I hoped you and Sam would be spending some time together."

"We are in a way." He explained the casino murder and how the owners had hired Sam as a private investigator. "We're bumping into each other constantly which is just adding to the strain." Jake filled her in on Murphy's dinner, the meeting with Internal Affairs, and his concern for her mental condition. "She's having nightmares, Abby."

"Sam can handle the strain. She's stronger than you think."

"It's more serious than just gossip, Abby." Jake swiveled the chair and propped his feet up on the desk. He told Abby about the case the department seemed to be building against Sam, the lack of evidence to clear Sam of Stu Richard's murder, and lack of leads.

"She must be frantic. Isn't there anything more that can be done?"

Jake told her how the case was given to Frank but right now the Smith case was taking up most of their time.

"What are her chances, Jake?"

He was silent for a while, mentally calculating the hours already spent on the case which turned up nothing. The rubber ball rolled slightly toward him and he picked it up, squeezed it.

"My," Abby said, "that bad."

"She's not taking it well either."

"I know if anyone can help, you can."

Jake bristled. There was that blind trust again that always bit him in the ass. He was no magician and that's what he would need to be to clear Sam's name.

"What about you, Abby? How's it going?"

"Wonderful. It is great to see friends again, but tonight we have a major meeting and I do have to prepare for it."

Abby promised to keep in touch and Jake hung up feeling like he let her down. It was one thing to admit to Sam that he had hit a brick wall on the Richards' case, but it was another to admit it to Abby.

He tossed the ball down and studied the photos on his desk.

They were snapshots taken from the videotape of the casino, specifically the bar area. One photo in particular was of an elderly man, gray hair and beard, tinted glasses. The hair and beard seemed to match the wig and beard found in Amid's apartment.

Jake walked over to the interrogation room with the one-way mirror to watch Carl interview Yang Chu, a Korean businessman in his fifties whose family of twenty-five had their stubby little hands in everything from jewels to artwork to drug trafficking and extortion.

Mr. Chu's dark hair was slicked back, revealing a well-defined widow's peak. On the table in front of him was a pocket calendar opened to a lined page.

"Anything?" Jake asked Lloyd as they watched Carl in action on the other side of the glass.

"He's claiming no knowledge of Reverend Smith." Lloyd chuckled. "The moment he sat down he started taking notes." They continued to watch and listen to Carl.

Carl asked to see Yang's wallet. Then he looked at his money, and brought up the subject of counterfeit money without letting on about the money they had found on Reverend Smith.

"What about Bartucci?" Jake whispered to Lloyd.

"Same. His money was clean; he knew nothing, knows no one."

"Right. Real church-going people." Jake moved toward the door. "I think I'm going to try something."

Jake walked into the interrogation room, introduced himself, and leaned against a wall while Carl kept his eyes on Yang.

Jake asked Yang, "Ever hear of the name Amid Gustaf?"

Yang bent over his notes. "Mitchell. Is that with one 'L' or two?" He looked up at Jake.

"Two."

Yang continued to write. "And can you spell this Ama Gusta?"

Jake cast a cursory glance toward Carl who shrugged. Jake pulled the notepad from Yang and looked at it. "Close enough." He tossed the pocket calendar back at Yang.

"I know no Arabs." Yang opened the calendar back to the note section.

"Iranian, to be more precise." Jake returned to the wall, arms folded across his chest. "What kind of combat knives do your guys carry these days?" Yang stared at him and leaned back in his chair. "Are they into fifteen-inch combat machetes?"

"I thought the papers said this preacher was shot?"

"But Mr. Gustaf wasn't. We have two homicides here, Mr. Yang, and we believe they are connected. Question is: Do you want to deal with us? Or with the Iranians?"

"I don't know a Gustaf," Yang repeated.

"They like young girls. Maybe you've sold a few and just didn't keep good records. If you think your family has cornered the market on terrorizing, wait til I drop the Yang family name in the Iranian neighborhood."

Yang huffed, sat up straighter and repeated, "I am a reputable businessman. My enemies spread rumors about my selling children to tarnish my reputation. We don't deal with any Middle Eastern factions."

Jake walked over and sat on the edge of the table. He offered Yang a cigarette but he decline. "What about local factions? Have a yen to muscle in on the riverboats? Maybe put a little pressure? Leave a few bodies? Cause some bad publicity until the owners give in?" Jake scratched the match several times til it flared, then dropped the match in the ashtray in the middle of the table.

Yang shook his head. "I have told you everything I know. I even show my good faith by coming here without my attorney. What else do you want?"

"For starters, you can keep your eyes and ears open. Maybe you have a renegade family member into some extracurricular activities you don't know about."

Yang looked insulted. "No one in my family makes a move

without my knowing it. There is honor."

Jake smiled. "Then we won't have a problem, will we?"

Yang leaned forward, eyes on Jake. "If I can help you, will you help my son?"

Jake knew Yang would bring up his son eventually, and that's what he was hoping for. Jayes Chu was nineteen and serving six years for drug trafficking. He unknowingly had set up a buy with undercover DEA officers a year ago. All the highly paid lawyers in Korea couldn't get the younger Chu out of it. It was the first member of Yang's family who had ever made it to prison, and Jayes was not having an easy time of it.

Jake moved off the table and toward the door. "We'll see."

Yang jumped up. "We can deal," he yelled.

Jake pointed a finger at Yang. "You bring me something."

"How long have you been doing this, honey?" Jackie slid into a booth at The Ritz, a garden room restaurant next to Chasen Heights' Ritz Carlton Hotel. It was open and airy, separated from the lobby of the hotel by huge areca palm trees. Yellow potted mums crowded the buffet table which was being restocked by the staff.

Across from Jackie sat a young waif, long straight blonde hair, Bette Davis eyes—what Jackie referred to as carp eyes because they bugged out like a fish—and a Madonna mole above her right lip.

Mandy Hunter lit a cigarette and tossed her Beverly Hills matchbook on the table. "About a year. How about you?"

"I've dealt mainly with private parties, if you know what I mean," Jackie said with a rolling laugh. "Right now, I need a little extra cash. Then I'm thinking of opening up my own business."

"Really?" Mandy's carp eyes got bigger. "Cool. That must be great."

They studied their menus. It was after two in the afternoon but this was when the girls normally got to eat. Prime time at Bev's was between eleven and two o'clock. That was how busy executives spent their lunch hours. And if you wanted to be around for the action, Mandy had said, you learn to eat after two.

The waitress came and they each ordered a grilled chicken salad and coffee.

"What about you? I'm sure you don't want to do this the rest of your life."

"I'm going to be a nurse." Mandy giggled. "Isn't that a trip? I'm going to college now. Work my classes around my gig schedule. I've already paid for two years of school."

"Is that what a lot of the girls do?"

Mandy shook her head. "Too many of them are on something. Just show up to make enough for their next fix. There's a big turnover in this business and Davud doesn't tolerate none of that shit."

"Guess that could be a problem."

Mandy gave a little laugh. "How ironic. Davud doesn't put up with the drug addicts but he doesn't mind a little blackmail."

Jackie's ears perked. "What do you mean?"

Mandy leaned forward, looked around the room, then whispered, "There's one room in particular, the executive suite, that's wired for more than sound."

"You're kidding."

"One girl, Tina, was fired. Word is she stole one of Davud's home videos. Was going to make a little money on the side, you know? Next time we see her, she has a black eye, her arm is in a sling, and she's standing in the unemployment line."

Jackie waited for the waitress to refill their coffee cups. "What kind of home videos could Davud have?"

Mandy smiled and leaned closer. "Think about it. Politicians, bankers, social elite, just oozing in money. Add up two and two."

Like sonar Jackie was aware that someone was staring at them. She leaned back and casually looked to her left to see an extremely handsome man, blonde hair pulled back in a ponytail, pale blue eyes, strong European features. Tall, well built, filled his suit out well. But his eyes were not on either her or Tina. She followed his gaze. He was staring at the matchbook.

24

“Please, gentlemen, have a seat.” Phil Brown, General Manager of the Holiday River Casino, thanked the young girl who left the tray of coffee and cups on the conference table.

The office suite was spacious, burgundy leather and brass decor, hunting scene border wallpaper running just above the half-paneled walls. The scenic view from the picture window was of the Indiana Harbor. In the distance, the Holiday River Casino inched its way to the breakwater and out into Lake Michigan. To the left, masts of sailboats seemed to jut out of the water, and the Chicago skyline was a welcome alternative from the smoke-belching steel mills to the east.

Phil sat down across the conference table from Carl and Jake.

“Nevada Resorts is a consortium of Vegas businessmen that owns Holiday River Casino. Is that correct?” Carl asked.

“Yes,” Phil replied as he poured the coffee. “They make it out here at least twice a year.” Phil studied Carl and then asked, “I’m curious, Mr. Underer, why the FBI would be involved in a local murder.”

“The Gaming Board wants to make sure there aren’t any organized crime connections.” It was a bit of a fib but close enough.

“The newspapers are suggesting some foul play on the part of competition, Mr. Brown. How do you feel about that?" Jake asked.

Phil smiled. "I think the Bordens are really stretching it."

"Your bosses did think they were going to blow the River Queen right out of the water but they've remained on top," Jake said.

"They could care less about the stats. They make most of their money in Vegas. This is just a little side investment. We have no reason to jeopardize any of our competition's businesses. Is that what the Bordens really think?"

Jake played with his wedding band, wondering why he hadn't run into Sam yet today. She seemed to have a habit of following the same leads.

"On the contrary, Mr. Brown," Jake started. "The Borden's are trying everything to diffuse those rumors. It would look bad on the entire industry, they feel, and have even hired a private investigator to prove those rumors wrong."

Carl walked over to the window and gazed out toward the lake, the boats dotting the horizon. From this distance, the murky lake looked as pristine as the waters off one of the Caribbean islands. Turning away from the window, he said, "Tell me, Mr. Brown, have you had problems with any of your accounts? Maybe all of you have something in common, like a pissed-off high roller."

"Nothing," Phil replied. "We deal strictly in cash here. No one is allowed to set up an account."

"Have you had an influx of counterfeit bills lately?" Carl tried to make it sound like a routine question. He returned to the table but didn't sit down.

"We get a few every now and then. More when we first opened but they were all of terrible quality."

"Did you have any run-ins with Reverend Smith?" Jake asked.

The intercom buzzed. Phil walked over to the huge desk and pressed a button. When he finished the call, he apologized, saying, "Wouldn't you know. The press is finally asking for an interview rather than printing innuendo. I have half a mind not to grant them one." He returned to his seat at the table. "Where were we. Yes, Reverend Smith. Fortunately for us, the River Queen was the first boat to open and it caught the brunt of the Reverend's venom. He had pretty much lost his fight by the time we opened."

"Has Reverend Smith ever been on your boat?" Carl asked.

"Not that I know of. Matter of fact, I'm surprised as hell that he even stepped foot on the River Queen."

"Can't you move these cars?" The lady behind the wheel of the Mercedes spewed forth obscenities directed toward the young officer who was trying to direct traffic from a crime scene area.

Ten minutes before, a call had come in to the Sixth Precinct of a dead body in a Salvation Army drop box by the Village Pharmacy. Lieutenant Mick Anderson just happened to be around the corner at Al's Deli having a late lunch.

Mick's tan trench coat flapped open in the autumn air as he fought to fasten the button over his basketball-sized stomach. The crisp air reddened his face as he hurried over to where the Mercedes was parked. Three squad cars and an ambulance had met him at the scene. He was not ready to deal with an irate lady with flaming red hair who wanted to park her vanity car and run into the pharmacy.

Earlier, two workers from the Salvation Army had backed their truck up next to the drop box, unlocked the door, and were just loading the bags of used clothing into the back of the truck when they found IT.

"Who's in charge here?" The woman with the red hair slammed her car door and stood with her hands on her plump hips. "HEY, YOU."

Mick looked over to see a forty-something lady who was trying to look twenty-something. She had stuffed her plump body into red stirrup pants and a red and green sequined sweater. She looked like one of Santa's elves.

Mick waved toward her saying, "Lady, move that car outta there or we'll tow it out."

"I need to pick up my prescription," she yelled back.

"Pick it up later. It ain't goin' nowhere." Mick turned to Detective Andy Branard and said, "Get those guys over to your car and get their statements." Mick caught sight of Benny and yelled, "Over here, Benny."

"I ain't movin', buster. I'll just park my car right here," the lady yelled back.

"Jezzus, I have got to find another line of work," Mick muttered as he stepped around the truck toward the Mercedes. "I'm callin' the tow truck now, lady."

"What the hell could be so damn important? What did you find? A dead cat?"

Mick reached down into the drop box, pulled out Amid's head by the hair and replied, "No, lady. We found a fuckin' head."

The lady gasped and crumpled to the ground.

25

"Shall we play the tape again, Princess?" Sam set the purple bear on the edge of the planter in the middle of the coffee table. Its legs dangled over the edge and its head cocked slightly, black eyes peering curiously. She kissed one of the tiny feet and touched the white flower on its chest. She made a mental note to make another trip to Spoil 'em Silly to get more Beanies™.

The tape hissed as it rewound. Sam had watched the condensed video numerous times and was still puzzled. The man who took the satchel was in the same room as Reverend Smith. From Benny's inspection of the entrance wound, there had been no powder burns. A silencer wouldn't have left much residue. But why did she have the sensation the killer was the man with the tattoo? Maybe he intended to kill him but the other man beat him to it?

The phone rang just as she pressed the PLAY button. It was Jackie. Sam carried her cellular phone to the kitchen and checked on the corn bread baking in the oven. Jackie repeated to Sam her conversation with Mandy.

"How can I get in touch with this Tina?" Sam asked, walking back to the study. She stretched out on the couch and kept one eye on the video. For three hours each day the baby seemed to suck all the energy out of her and it took every ounce of strength to keep her eyes open. Sometimes she just didn't fight it. Since this sounded like it might be a lengthy phone call, Sam pressed the slow motion button on the video recorder.

"I got that one covered, girlfriend," Jackie replied. "I offered to watch the front desk for Holly tomorrow while she takes her morning break. Then I'll take a peek through her files."

"What time will that be?"

"Around ten. Davud likes her to be there during the eleven to two rush."

"Good, I'll meet you."

As Sam listened to Jackie, the video, still on slow motion, lost its picture, which was at the point of the power outage. This was the section of the video that Jake and Carl, and which Sam, too, had been fast-forwarding through since they assumed there wasn't anything to see.

The lights in the casino flickered as the generator kicked in. Then the lights went out again. Sam blinked heavily as she watched. Now in slow motion, a strange light appeared on the screen. It was a red beam, tiny, flashing from the main casino into the room where Reverend Smith sat.

Sam bolted to a sitting position.

"Listen, Jackie, I have to go."

"Sure, thing, Hon."

Sam rewound the tape and played the segment during the power outage in slow motion. She rewound the tape to the segment that showed the main casino, the camera angle from above one of the crap tables. Red beam, laser sighting. What usually couldn't be visible to the naked eye was enhanced by a slow motion film and the smoke and dust motes floating in the room.

She knew the hunch she had the night of the murder was correct. Sparrow was the shooter. Or was supposed to be the shooter. But Amid got in the way and Amid was too close to Smith for Sparrow to take a shot. The tape continued and she watched as

Sparrow trailed Amid out of the casino. Were they working together? She doubted it. Was Sparrow the one who was supposed to take the satchel? Would have been difficult for him to walk over to a dead man to take something off of him. Sparrow would have no way of knowing where the Reverend's body would end up. Maybe at the feet of another gambler. There would have been screams, commotion, security would have been called. And the way Sparrow's eyes had zeroed in on the thief gave her the impression things did not go down the way they were supposed to.

Tim's study was next to his bedroom on the second floor of his parents' four-bedroom house. The walls were papered in Star Trek paraphernalia, James Bond movie posters, and posters of R2-D2 from Star Wars. Royal blue carpeting was littered with scraps of computer paper, which Tim usually cleaned up by the end of the day.

Tim was in an accelerated class at school and found his day over with by one in the afternoon. He did not partake in extracurricular activities. No sports, no debate classes, no band lessons. Just school and his computer.

His father had purchased Tim every on-line communication service available. Tim could access libraries, join in chat rooms, and illegally hack into a number of business and government programs. He had been hired by a few businesses to develop and maintain their Web sites, all fees which would be useful toward paying his college tuition. He had spent his summer taking college courses. That, and the evening courses Sam had talked him into, would enable him to complete college in two years.

Tim read one of his E-mail responses to his search for Sparrow. "Pea brain," Tim muttered as he deleted the obscene response. When a search through the electronic bulletin board proved fruitless, he tried an Instant Message. The message came back that the user was not signed on. That could mean either that Sparrow was not an America Online user or that he was but not signed on at the present time. And there was a third possibility. Sparrow could be the password he used when signing on or signing messages but not necessarily his user name.

Tim said out loud, "Looks like I'll have to unleash RoboSpy." Tim had written a program that was like an information-seeking robot which could search through databases for employment data, arrest reports, even government records. Tim's RoboSpy could not only search the intricate highways of the Internet, but it could also tunnel through the kill files and read any records that were supposedly deleted in search of whatever he asked of it.

He pushed up the sleeves of his sweater, weaved his fingers together, cracked his knuckles, and typed his command. When the command was completed, he went downstairs to eat.

By the time Tim returned, his software program had found hundreds of passwords using Sparrow, but only one person with a password and deleted messages signed by Sparrow. The E-mail address was SPIZELLA@AOL.COM. Tim knew from biology class that Spizella was the genus of several small New World birds, such as the sparrow. His heart quickened. Tim sat down and composed a message to Sparrow.

26

The gavel was loud, pounding several times to silence the fifteen hundred voices in the school auditorium. The Eagle Ridge Reservation was located just east of the Black Hills, southeast of Rapid City, near the South Dakota/Nebraska border. The high school gymnasium was filled to capacity. Additional folding chairs lined the front of the bleachers to accommodate the audience.

The seven Council members sat behind a long table against the back wall where a large blue, white, and black school flag hung. The Council Chairman, Foster Two Bulls, wielded the gavel like a carpenter faced with a stubborn nail. The members were a mix of Stetsons and flannel shirts. Microphones dotted the room and lined the press table where several local reporters and photographers sat.

There were a number of issues that the Chairman and Chief Big Crow disagreed on but the Chief had always respected the fact that the people had spoken when they voted for Foster Two Bulls. And the issue of casino gambling had been a controversial issue since the first hint of a casino on the reservation.

The Eagle Ridge Casino was scheduled to open in six months and the issue of profits was still being debated. Tribal members argued over what to do with the profits: share them among all those currently living on the reservation or use them for economic development. The residents would be voting next week.

"It's a good turnout," Cora said as she gazed around the auditorium, fingers locked around the straps of her bib overalls.

"Yes, it is," Abby agreed, waving at familiar faces as they made their way down to their seats next to Chief Big Crow and his wife, Agnes.

"Why do we always have to sit in front?" Alex grumbled.

"To keep you from napping," Cora countered.

Chief Big Crow hobbled over to greet them, his face as tarnished and weathered as the cane he leaned on. Tired eyes smiled at them from behind thick glasses. A bola dangled from the thick silver conch at his shirt collar.

"Best seats in the house," Chief Big Crow rasped.

Agnes patted the seat next to her and whispered to Abby, "I've got all the goodies." She pointed with a gnarled finger toward the large tin sitting on her lap. Folds of skin sagged under her eyes and her white hair was gathered in a knot at the top of her head. "Do you plan to speak tonight, Abby?"

"They don't listen to me anyway. I am only here to listen." Abby gathered her fringed shawl around her before sitting down.

Alex chuckled. "Right." He leaned to his left where Cora sat. "Ten bucks says Abby is on her feet in ten minutes."

Cora shook her head. "She means it this time. She is only here as an observer."

"Twenty bucks."

"You're on," Cora whispered back.

The gavel pounded again, louder and longer this time. Foster Two Bulls read the minutes from the last meeting then opened the floor for comments. Chief Big Crow hobbled to one of the microphones and waited for silence before speaking.

"You know where I stood on casino gambling," Chief Big Crow started. "I did not feel it was the type of industry we want or should have on our reservation. But I let the people speak. It would bring jobs. It is close to the Black Hills and would draw from the many tourists who come through here. It is close to the interstate. It is a fact of life. Many of you will be starting classes soon to learn the gaming business.

"Now we are fighting over the profits we haven't even seen yet. I have a word of caution. The Hon Payta Tribal Council in Wisconsin, who last year approved the distribution of per capita payments, has had nothing but trouble. Residents who had moved off the reservation are now trying to move back in order to share in the profits. It is pitting brother against brother, father against son. Do you want this to happen here?"

A gentle murmur ran through the crowd as Chief Big Crow returned to his seat. A baby started crying and was soon silenced with a bottle. Latecomers were restricted to standing room only, their faces hidden in the shadows.

From the opposite side of the room, a young woman approached a microphone, her hair pulled back in a long braid. Louise was Foster Two Bulls' daughter. She had attended college off the reserve and returned to teach English at the reservation's high school.

She spoke about honor and loyalty to one's community. "If people choose to leave family and home to live in the white man's world, then they should not be allowed to benefit off of our fortune." A sea of bronzed faces nodded in agreement. More speakers echoed Louise's feelings, talking of independence through casino profits, how they could live more comfortably, live in bigger houses, have luxury cars.

Abby clenched her hands in her lap, the knuckles turning white. She shook her head in utter amazement at the comments. She had heard enough. The moment Abby stood, Alex held out his hand to Cora, palm side up, for payment on their bet.

Abby approached the microphone and waited for the droning murmurs to die down before speaking. She gathered her shawl around her, a striking black and rose-colored fabric which matched her dress. Her jewelry was a walking advertisement of Alex's handiwork—a squash necklace and wide-band bracelets in mother-of-pearl and onyx. She needed no introduction. They knew of her work with President Whittier for the return of the Black Hills to the Sioux and of her appointment to the Bureau of Indian Affairs as a Midwest Representative. Everyone knew *wicasa waken.*

"There is more here than just a question of greed," Abby started. "You would need approval from the Department of Interior to use the profits in any way other than to fund tribal government programs, provide economic development, welfare, and fund operations of local government agencies. What you also don't understand," and this time Abby looked toward Louise, "is that per capita payments would be subject to federal taxation. You are not looking at the big picture. You are only looking at tomorrow."

Now Abby turned and let her gaze fall on the audience as she continued. "Competition is coming closer. There are riverboat casinos in many of the Midwestern states. There won't be a need for people to travel to South Dakota for their gambling.

"Because of our proximity to the Black Hills and the possible, no, probable and ultimate return of the Black Hills to the Lakota, we stand a good chance of having a flourishing business. But we can't look at it as an end to all means.

"Needy families would have to give up any other assistance they currently receive such as general assistance benefits, welfare, food stamps, and Social Security, and possibly end up worse off than before." The audience talked among themselves forcing Chairman Two Bulls to gleefully pound the gavel again.

Abby returned her gaze to Louise. "You, of all people, know how desperately we need a college. Profits should be used to create an economic base on the reservation, for building our own hospital, shopping center, library, nursing home, housing, and recreational facilities."

Louise bristled at being singled out. She looked around the room as she felt her father's position losing ground, then pointed a finger at Abby. "Those are strange comments from someone who does not live here, someone who drove into town with a shiny new van, who doesn't have to worry about where her next meal will be coming from."

Sidney Harris, the youngest of the Council members at forty-four and one who had not yet sided with either position, pulled the microphone from the center of the table. "Abby has been very generous when it comes to contributing to the Native American College Fund and our building fund."

"Sidney," Abby said, then thought best of telling him she could defend herself. Instead, she just shook her head no, not wanting him to cite some laundry list of do-good things she and Sam had done in the past. No matter how much Abby grimaced whenever Samantha took a vocal stand on issues, it was difficult for her to admit sometimes that Sam was just being her mother's daughter.

Abby continued, "I will not apologize for my way of life. I have fared better than many of you mainly because I did not stay on the reservation. But you can do better. Look around you." She paused, letting the congregation follow her gaze. "This high school is in deplorable condition. The pipes freeze in the winter. The bleachers you are sitting on are warped and brittle." Heads bowed, examining the wooden seats. More murmuring. Another crash of the gavel. "Eagle Ridge needs many improvements. Our elderly should not have to go without heat or food. Our children cannot learn in schools that are crumbling around them. And medical care should be available for everyone. I left thirty years ago because of the greed, alcoholism, and lack of tradition. That is what kept me away. But the youth and their eagerness to learn, the elderly who we need to make sure share their history and our customs, and the willingness of some of you to strive for sovereignty and unity, that is what keeps me coming back."

A thunderous applause echoed as many in the audience jumped to their feet. When it died down, Abby added, "Many of you, and you know who you are, care only about where your next drink is coming from, not your next meal. Many of you are more concerned about your next drug buy with little regard for whether your children need medication or clothing. To achieve true sovereignty we must teach people to be self-sufficient, not how to go to the mailbox every month."

Alex leaned toward Cora and whispered, "The more Abby complains about that man on the radio, the more she sounds like a ditto head."

"Many of you," Abby continued, "although somewhat justified, focus too much attention on what non-Indians are naming their sports teams or who they are using as mascots. People are trying to focus your attention away from the more important issues, the relevant issues that determine the future of our tribe.

"When you vote next week, you should think of what is good for the entire community, not just your pocketbook." Abby looked at the Council of seven men who were whispering among themselves. "I also would suggest that the Council appoint members to fill the two vacancies as soon as possible. I would like to nominate Cora Chasing Hawk and Louise Looking Elk. They have strong but diverse opinions. But diverse is good. It lets people see more than one side of an issue. This Council has been male-dominated for too long. We need youth, we need women. Perhaps if they made up their minds tomorrow, the Council can cast aside their old codger ways and bigotry against women. This could be the Council's ultimate giveaway."

The crowd jumped to its feet. The look on Louise's face was shock. Then slowly, she, too, began to applaud.

Abby searched the faces in the crowd as she returned to her seat, feeling good about the positive response. As she sat down, she whispered to Alex, "Was I too preachy?"

Alex ran a thumb and index finger at the corners of his mouth, a sober gesture which served more to halt the smile turning up the corners of his mouth. "Nah," he replied.

Cora asked, "Why Louise? I thought she would be the last person you would recommend. And to serve with me? It's like oil and water."

Abby smiled, patted Cora's arm and replied, "Abraham Lincoln once said something about, *the best way to eliminate an enemy is to make them your friend.*"

27

At five minutes to ten the next morning, Sam was back at Beverly Hills at the pre-arranged time. Tim's computer search had found several inmates using the nickname of Sparrow but they were all still incarcerated. But she was confident Tim's newest hacking software would be successful.

Holly sat at the front desk, the telephone pressed to her ear. She hung up the phone and asked Sam, "May I help you?"

"I'd like to see Jackie," Sam said.

Holly looked at her watch and grabbed her purse saying, "She should be out any minute."

Ten seconds later, Jackie emerged from behind the mystery door wearing a black satin tuxedo jacket that came within a few inches below obscenity.

"Take your time," Jackie said smiling as Holly left on her break. Jackie raked her talons through her dark hair and shook the curl back into it.

Sam studied Jackie's outfit. "You really get into this stuff, don't you."

"I like to make people feel good, what can I say?"

* * *

While Sam and Jackie thumbed through the personnel files in Holly's desk, Yung went through the motions of a sexy dance on a coffee table in Room C. Her eyes were mysterious, her black hair long and shiny. She slithered out of a peach satin dress, taking her time, letting her fingers seductively slide over the fabric.

Her audience was a good-looking man, blonde hair pulled back in a pony tail, pale blue eyes. He was tall with a nice build, good American man. Why can't she find a nice American man?

Yung didn't mind being Davud's lady. He bought her presents, jewelry, made her feel important. She did for him what she had been taught in her youth to do for a man.

"Did you want to touch?" Yung whispered.

The man's eyes were fixed on her naked body. He didn't unzip his zipper. Didn't run his hand across his crotch. For the past twenty minutes he had just watched with those mesmerizing eyes.

"No," he finally answered.

"Just want to watch?"

The man nodded.

Jackie held the personnel file on Tina Kaz in her hands. Sam wrote down the address. The two stood up and tried to look innocent as Yung emerged from the doorway and walked past them muttering something in Filipino.

Jackie nodded toward Jung and whispered, "That's Davud's main squeeze."

Sam winced. "A little young, isn't she?"

"As I said before, girlfriend, men today want jail bait."

They heard the back door close, watched as Jung carried the mail into Davud's office. No more than three minutes later, Yung came running out of Davud's office screaming, "*Daliri, daliri*, Eeeeeyahh, *daliri*."

"What on earth is she screaming about?" Jackie asked as she

and Sam ran into Davud's office. On the desk, next to his stack of mail, was a small brown envelope Jung had just opened. Next to it was a finger.

"I guess we now know what *daliri* means," Jackie said.

Sparrow sat in his car in the back parking lot of Beverly Hills. He had stopped by to drop off another little present for Mr. Menut. He usually didn't frequent such places but every now and then he was curious, curious as to whether or not a woman could ever excite him again. But his libido had been killed long ago.

He leaned back against the headrest and closed his eyes. The newspaper articles about Reverend Everett Smith bothered him. He had never before received false information about a target, always prided himself in relieving the world of a few unimportant scum. But a reverend? Sparrow was not a religious man. Had never been to a church, that he remembered. He had read numerous articles of the TV evangelists who bilked people of their life's savings, but even that crime wasn't worthy of a contract hit. Menut and his bosses had used Reverend Smith just as they had used him.

The headache was almost blinding. Sparrow raked his hands through his hair and pressed tightly against his scalp. The headaches were becoming more frequent. And with the headaches came the flashbacks. Dark rooms, sweat, needles, lightning, the smell of burning flesh.

He opened his eyes and saw her, the woman he observed going through the receptionist's files. Why? Did she know Menut? Did she know about the counterfeit plates? She had cop written all over her. But, god, she looked like Jennifer. Same willowy figure and blue eyes. Who was Jennifer? The pain shot through his head again but he clenched his jaw and fought it.

From the visor above his head he pulled out a pad of paper and pen and wrote down the license plate number of the Jeep.

* * *

Sam hadn't quite figured out the connection yet. Just follow the paper trail is what her head was saying. And the paper trail started with a matchbook and ended at Menut's back door. From there it branched out to Reverend Smith, the satchel and whatever its contents might be, Amid, and an unknown face with a strange name—Sparrow.

The Reverend's mission that night seemed that of a courier. He was to pass off the satchel to who? Amid? Amid seemed to know the lights would be taken care of because he waited for the right time to approach Smith. But Smith could have passed the satchel on to Amid in a darkened parking lot. Why the riverboat casino? Maybe with all the nationalities on board it would be hard for anyone to give the police Amid's description. Maybe it would be easier for him to fade into the background. But now Sparrow had the satchel. A double-cross?

The apartment Sam stood in front of appeared to be a new complex, three stories, six units, in a nice section of town. The way Mandy had described her living conditions to Jackie, Sam had expected Tina to live in a rundown section of town with the rest of the socially addicted.

The door opened and Sam stared into a rather attractive face, if it hadn't been for the bruised cheekbone and half-rings of purple under the left eye. The cast on her right arm stopped just below the elbow. All of the fingers jutting out from the cast were bruised and swollen.

"Miss Kaz?"

Tina nodded while her eyes gazed around Sam's shoulder into the hallway.

"Yes?"

Sam handed a business card to Tina but Tina made no movement to let her in. Sam explained, "I have some questions about your former employer, and I don't think you want me to ask them out here." Tina took a small step to one side and Sam entered.

Tina closed the door. "I have nothing to say." One large suitcase sat in the middle of the living room.

She was a waif of a girl and Sam could see where it would be easy for someone to toss her frail body around. Sam found herself wondering if the ample cleavage pouring out from Tina's sequined bustier was real. Black suede boots kissed the bottom hem of Tina's matching suede mini-skirt. Sam imagined Tina did some major damage to her credit cards especially if she needed money for drugs.

No furniture, television, dining room table. Just wall-to-wall carpeting. Probably the one thing Tina couldn't sell to supply her habit. Sam found herself searching Tina's arms for track marks.

"Going somewhere?" Sam asked.

"On vacation."

Sam slipped out of her blanket coat and searched for a place to lay it. The carpeting seemed clean so she tossed the coat on the floor. She sat down at the window seat and looked out on the yard between the buildings. Tina lived on the third floor and had a somewhat pleasant view of a pond and surrounding weeping willows. She saw Tina surveying her medicine bundle and earrings.

"Nice jewelry," Tina said as she sat down across from her.

Sam asked "On the run?"

Tina nervously lit a cigarette, her hand shaking, her eyes wincing from the pain. "Who sent you? Davud?"

"I'm investigating a murder."

"What makes you think I can help?"

Sam slid off the window seat. "Do you have anything to drink?" She walked into the kitchen and opened the refrigerator. No food. Just condiments, two cans of beer, half a loaf of bread with an unsightly growth on it, and two bottles of orange juice. Sam brought back both bottles of O.J. and handed one to Tina.

Tina's untrusting eyes were yellowed, teary, sunken. Her breathing came in quick spurts. She painfully kneaded her good hand in her lap. Whether the pain was from the broken arm or internal, Sam wasn't sure. She unscrewed the bottle of juice for Tina and wondered if her pain was more internal than external. Especially since Mandy said Tina was a cocaine user.

"Menut is into a lot of things, I think. I was hoping you could fill in a few blanks." Sam opened her wallet and pulled out a stack of greens. That got Tina's attention.

"Knowing too much is what made me a physical wreck," Tina replied, not taking her eyes from the money.

"Whatever you say to me will be in the strictest confidence."

Tina let out a laugh. "Where have I heard that before?" She winced at the pain in her face the laugh had caused. She took a long drag of her cigarette, her gaze riveting back to the money. After a long silence she explained, "Davud has a camera set up in one of the rooms. It's the VIP room, people who he assures the utmost in secrecy. They make reservations under assumed names but Davud knows who they are. He makes it a point to know. They have favorite girls. You see things, pictures in the paper, you know? You just know you're dealing with someone important."

"What did Davud do with these videotapes?"

Tina shrugged. "Kept them in a safe in his office for future reference should he need assistance with politicians. I heard him on the phone one day asking for assistance with a Customs agent. He needed to get something into the States."

"Did he say what?"

Tina shook her head. "Whatever it was, he needed the help of someone who Customs would never suspect. That person was one of Davud's customers. I think he blackmailed him into running this errand for him."

Sam looked at Tina's broken arm. "How do you fit into this picture?"

"I needed money for, you know." She took another drag from her cigarette. "I saw the safe unlocked one day and took the video. Thought I'd get a copy made real quick and do a little blackmailing on the side. But Davud found out, thanks to Yung, that little cocksucker."

"You're lucky he didn't have you killed," Sam said. "Menut runs with a rough crowd."

"Tell me about it." She took another drag and blew the smoke out slowly. "The customer was nice though, you know? I'm not sure I could have gone through with it. As it was, the guy was devastated that Menut was threatening to make the tape public. It would ruin him."

"Exactly who was this customer?" In an act of inspiration, Sam started to slowly count out the money on the cushion between them. Tina's eyes widened as Sam kept counting past three hundred, four hundred, five hundred.

"The preacher," Tina said. "Reverend Everett Smith."

28

The council lodge wasn't as large as the school gymnasium but at least it was larger than the Zell's two bedroom house. Folding chairs had been set up for viewing; long tables had been placed against the wall for food and drinks.

In the back room, a closed casket containing the remains of Ramon Zell, rested against a wall. A framed picture of the deceased in his Army uniform had been placed on top of the casket. The young man was handsome, dark features, full lips. Around the picture his mother had placed Ramon's dog tags. There were few tears. Colette had cried them all when she first heard the news. But all hope had died more than twenty years before. The love for their only child was still there, but the pain and grief had lessened with each passing year.

The room was filling with well-wishers, not mourners, because they all knew this was a time of rejoicing. They came bearing treasures for the giveaway, some with hand-woven blankets, jewelry, pottery, pipes painstakingly carved. One of the tables was filled with cakes, fry bread, cheese, smoked fish, pastries, and punch.

The lodge looked more like a log cabin and had been built by hand by twenty of the tribal members. Rugs and artwork created by some Eagle Ridge artists adorned the walls.

Abby and Alex entered the already crowded room, followed by Cora. Abby looked toward the picture on the casket. She walked over and wrapped her arms around Colette.

"It is better now. His soul has returned home," Colette said smiling.

"Grief knows no boundaries or nationalities. There are many families this week who will grieve with you," Abby said. They stepped away from the door as Colette went to greet more arrivals.

"Did you tell Jake to make sure the lawn service came out to trim the hedges?" Alex asked Abby.

"Yes, I did."

"But not to take more than a third off," Alex clarified.

"Alex, Jake is capable. Trust me." Abby gazed out the window to the lot next door with its junk cars and broken down fence. "See?" she said nodding toward the window. "That is what we need to use the money for." She shook her head. "People show more pride in their possessions when they have hope. They can't find hope in a bottle."

"You are right, Abby," a voice from behind them said.

Abby turned to see Louise Looking Elk. She could be attractive if she smiled more. But she always had a look of someone ready to pick a fight. Today something had changed.

"About what?" Abby asked.

"That." Louise nodded toward the window. "What you said about the casino profits. I thought about it a lot last night. Spoke to my father. You are right. There are many programs we need the money for that would benefit everyone."

Abby nodded slowly, watching as the Council members walked into the room. "How did your father take it?"

She smiled slightly, almost triumphantly. "I think you will be surprised."

Abby motioned for Alex, who came over carrying a large box. Abby sifted through it and then pulled out a piece of felt which she handed to Louise.

"This is for you."

Louise unwrapped the cloth. Inside was a square piece of jewelry containing inlaid coral, onyx, and turquoise. It hung from a leather cord. It was one of Alex's finest pieces.

Louise's eyes lit up. "This is magnificent!"

"Wear it and think of our common struggle."

Louise quickly put it on and hurried to a mirror.

Abby turned to see Cora's face. "Now, stop brooding," she scolded as she handed Cora a box.

Opening the box, Cora said, "For me?" She slipped the leather and coral wristband over her hand.

Abby smiled. "You've been drooling over it for two years, although I'm not sure it will go with your bib overalls."

"Thank you." Cora gave Abby a hug.

It was almost like Christmas in October. Packages and bundles were being exchanged. Food was being consumed. And word soon spread throughout the congregation that the Council would have an announcement later in the day.

29

Lloyd pounded and jerked until he finally managed to pry open two of the windows in the conference room. Because maintenance had not found a way to control the heat, it was a sweltering eighty degrees in the office. Wiley pinched the bridge of his nose and yawned. He shook his head of wirey hair, stood and stretched.

Carl, Jake, and Frank were seated at the adjoining conference table buried in stacks of newspapers from Reverend Smith's demonstration days and printer reports on the Chu and Bartucci families.

"Anything yet, Wiley?" Carl asked as he wiped his neck with his handkerchief.

"These are good," Wiley finally said. "Not quite the paper Crane uses but a good cotton and linen blend," Wiley replied. "Shouldn't be hard to track down once I pinpoint the flaw." Crane and Company had been manufacturing the paper used for currency in the States for more than a hundred years.

Frank opened the door for Janet who was bringing in cold cans of pop. She set them on the table and left. "I don't understand," Frank said. He popped open a can of Pepsi and chugged half of it. "It takes a ballsy person to try to pass off counterfeit money on a casino boat."

"Hey, look at this." Lloyd stood by the monitor where a videotape was playing. He pointed at the man seated at the bar who was wearing what looked like the wig and fake beard found in Amid's apartment. "Isn't this guy seated where Sam picked up that glass she wanted checked for fingerprints?"

Jake sifted through the photos on the table. "We noticed that yesterday. It could be a coincidence but the wig and beard seem to be identical." He grabbed the remote. "And here's something else interesting." Jake pressed REWIND.

The tape whirred and then stopped. The men watched as Amid sat in the same seat prior to the elderly man sitting down. Amid left the bar and strolled over to the non-smoking room, all the time keeping a close eye on Reverend Smith. Soon, the bearded man appeared. He sat in the same seat that Amid had vacated and ordered a drink.

"The guys in the computer lab are working on this picture. They are going to remove the glasses, wig and beard and give the old guy blonde hair and a cap. My bet will be it matches the engineer with the fake I.D."

Carl nodded in agreement, the puzzle pieces falling into place. "Now the question is: Did they know each other?"

"Could you give something to Jake?" Sam placed two envelopes on the counter in front of Sergeant Scofield. Tina had gladly accepted Sam's money. Although she had paid the price for stealing the tape from Davud's safe, what Davud didn't know was that Tina had made an extra copy. Unfortunately, with the Reverend's untimely death, the tape was useless. So Sam had purchased it from her for another five hundred dollars.

"Why don't you take it in yourself?" Scofield nodded toward one of the conference rooms.

"That's okay." She tucked a note in one of the envelopes and wrote *OPEN FIRST* on the larger of the two.

* * *

"Did she leave?" Jake asked as Ed handed him the envelopes.

"Had some place to go, I guess," Ed replied.

Once Ed left, Jake ripped open the first envelope. Enclosed was a videotape and a note that read:

Let me know if you need
my help.

S

"What is it?" Frank asked.

"I'm not sure, but we're about to find out." Jake popped the video in the recorder and pressed PLAY.

"What the hell...?" Frank mouthed as Reverend Smith came into focus. The men groped for chairs while Wiley scooted his chair back for a closer look.

On the screen a young girl slowly stripped while speaking in a sexy voice to the Reverend who was mesmerized. The good Reverend fumbled with his belt buckle, then his zipper. When he started to have carnal knowledge of his body, Frank said, "Shut it off." He grabbed the remote control and pressed the STOP button.

"Where did Sam get this?" Carl asked.

"I'm not sure." Jake opened the second envelope and tipped the contents out on the table. Wiley and Frank jumped back as Amid's finger thumped on the table. "Jezzus."

"I want that young lady back here NOW." Carl pounded his fist on the table.

Jake dialed Sam's cellular number but wasn't surprised that all he received was the recorded message. She hadn't been leaving her phone on lately. He picked up the receiver on the wall and called Ed.

"Have a car follow Sam's Jeep and report back," Jake ordered.

* * *

Jake had to weave his way through one hundred demonstrators in the parking lot of the River Queen Casino. At the head of the pack was Myla Smith, Reverend Smith's daughter. Cameras were rolling as she chastised the casino for murdering her father. The demonstration didn't stop the customers from entering the casino.

As he followed the gamblers, Jake called Frank on his cellular phone and told him about Myla. Frank was on his way.

The pavilion lobby was crammed with people, some lined up for the inexpensive buffet, some making their way to the off track betting parlor, others gawking at the items in the gift shop window.

It hadn't taken long for the beat cop to report that Sam was headed toward the River Queen Casino. Jake approached a woman at the Information Desk. "I'm looking for a Sergeant Casey." He flashed his badge.

The white-haired lady peered over her rhinestone glasses at the badge. "About five-seven? Blue eyes? Lots of feathered earrings?"

Jake nodded.

"She's in a meeting with William Borden, Jr." the lady reported.

Jake followed her instructions and took the elevator next to the gift shop. A security guard met him on the second floor and led him past gray modular workstations, down a long corridor past executive offices, where he stopped at a solid oak door.

As the guard knocked, Jake reached over, turned the knob, and walked past the guard before Borden had a chance to open the door.

"Mr. Borden," Jake called out as he approached a table near the picture window overlooking the river. The suite carried the safari motif, boasting a rattan table and chairs, a wet bar, floral cushions, faux palm trees, and solid oak floors with a thick green and tan area rug.

"Sergeant Mitchell." William Jr. flashed his million-dollar smile. "Hope you're here to cart those demonstrators away."

Jake swung his gaze to Sam. She had a coy smile on her face, triumphant, a little devilish. A pot of tea was on the table in front of her.

"I need to borrow Sergeant Casey."

Jake pulled out a seat and sat down.

"Bill, have you met my husband?"

"Husband?" Borden reached across the table and shook Jake's hand. "Yes, we have met but I had no idea you two were married." He looked from one to the other and asked, "This doesn't cause a problem with the case, does it?"

"Not at all," Sam said. "He follows his instincts, and I follow mine."

"I would like to thank you, Sergeant Mitchell, for getting our casino up and running so quickly. I was afraid your FBI Director was going to cordon the boat off indefinitely."

"We had all the information we needed. It didn't seem fair to keep you from operating," Jake replied.

After a few strained seconds, Borden said, "I was just getting ready to make your wife an offer."

Jake's eyebrows shot up. "Excuse me?"

Frank pushed through the crowd and grabbed Myla by the arm. Sun reflected off of his sunglasses and a black felt hat kept the chill off his head.

"Get your hands offa me," Myla screamed, shaking her head of beaded corn rows.

Once she was away from the cameras Frank said, "You are making one big mistake, Missy."

"I don't see the cops finding out who killed my father. And if it takes headlines in the press every day, I'll do it."

"Your attitude is excess baggage, so lose it."

Myla stood with her hands on the tops of her black leather

pants. "Ain't nothin' wrong with my attitude."

Reporters were trailing close behind and Frank had to lean close so they wouldn't hear. "You don't know what the hell you are talking about. These antics of yours are going to make the press even more curious. And that's the last thing you need."

"What are you talking about?"

Frank grabbed her arm and steered her toward his car. "I have something to show you. Then you can decide if you want to carry on with your grandstanding."

"No more," Myla said wiping her eyes with the tissue Frank offered.

Carl pressed the STOP button and leaned back in his chair. "As you can see, this is a very delicate situation we are in."

Myla turned on them. "You fabricated this entire tape. It was a set up to get my father."

"HEY." Frank stood, slapping both hands on the conference table, leaning toward the young woman. "I told you before to leave your baggage out at the curb."

Myla crumped, like a scared little girl, a girl who missed her father. She buried her face in her hands and wept.

"There was no mistaking that the man in the videotape was your father having hands on experience at self-gratification." She started to cry even more. "Think about it, Myla," Frank said. "You stage these demonstrations, make the press curious, and sooner or later some reporter looking to make a name for himself is going to dig until he finds something he can sell to the first sleaze paper who offers him money."

Myla's hands started shaking. "Why," she whispered between tears, "why would he do something like that?"

Frank shook his head. "I don't know. Maybe he led too structured of a life. Maybe his work wasn't exciting enough for him."

"Or maybe my mother wasn't?"

Carl and Frank didn't say anything. They let her spend a few minutes composing herself. Carl folded his hands together and said, "Once this case is closed, I'm sure the CHPD would be willing to destroy this and any copies of this tape they might find."

"Copies?" Myla's eyes widened. "There might be copies?" Her beads jangled as she whipped her gaze from Carl to Frank.

"It's possible," Frank replied. "I'm going to check it out as soon as possible. In the meantime, if you or your mother can think of anything useful your father might have said, might have written down, anything about his last trips abroad, it might be helpful."

30

Several minutes after a squad car left to take Myla home, Jake and Sam walked into the conference room.

"It's about time." Carl stood up.

Sam tossed her coat on a chair and smiled when she saw the opened envelopes on the conference room table. "Did I hear you gentlemen needed some help?"

Carl demanded, "Where the hell did you get the tape? And the finger? How did you...?"

Sam ignored Carl's rantings and did a slow survey of the room, the pictures on the wall, the photos of Amid and the elderly man she knew as Sparrow. Then she walked up to Wiley's work table, glanced at the hundred-dollar bills.

"Sam," Jake said, pulling out a chair at the table, "would you please have a seat."

She glanced briefly at the chair, then held one of the bills in her hand, felt it, held it up to the light. She cast a puzzled look Carl's way.

Carl glared at Jake, as if to say, "Your problem," and then sat down. Jake leaned against the wall by the door.

"I'm not going to play twenty questions with you, Sam." Jake rolled the sleeves up on his shirt and shoved his hands in his pants pockets.

She held his gaze as she crumpled the currency in her hand. Her eyes caught a quick glance of Wiley's Treasury Department I.D.

"Counterfeit?" Sam asked.

"Sam." Jake gripped the back of a chair, pulled it out further. Reluctantly, she walked over and sat down. He returned to his post by the door.

"Reverend Smith had fifty thousand dollars in counterfeit bills on him," Jake explained.

"Interesting. They blackmail him with the tape to bring the phony plates into the country," Sam said.

"Printing plates?" The men said in unison.

She enjoyed the surprised looks on their faces. Lloyd's pipe moved around his mouth as if on a track. Frank ran a hand across his cropped beard and gazed quickly at Jake. Carl sank back in his chair and folded his hands across his chest. Wiley let out a giggle. Jake was stoic, his lips pursed.

"How do you know there were plates?" Frank asked. He seemed to ponder his own question, gave a wave of his hand and said, "Forget it. Do I really need to ask?"

"I saw them. I mean, the vision came to me when I was in Amid's bedroom, something heavy, metal, two objects. But it all fits now that I see the counterfeit money," Sam replied.

"Vision?" Wiley perked up, searched the other men's faces. "What does that mean?"

"How did you find out about this tape?" Jake asked.

Sam showed them the matchbook, explained Jackie's involvement, about meeting Davud, and her conversation with Tina.

Frank read the matchbook and giggled, saying, "Listen to this. *Beverly Hills, Where The Customer Always Comes First*." Then he laughed even harder.

"Shit," Carl whispered, grabbing Smith's appointment calendar. "Reverend Smith must have picked up the plates during his last trip to Africa. Either he made a side trip to Iran or he met someone in Africa."

Wiley raised his finger. "I'm still trying to understand the vision part." They all ignored him.

"But how could he get it through customs?" Frank asked.

"Money talks," Lloyd offered.

"Only one problem with this scenario." Wiley wheeled his chair closer. "Plates are going in the wrong direction. It's the foreign countries making the majority of the counterfeit U.S. currency. They should be keeping the plates over there."

"Not necessarily." Carl pulled off his horn-rimmed glasses and set them on the table. He steepled his fingers and tapped them against his chin in thought. "Amid was Iranian and right now Iran is being watched too closely. They are feeling the pressure. Could be they needed to get the plates out of the country, maybe sell them to China, South America. Definitely not any country in Europe or there would be no reason to haul them over here."

"Makes sense," Wiley agreed. "And with the value of the American dollar right now, these plates are going to go for big bucks."

The men nodded in agreement. Jake walked over and closed the windows from the cool air. The sun was setting and maintenance had finally found a way to turn the heat off.

"Are there more copies of the videotape?" Frank asked.

Sam said, "Just the original which Davud keeps in a safe. But Jackie and I can get our hands on that copy."

Jake said, "And you had to involve Jackie?"

"Damn," Lloyd chuckled. "This is better than a soap opera."

"Yes." Sam replied with a shrug. "She took a job as a dancer to keep an eye on things for me." With a hint of a smile she added, "Unless you would rather I be the one doing the stripping."

"Who's Jackie?" Wiley's head swiveled from one face to the next, none of his questions being answered.

Chief Murphy burst into the room and glared at Sam. "I hope you have a good reason for being here." A heavy dose of aftershave followed him in.

Sam looked up at Jake. "Visiting my husband," she replied.

"Oh, yes." Murphy's gaze moved to Jake. "Life is full of surprises."

"Chief Murphy." Carl stood and shook hands. "Sergeant Casey has been hired by the owners of the River Queen Casino. She's just sharing some information that might help our investigation."

"Is that so?" Murphy moved around the conference table, his gaze roaming over printed reports and settling on Amid's finger. "Jezzus. What the hell is that?"

Before anyone could answer, a massive shadow filled the doorway. "Chief." Captain Robinson entered the room. He moved gracefully for a man of his bulk, nodded his hello to Sam, saying, "Congratulations on your marriage." To Murphy, he said, "I need to go over some budget figures, when you have a moment." He stepped back and let Murphy pass him.

Robinson gave Sam a parting wink before returning to his office.

"What the hell was that all about." Carl sat back down while Jake closed the door.

"I don't think Robinson has a budget to discuss with Murphy. He was just trying to avoid bloodshed in his precinct," Jake said.

"I'd like to be gone before he comes out again." Sam stood.

"Not yet, young lady." Carl pointed toward the finger in the center of the table.

"Oh, that was the second one Davud received."

"All right." Carl pushed away from the table, stood, fingers tapping the back of his chair. For a while, it was the only sound in the room. He lifted his head and stared at Sam. It was stern but quizzical. He was a man who didn't mind learning something if it helped solve a case. "Give us your scenario," Carl finally said.

Sam could feel Jake's eyes on her and for a moment she finally felt back in her element. This was where she belonged and she hadn't felt that way in a long time. "Reverend Smith is blackmailed into bringing the plates into the U.S. To keep his part in the scheme quiet, they hire Mr. X to kill him."

"Amid?" Frank asked.

"No." Sam picked up the picture of the elderly man in the tinted glasses. "Him." He goes through this elaborate plan to sabotage the power on the boat but he hesitates."

"Why?" Jake asked.

Jake had been too quiet for too long, digesting the information, probably fuming at her coyness. Any minute now she expected him to start squeezing that damn rubber ball.

She retrieved one of the tapes on the table and shoved it into the VCR. "Tim made a copy of one of the tapes you brought home."

"Geez," Carl muttered, another sharp look at Jake. Frank smiled and shook his head.

She held the remote and pressed FORWARD, explaining, "I received a call from Jackie while I was about here on the tape, just before the power outage, so I put the tape on SLOW. Now watch." The monitor went black. "This is when the power was first cut. Then you'll see the generators kick on." The monitor showed the main casino in a dim light. "Now keep your eye on the bar where Mr. X is sitting. The power will shut off for good." The monitor went black. Then they saw the beam of red.

"Infrared," Lloyd said.

"Night scope on the damn gun, too. Would have to be." Carl added.

"I think the shooter saw Amid through the night scope. Amid probably crossed right in front of Smith, shot him, and took the satchel. The shooter saw it all." Sam pressed the STOP button and turned to the men. "I don't think things happened the way they were supposed to. If they had, there would have been no need for the shooter to follow Amid, kill him, and take the plates."

Her audience was silent, mulling over the scenario, creating new questions. She let them chew on the facts and after a while said, "Don't say *thank you* all at once."

Jake sat down in the chair she had occupied. "We'll say thanks if you can give us the name of the shooter."

She leaned against the table and smiled. "Sparrow."

Carl jerked away from the chair, not sure he heard her correctly. "Sparrow?"

"Yes. He has a tattoo of a bird on his hand and the word *Sparrow* written below it."

"Have you heard of him, Carl?" Jake asked.

Carl snapped his phone open. "Yes. He's on Interpol's Top Ten list."

Hot lights, arms stretched as he hung for hours, flashes of white lightning, pain, unbearable pain, then nothingness. Sparrow woke with a start, his clothes dripping in sweat, his breathing labored.

Sitting up, he felt nauseous, then realized the pain wasn't in his dreams. He fell back on the bed, his hands holding his head as he writhed from side to side. With all his strength, he fought the pain, blocked it out.

He hated white walls, even refused to stay in hotel rooms that didn't have some patterned wall paper. The pain seemed to intensify when he had to stare at white walls. And no ceiling lights. Ceiling fans with multiple lights didn't bother him. But one dome light that hugged the ceiling was too much of a reminder.

After a while he dragged himself to the bathroom, took two pain pills and climbed into a cold shower. As he shaved, he stared at himself in the mirror. This job was taking its toll. The lines around his eyes were becoming more pronounced. His hair had a hint of gray flecks. Although he still had a muscular body and a quick mind, the headaches and flashbacks bothered him. This would be his last job. He made his decision. He'd find a buyer for the plates and then retire.

Feeling refreshed, Sparrow dressed, made himself a cup of coffee, ordered dinner from room service, and sat at his computer.

From his briefcase he retrieved a black notebook. He had decided there were only three organizations stateside he cared to make his offer to: The Karankos family out of New York, Yang Chu in Chicago, and Martinez in California. He still had not ruled out the possibility that Menut would bargain. If all else failed, he would try Libya, Syria, maybe even Moscow.

But time was a factor. He had heard that Dino Karankos, the baron father, was ill. Dealing with anyone but the father was unfathomable. Martinez was too far away. He would have to Fed Ex the samples and wait for them to send the money in person. His only choice for a quick sale, next to Menut, was Yang Chu.

Thanks to modern technology, all were available through the Internet. His message was cryptic: *The eagle has flown. Need five to bring him home. Samples upon request.*

Sparrow checked his file for other messages. In the lower right hand side, a small icon in the shape of a spy glass flashed. It meant, *Intruder Alert.* Any time anyone tried to access programs Sparrow had signed on to, it would alert him that someone had intruded into his file space.

He typed in a command to trace the intruder.

"You have a beautiful home." Carl stood in front of one of the window seats in the dining room viewing the back acres of Sam's property.

Dusk was closing in quickly, the distant acreage already in darkness. Jake and Frank were out on the patio grilling steaks. Lloyd was keeping watch, puffing on his pipe. They had tabled their meeting after Jake invited everyone over for dinner. Notes and files were carted along. Wiley declined the offer since his wife had invited friends for dinner and he still had to stop by his office in Chicago.

"Thank you," Sam said, setting the salad bowl on the table. She joined Carl at the window. Her gaze rested on Jake who seemed at ease standing over a grill, beer can in hand. Frank was dancing, she could only guess he was doing his own rendition of a table dance, pretending he was at Beverly Hills. That got Jake smiling, laughing, shaking his head. His features softened and she found herself remembering ways she had gotten him to smile.

She studied Carl. He looked as if he may have been a real lady killer in his youth. Still trim, healthy looking, moved as though his joints didn't ache, but then sixty something is not considered elderly these days.

"He's a good man," Carl said, his head nodding toward the patio, eyes on her. "I was the one who kept everything under wraps on the Hilliard case. Jake was just following orders."

"You taught him well." Her comment could have been taken two ways. It sounded like a compliment but there was an edge of cynicism in her voice. "Would you have kept information from your wife, Carl, if you had been married?"

Carl seemed to think long and hard about that one. Took a swallow of beer. "From the woman I might have married, I kept a lot of things. Even kept her existence a secret just to keep her out of harm's way. Those were rough times back then." He gave her a long, hard look, an affectionate gaze. "You were a different story. Always handling things your own way, never following orders. You were a loose cannon. Could have blown the entire operation. It was a decision call. As much my decision as Jake's. I'm sorry if you interpret that as betrayal, Sam."

He gave her arm a gentle squeeze, turned away from the window, took a seat at the head of the table, near printed reports and notepads. This was going to be a working meal.

Jake brought in the steaks, Frank the potatoes, Lloyd the tin of grilled onions and mushrooms. A fire was blazing in the living room fireplace, coffee dripping in the coffeemaker. It was boarding-house reach, grab and pass. Steaks were perfect and, although Sam thought a glass of red wine would go just perfect, she opted for a glass of iced tea instead.

After fifteen minutes of eating and small talk, the conversation turned to Sparrow. "The man has been a thorn in Interpol's side for the past twenty years," Carl reported. "He has never been seen out of disguise, slips in and out of countries with ease, can't begin to count the number of aliases he uses." Carl poured himself a glass of wine and passed his empty plate to the far end of the fifteen-foot-long table. "I'll call my office."

"Former office," Lloyd corrected him.

"Yes, former office, and have Marcel fax us the latest Interpol report on him. My best guess is he's a mercenary, sells himself to the highest bidder."

Sam brought in the coffee and cups, then one of Abby's cakes. She tried picturing Sparrow without his disguise, and wondered if even the blonde hair peeking out from under the cap he had worn to gain access to the hold of the boat was his natural hair color. She cut the cake and passed plates around the table, still thinking about the personality of this killer.

The fork hovered, just inches from her mouth, as she thought about Sparrow, the youthful face boarding the employee entrance to the boat in contrast to the frail man leaning on a cane. The conversation around her faded in and out as she wondered how much anger it would take to decapitate a man. And why torture him first by cutting off his fingers? Did he cut them off one at a time or all three together?

"Lloyd, what's your take on this guy?" Carl asked.

Lloyd took his time, refilled his coffee cup, rubbed his fingers back and forth across his chin. "He's not your standard profile," Lloyd finally said. "Just by the way he killed Amid you can tell someone had tried his patience. Goes against his previous profile of being organized and researching his targets, selecting a crime scene, patiently waiting for a specific time. Then he snaps and brutalizes Amid. At first, I would have thought there were two distinct killers here."

Frank's head swiveled from Carl to Lloyd. "So, what made him snap?"

"He was double-crossed," Sam offered.

"So why hire Sparrow in the first place if you're going to have someone else kill Smith?" Jake questioned.

"He's a good diversion," Carl said, standing and stretching. "Police focus on a terrorist hit and no one suspects counterfeit printing plates."

"But they would have paid him first, right?" Frank asked.

"From what I recall, Sparrow always demanded money up front." Carl grabbed his glass of wine and finished it in one swallow.

Sam stared across at Jake, locked eyes. She could see the wheels turning in his head, the facts tumbling until he got everything right side up. And she must have come to the same conclusion at the exact time he did. He smiled slowly.

Jake said, "I don't think he got genuinely pissed until he saw the printing plates. He was curious what it was Amid had taken from Smith. So he followed him. Then he figured it out. The fee he was paid was counterfeit."

31

Smoke curled around the windows as fire licked and sputtered, filling the Jeep, melting the steering wheel. Sam pounded her fists on the glass, screamed out in pain but she couldn't hear herself above the whine of the sirens. Her throat felt raw, automatically constricting, refusing to inhale the poisonous gas while all around her debris crashed. She stood in the middle of an inferno, unable to move, with only the car window which she continued to beat with her fists.

"SAM, STOP!"

Sam's eyes jerked open. She was sitting up in bed, her fists being held by each of Jake's hands. The bedroom was dark and all she heard were her gasps, deep ragged breathing like someone who had been suffocating and just now coming up for air.

"Oh, god." Her body started to shake.

Jake gripped tighter, forced her to lie down. "I should call the doctor." He reached for the phone.

"NO!" She grabbed his arm. He was silhouetted against the dim lights filtering in from the hallway. She didn't know what time it was, only that it wasn't daylight. But Jake must have been in his bed down the hall and jostled from sleep because all he had on was a pair of gym shorts. "He can't help me. No one can help." She drew herself up, hugged her knees to her chest and wept. She felt the bed move as Jake got up and walked out.

Serves me right, Sam thought. She had been pushing him away, why should she expect him to console her now? The dreams had only been snippets before or she had always been able to jerk herself awake before realizing the full message in the dream. Not this time. Now she knew what had been bothering her. Sobs racked her body, as mounds of hair fell over her arms, cascading down the back of her cotton nightshirt. She heard the rattling of a spoon against a cup. Jake had returned with a cup of tea.

He pushed a button behind the headboard and the overhead bridge light clicked on. He handed her a tissue in one hand and the cup of tea in the other. Sam wiped her eyes and her nose and tried to grab the cup but her hands were still shaking.

"Wait." Jake set the saucer down, sat down next to her, and helped her hold the cup.

Sam noticed he had taken time to throw on a pair of jeans. His hands were warm which reminded her of how warm his body always felt. She gulped the tea, not caring how hot it was. Jake just kept staring at her, those worry lines creasing his forehead, his eyes clouded with concern.

She knew he wouldn't force it out of her so when she remained silent, Jake reached over to turn the light out, saying, "I'll let you get back to sleep."

"Don't..." she grabbed his arm again and took a ragged breath. "Stay a little while." She didn't know why she did it but she moved over so he could lay next to her, so she could feel warm and safe and maybe sleep without the nightmares haunting her.

Jake obliged. He laid down and pulled the comforter over her. Sam settled in, smelled his aftershave, felt the warmth of his skin, and clung to him. Her body shook, like waves of adrenaline that would settle down briefly and start right up again.

"I keep seeing the explosion in my dreams," she started.

"When your father died?"

"No." She felt his arm around her shoulder, his fingers sifting through her hair. All so familiar. And it felt wonderful. "When Chief Connelley died. At first I always thought my nightmares were about me trying to get out of the burning Jeep. But actually I was trying to help Connelley get out. And I couldn't. I can see him behind the glass, the Jeep is in flames, and I can't break the glass or open the door."

"Everything happened too quickly for you to do anything, Sam. Besides, you were in no mental state to help anyone."

"But I should have." Her lids were heavy as the tea warmed her insides and Jake's skin warmed her outside. "I knew something was going to happen. I felt it. And I didn't warn him. He didn't have to die that way, Jake." The tears started up and she held on tighter to him.

"Abby said that all you felt was Cain's presence. You had no idea how or when it would happen. There wasn't any way you could have known there was a bomb in your Jeep."

She felt herself drifting, her head rising and falling with Jake's breathing. Outside, branches brushed the outside railing and crisp leaves scraped against the patio windows.

"Jake?" She wasn't sure if he was asleep and if he was, a part of her didn't want him to awaken. She was too warm and cozy to move.

"Hmmm?"

"Can we go out?"

Silence. Then he said, "Out?"

"Yes...like on a date." She heard a soft laugh and could almost feel him smiling in the dark.

"Where would you like to go?"

She buried deeper under the covers and snuggled closer. "You pick."

He stuck his feet under the covers, burrowed in, and whispered into her hair, "One date coming up."

* * *

Tim eagerly crawled out of bed, fumbled with his glasses and stumbled to his computer. His Chicago Bears jersey served as a pajama top, his blue and white gym shorts were his pajama bottoms. His mother kept stocking his dresser with fancy silk pajamas but he kept shoving them to the back of the drawer.

Classes for him were seven in the morning until one o'clock. He didn't have to get up at five but it gave him an hour of computer time before having to jump into the shower.

He turned on his computer and waited for the screen to clear. Signing on to AOL, he waited for the mechanical voice to announce, "You have mail."

He scanned through several messages and digests until he found the one he had been hoping for. He clicked on READ.

"Who am I?"

Sparrow

Tim's heart raced. A hoax, maybe? Maybe not. He thought of picking up the phone and calling Sam but stopped. It was too early. And besides, he was the one looking for Sparrow. So how did Sparrow find him?

Tim pondered that thought. Sparrow was giving him a challenge. All he could do was play it out and see where it led. He quickly typed a response.

Assignment accepted. Do I
have a time limit?

Bond

Tim hadn't been this excited since his father purchased him a flight simulator for his birthday. An avid fan of James Bond movies, he thought it only fitting he sign his message as *Bond.*

For Sam to want his help, this Sparrow guy had to be someone important. The thought of unleashing his RoboSpy program through a major network was exhilarating. He pushed the intercom and told his mom he was running late and asked if she could bring his breakfast upstairs. She wasn't too thrilled about the idea but eventually agreed.

Before jumping in the shower, he set his program loose through the CIA and Interpol files.

32

"What is it you are bothering me with so early in the morning?" Yang Chu pattered over to the desk in his silk robe, his hand cradling a teacup and saucer.

Li Chu, his twenty-five-year-old son, eldest of his six children, sat at the computer in the home office of the Chu palatial estate. A very prolific business acumen on the part of Yang and his three brothers had allowed them to acquire a twelve-bedroom house on the outskirts of Chicago's Little Korea, the Korean counterpart to Chinatown.

Being a family man, Yang insisted the brothers, their wives and children, the parents, and even the parents of the wives, all move in. One big happy family under the roof of Al Capone's former hideaway. There was a large outdoor pool, a smaller lap pool indoors, guards posted at the gate and at two points along the ten-foot-high brick fence, and a staff of six servants from the homeland. The house was large enough that the families didn't collide and sometimes met only at dinnertime.

"Look at this." Li pointed to the screen where the message from Sparrow appeared. "What do you think this eagle has flown means?" Li was a carbon copy of his father in height and build as well as business sense. And Yang had a wish that his two sons follow in his footsteps. His eldest daughter was married to a shiftless husband who lived off his wife's fortune. His three remaining daughters were still in school. "Printing plates?"

Yang pulled up a chair and sat down. "Has to be. The FBI was there when I was interrogated and the man kept focusing on counterfeit money. The eagle has to be the plates. Think what this could mean."

Li slowly shook his head in the negative as he considered this. "No, father. Think of how much we can get if we sold them to one of our contacts in North Korea. Think of how much money we can print if we keep the plates."

Yang jerked his head toward his eldest. "NO! What about Jayes?"

Li snorted. "You are going to pass up the millions we can make? My brother isn't worth that much."

Yang slammed his cup and saucer on the desk, splashing tea on the keyboard, screen, carpeting, and Li. He stood up and slammed a closed fist into his hand. Li pushed his chair away from the desk, away from his father, and up against the bookcase.

"YES! Even you would be worth that much to me," Yang bellowed. He had never struck his children, but that didn't mean he hadn't ever wanted to. This was one of those times. Yang bent over and pointed a finger an inch from Li's face. "Above all, family comes first. The FBI is aware of the phony plates. All the government would have to do is change the plates, print a new series and ours would be totally worthless." Yang slowly straightened up, waved toward the screen and said, "You reply to him that we want to see samples." He patted his son on the shoulder as if apologizing for his outburst. "We will play along as the police asked. We will do whatever it takes to get our family back together."

"You didn't think I'd forget you, did you?"

Davud grimaced at the sound of Sparrow's voice on the speaker phone. "How could I? You keep leaving me those little presents."

He looked across his desk at a Goliath-sized figure. Davud had brought Gholam to the States five years earlier. He was supposed to return but Immigration had yet to locate him. He was not a figure people wanted to mess with. Standing just under seven feet, Gholam weighed four hundred pounds, and had a face that scared his own mother—large protruding forehead, bulging eyes, a mouth full of mismatched teeth. They usually don't make them big in Iran.

"I want my two hundred thousand dollars, Mr. Menut."

Davud watched as Gholam tried tracing the call.

"I will have it for you tomorrow, Mr. Sparrow. We should discuss the exchange."

Sparrow laughed. "Exchange? I don't think so. The two hundred thousand is a show of your good faith. Then we negotiate the price of the plates. And I should warn you. There are more bidders in the race."

Davud's face reddened. He hadn't even told his superiors about the plates being stolen. If someone were to buy them before he could get them back...he didn't even want to think about the consequences.

"NO!" Davud screamed into the phone. "It is my property. There is no need to bring any other parties into the matter."

"I will call you tomorrow morning with instructions."

Davud slammed the phone down and looked at Gholam's unsmiling face.

"Cell phone. Can't trace it," Gholam said with his deep, nasally voice.

Davud leaned back and rubbed his bad eye. Gholam may be big and slow, but he could pull the wings off this Sparrow's body before he knew what hit him.

"Let him play games. Tomorrow we will pay him his two hundred thousand dollars. You will follow close behind and then tail this insect. Once I have my hands on the plates, you can have his money."

* * *

"I don't believe it." Sam studied her face in the visor mirror. She turned to Jackie and said, "Look at this." Her finger pointed to a patch of bumps on her chin. "I'm breaking out," Sam whined.

Jackie studied the area, squinted, backed away a few inches and cocked her head to one side. "Those little things? Honey, you have no idea what those raging hormones are going to do to your complexion."

Sam returned to the mirror, surveying every pore.

"What on earth is that?" Jackie said.

Studying her chin closer, Sam said, "I told you the blemishes were getting bigger."

Jackie pulled on Sam's sleeve and pointed toward the entrance to Bev's. "I mean THAT."

Sam flipped the visor up and stared at the monster trailing Menut. The two men climbed into a Lincoln Town Car and sped off.

"Never saw him before and I don't think I want to," Sam said.

"I bet he's the one who did a number on Tina."

The two women crossed the parking lot to the back door of Bev's. In mid-stride Sam stopped and raised her head as if listening. She took time to survey the parking lot and look back at her Jeep. Sunlight danced off car windshields. She looked for movement, someone ducking behind bushes. But there wasn't a soul in sight. No one standing by a car. No one watching from a parked car. But she still felt eyes on her.

"Don't go pulling this spooky shit on me now," Jackie said, her hands on her hips, her eyes shifting from Sam to the parking lot.

"I feel like someone is watching us."

Jackie grabbed her by the arm, saying, "Well he or it ain't going to be watching for long." She steered Sam through the back door and toward the first door on the left. "Stay here. I'll find out where Yung is." Jackie left Sam standing in the corridor.

Sam strolled down the corridor and put her ear to Davud's office door. She made her way to a staircase to the second floor where she assumed Davud lived. The corridor was dimly lit and smelled of cigar smoke.

Jackie emerged and waved toward her. Sam hadn't noticed before because Jackie had kept her leather coat on during breakfast, but today she looked more like an executive with her pink suit and black silk blouse.

"Aren't you working today?"

With a hand on each of the lapels, Jackie pulled the suit coat open to reveal a see-through blouse. Jackie wasn't wearing a bra.

"I also have on a garter belt, just a garter belt. Thought I might call it the businessman's special," Jackie said with a raucous laugh. "They will never look at the ladies in their office the same way."

"What do you do in a locked room if a guy gets too, you know..."

"I didn't take self-defense classes from you for nothing," Jackie replied. "But there's also mace and a panic button." Jackie pointed toward the office. "Yung will be with a customer for the next twenty minutes, so the safe is all yours."

The safe was a floor model, about the size of a two-drawer filing cabinet. Most people don't like to rely on their memories for combinations and usually use a number they are familiar with. Thanks to Jackie, Sam had learned Davud's birth date and social security number. She had the safe opened in less than a minute.

She pulled out a blue notebook and thumbed through it. It was an accounting ledger of daily receipts, which she found confusing since he had a sophisticated computer that hooked him up with his mother country. Unless he was keeping separate books.

It took every ounce of restraint not to take the notebook. She set it aside and pulled out the videotapes. Reverend Smith's was right on top. There were four others marked: Palmer, Brewer, Reise, and MacGrady. She knew of a councilman named Palmer, and MacGrady was the family name of a string of banks. The other two names weren't familiar.

From a supply cabinet Sam retrieved five blank tapes, marked each one and exchanged them with the ones in the safe. She shoved the five tapes into her tote bag and closed the safe.

Tillie Novak parked her car just outside the gate to Sam's house, got out, walked over to the gate and pushed the button that closed it. She climbed back into the car and checked her purse. Just over five feet tall, Tillie's feet barely touched the pedals of her Ford Crown Victoria. For the past ten years she had cleaned for Abby and Sam. She was a perfectionist and cleaned the old fashioned way—tables were polished instead of dusted, floors were scrubbed on her hands and knees, and twice a year she took down every book on the shelves in the study and dusted them. Contents of the kitchen cabinets were removed three times a year and the cabinets washed down; closet floors were vacuumed every week; the chrome on the exercise equipment was polished once a month. Sometimes Tillie brought her niece to help out when her niece needed money for school.

Tillie shoved the car into gear, not paying any attention to the squad car tailing her until he put his lights on. "Oh, no," Tillie moaned as she parked the car at the curb.

The officer walked over to the driver's side as Tillie rolled down her window. He had a nice smile, short blonde hair, and mirrored sunglasses that hid his eyes.

Tipping his cap toward her, he said, "Morning, ma'am."

"I'm sorry, officer. Was I speeding?"

"No, ma'am. But I think you have a taillight out."

"Do I?" Tillie climbed out of the car and walked to the rear. The sleeves of her flannel shirt were rolled up from cleaning. Not one to dress like June Cleaver, she always preferred blue jeans and one of her husband's shirts, whether she was cleaning or puttering around her house.

"It's the left one. Why don't you step on the brakes while I watch it."

Tillie obediently returned to the driver's seat and pressed the brake pedal.

"Can you pop the trunk open?" The officer called out. "You may have a loose wire."

Tillie reached into her glove box and pressed the yellow button. Once the trunk popped open, she climbed back out to find the officer's hands in a maze of wires.

"This is so nice of you, Officer," Tillie said as she watched him attach and reattach wires.

"How's Miss Casey doing?" the officer asked, nodding toward the property beyond the wrought iron fence.

"Oh, you know Sergeant Casey?"

"Heard a lot about her."

"It's a shame about her suspension, though," Tillie said, explaining further. "I know once she has her hearing she'll be cleared of those murder charges. There's no way she would ever kill a fellow cop. She was set up, pure and simple."

"How long until her hearing?"

"Four months, I believe. But she doesn't let grass grow under her feet, no sir. She has already been hired by some people to do some work for them. Working on a case now."

"There. That should do it." The officer straightened. "Try the brake pedal again."

Tillie smiled and climbed back into the car. She pressed the pedal twice.

"It's all fixed now, ma'am."

"Thank you so much, Officer." She squinted in the sunlight as she looked for his name tag. He didn't have one.

"Jones, Randall Jones," the officer said. "Drive safely now," he added before turning and walking back to his squad car.

As Tillie drove off, Sparrow lowered his mirrored sunglasses and tried peering through the wrought iron fencing. But vines and trees made it impossible. He backed the squad car up to the main gate and peered down the long driveway. Impressive. Very good alarm system, too. Complete with video camera.

By running the license plate number of the Jeep through the computer, he had obtained Sam's name and address. He had a feeling she was a cop. He didn't have any interest in breaking into Sam's house. He had plans to meet her elsewhere.

The car was on loan from a restaurant parking lot and the uniform was from his suitcase. He would have the car back before the owner was through eating lunch. Sparrow had one more trip to make.

33

Frank's eyes moved quickly over the airline log sheets of passenger cancellations for the night of Reverend Smith's murder. Once it was determined Sparrow might have changed his plans and stayed in town, the next step was to find out who might have made last minute flight cancellations.

"This is useless," he mumbled from behind his cup of coffee. He looked across the table at Lloyd.

"How do you think I feel? I'm supposed to be fishing right now." Lloyd looked at the skin on his thin arms. "Instead, my skin is getting heat burn from the damn thermostat in this place." Even his face was pink, the color enhanced by his pale eyes and white hair.

"I've got thirty cancellations on my list," Frank reported. "By eliminating the women, it leaves us with twenty-two to check out."

"I have twelve," Lloyd said, casting a glance through the plate glass window. "Let's give the lists to some grunts to finish up. We've wasted too much time already."

From across the room, Wiley tossed back his head and laughed, his clenched hands pumping in victory. "Gotta love it! Do you think that little brunette out there would run a library search for me?"

* * *

Yang Chu, dressed in his best silk suit and shirt walked in and bowed to the men in the room. "I have received contact," he announced once Jake closed his office door.

"From?" Carl asked, eyebrows raised.

Yang unfolded the computer paper and handed it to them.

"The eagle has flown," Carl read. "And it's signed by Sparrow."

Yang said, "I wanted to find out from you how I should respond." He sat down and pulled out his pen. "I told him I wanted to see samples."

"Good, that's good," Carl said. "But you probably shouldn't come here any more just in case you are being followed." Carl wrote down the number to Jake's cell phone and handed it to Yang. "Use only your cell phone. Call us when you get the samples and we will tell you how to proceed. Negotiate down to three million. He'll probably settle on four. My department will get you the four million."

Yang nodded in agreement, looking at each of their faces. "And?" When none of them answered, Yang said, "My son. I want your word you will help my son."

"Although he was sentenced to six years, he should only have to serve two," Jake explained.

"Two is too long," Yang said.

"All right. For your assistance, we'll try to lower it to one. If we succeed in apprehending our suspect, then I will get a suspended sentence on good behavior. You have my word on it. But he may have to do community work with drug rehab centers."

Yang jumped to his feet and bowed. "I will contact you as soon as I hear something."

* * *

Carl and Jake returned to the conference room, followed close behind by Wiley who was still chuckling and shaking his helmet of black curly hair.

Wiley spread a newspaper out on the conference room table. "You won't fuckin' believe this." He pointed at the front page. "See this picture of the Iranian demonstration against the U.S. years ago?"

In the center of the front page of the *New York Times* was a sea of protesters chanting, holding up pictures of Bush and Reagan, pictures of a pig. The men circled the table and studied the picture.

Wiley pointed. "See the emblem on the flag with the pig?"

"They were not too artistic, were they," Frank said. "So, the flag has a pig with a brand GCP. What does that stand for?"

Wiley laughed again. "I love it. I told you every artist likes to put his little trademark. GCP stands for Greedy Capitalist Pig. Now look at this." He curled his finger and led them to the microscope.

"You found a flaw," Carl said smiling. He peered into the lens. "What am I looking for?"

"The microprinting in the border around the picture of Franklin. It should say *The United States of America*. But this one has a small GCP after America." Wiley howled with laughter again. "Ain't that a fuckin' riot?"

Carl stepped aside to let the rest of them have a look.

"Good work, Wiley," Lloyd said.

"Is it the same for the fifty-dollar bill?" Jake asked.

"Yes," Wiley replied. "And you'd never catch it with one of those hand-held magnifying glasses."

An hour later, Sam appeared in the doorway and Wiley motioned her over with the excitement of a three-year-old. She peered through the microscope and smiled when she saw the GCP.

"What now?" Sam asked as she set her tote bag on the table.

"I'll have my department issue a notice to banks and the casinos on what to look for," Wiley explained.

"Once this case is closed," Carl said, "we can put out a release to the media about the counterfeit bills and how they can be identified. That should keep anyone from trying to pass them out since they will know we're aware of them."

"Where's Lloyd?" Sam asked.

"Had a phone call," Carl said.

Jake felt Sam looked more rested. He had returned to his own bedroom before dawn. Somehow, it was difficult to get to sleep feeling her body next to his. Today, physically, she looked fabulous and even had more color to her cheeks. But he was still worried about her mental condition.

Sam's medicine bundle brushed the tabletop as she sat down. Pulling the videos from her bag she explained her trip to Davud's and the tapes she found.

Studying the labels, Jake asked, "You didn't steal these, did you?"

"Borrowed. I replaced them with blank tapes that I labeled the same as these." Sam then explained the ledger she found.

"Double dipping?" Frank asked.

"I say we have IRS check out this guy. We might be able to get him on income tax evasion," Carl said.

"I'll call Myla and let her know we will be destroying the original and the copy of these tapes," Frank said.

"What about the rest of these?" Sam asked as she picked up the videos. "I recognize the names Palmer and MacGrady, but I don't know who Brewer and Reid are."

"We'll check them out," Carl said.

Wiley started packing up his equipment. "Make sure I get all the money to take with me guys. It's been a slice."

Sam moved toward the door. "I'll leave you boys to your fun."

"Good work, Sam," Carl called out as she left.

Jake followed and walked her to the elevator. He pushed past Brandon, a beat cop with an axe to grind.

"Lock up's downstairs, Mitchell." Brandon worked a toothpick around his teeth as he leaned against Scofield's desk.

Sam pushed the button on the panel and turned to face Jake. "You're taking a big chance being seen with me, Sergeant Mitchell."

He looked around the office at the heads turned in their direction, the stares from the clerical help, the glare from Brandon.

"My reputation wasn't that great to begin with."

As the elevator doors opened and Sam stepped in, Jake tucked a note in her pocket.

Once the elevator doors closed, she pulled out the slip of paper. It read:

Serengeti's Steak House
Dinner Saturday - 6:00 p.m.

34

"Good news," Yang said to his eldest son. Li took his father's trench coat and hung it up. He followed his father upstairs to their office as Yang explained his meeting at the police department. "You do not breathe a word of this to anyone, especially your mother. I don't want to get her hopes up." He walked over to the credenza in back of his desk and poured himself a glass of water. His eyes were drawn to a white envelope leaning against his calendar. It had his name on it, and where the return address should be was the name *Sparrow*. Picking up the envelope, he asked, "Where did this come from?"

"I have not seen this before."

"Who was here today? Did someone drop this off?" Yang headed for the door saying, "Gather everyone downstairs in the study. NOW!"

Yang was checking the counterfeit bills Sparrow had placed in the envelope when everyone walked into the study. They lined up like Army recruits waiting for inspection. Holding up the envelope, Yang demanded, "Where did this come from?"

The guard from the gate and the two from the brick fence looked at each other. The butler, cook, gardener, and three maids shook their heads.

"No one?" Yang bellowed. "This shows up on my desk and no

one knows who put it there?" He walked up and down the line of faithful servants. Could Sparrow have bought someone off? Was there a spy in his midst? "How clever is this person who can walk past my guards?"

Tokey, the bald, wrestler-sized man whose post was the main gate, opened his mouth in surprise. "The policeman," he breathed. The other two guards nodded as they remembered. "A policeman stopped by to see you. Asked if he could wait."

"You let him roam the house?" Yang asked.

Tokey shifted his weight and quietly said, "Your wife, sir."

"Mae Ling?"

"Yes, sir. She took him upstairs to make him comfortable. She had Cook make him some tea."

Yang slowly sat down, studied the envelope. "He was the only stranger in the house today?"

They nodded. Yang had them describe the police officer. The FBI man had been right. He should use his cell phone. He should be careful. If this Sparrow can show up on his doorstep, who's to say he isn't watching him right now? He couldn't do anything to jeopardize his son's life.

"You are all dismissed." After the servants left, Yang made a call from his cell phone.

Usually Tim loved school. It was challenging, his teachers were supportive, classes were interesting. But now it was a distraction from his mission. All he could think of all day was Sparrow.

As soon as he got home, Tim threw his books on the bed and ran to his computer. There was only one message:

I'll give you forty-eight hours.

Sparrow

Next he accessed his RoboSpy program for a status report. The Interpol search yielded reports on possible mercenary activities by someone known as Sparrow. It listed possible aliases but there was no verification of his true identity.

Some of the operations he was considered responsible for included the 1993 murder of Paco Batiste, a Columbian drug lord who alienated several drug cartels by trying to expand his territory too far; and the murder of a Sicilian Mafia family head whose own sons reportedly hired the assassin.

Tim was too excited to sit still. He decided to send a message to Sparrow with the list of his aliases and an added note that he was still searching for his true identity. Then he picked up the pages from the printer and pedaled his bike over to Sam's house.

"Are you sure you have everything?" Jake asked Lloyd as they checked the study.

Lloyd inspected his briefcase and nodded. "I have my computer, my phone, my briefcase. My suitcase is in Frank's trunk. I'd say I was ready."

"You're sure you have to leave?" Jake asked.

"Yes. The last of the bodies of the unidentified MIAs just arrived at our facility in Virginia." Lloyd turned to Carl. "I'll call you as soon..." Lloyd stopped, glanced at Jake and Frank. "Well, I should get going."

It had been an hour since Frank left to drive Lloyd to the airport. Carl sat at the kitchen table and stared out into the back yard, hands pressed together prayer style. Long after the sun faded and the landscaping lights clicked on, Carl was still staring out, eyes focused on nothing in particular.

"Want to tell me about it?" Jake finally asked.

Carl nodded but it took him several minutes before he spoke. And then he told him briefly about Judith and Charlie. "I loved my work. But looking back, I have regrets. Guess there're regrets in everything we do. If I had quit the Bureau and made a life with Judith, I would have regretted leaving the work I love."

"But at least you spent time with them," Jake said.

Carl smiled. "I have to admit, being secluded four weeks out of the year was almost like being on a mission, wrapped in secrecy. It probably added to the excitement."

Tim appeared at the patio door.

"Come on in, Tim." Jake slid open the screen door.

Clutching an envelope close to his chest, Tim asked, "Is Sam home?"

"Not yet." Jake introduced Tim to Carl. Jake got Tim to sit down and take a few deep breaths.

"What has you so flustered?" Jake asked.

Tim clutched the envelope tighter, bending the corners.

"Is it okay if I just wait a little while for her?"

"Sure." Jake gave Carl a pat and said, "I'll go check on that report."

Carl studied Tim, the envelope he carried, and asked, "What are you studying in school?"

"Computers. Mainly computers. I'm in an accelerated class right now. I'm on half days so I get out at one o'clock."

Carl smiled at the youth's enthusiasm. "It's great that your parents support your interests."

"My dad is fascinated with computers and I taught my mom how to use the one at home. Dad wants to help me market some of the programs I've written."

"What kind of programs?"

Tim's eyes shifted as he grinned and clutched his envelope. "Just games, stupid games, really."

They talked about favorite vacation spots and family get-togethers. As they spoke, Carl was reminded of another teenager...Charlie. Carl couldn't help staring at Tim. Except for the glasses, he looked quite a bit like Charlie did the last time he saw him.

"What are your plans for the future?" Carl asked the youth.

"I'd like to be in the FBI, or CIA. Get involved in spy stuff."

Carl laughed. "I made the Bureau my life and look where I'm at. No, son, you don't want to be a spy. There are many other departments within the FBI you could get into that could use your expertise in computers. With your talents, you can do some pretty good sleuthing through a computer and not have to put your life or your loved ones' lives on the line."

Jake walked in from the study carrying sheets of printer paper. "Here's the report from Interpol."

Tim's shoulders sagged. "I have to go," he stammered. "Could you ask Sam to give me a call?"

He was out of the door and on his bike before the two men realized it.

As Tim raced down the street and up his driveway, he didn't notice the car parked across the street, or the man sitting behind the wheel.

35

The men were gathered in the study when Sam returned home. Carl looked up from his seat at the bar. A glass of beer in front of him. "Did you get it?"

"Yes," Sam replied. Yang's wife delivered the envelope to Jackie at Beverly Hills and I dropped it off at Wiley's office. He said the bills are identical."

"We're ordering pizzas," Frank said, telephone in hand. "Have a preference?"

"Anchovy and black olive," Sam replied

Frank shuddered

Sam asked, "Where's Lloyd?"

Jake straightened up from behind the bar where he had been searching through the refrigerator. "He had to fly back." He explained to Sam about Carl's son and the remains found in the Iron Triangle.

"Carl, you had a son?" She listened as Carl spoke of the son he barely knew. It was a well kept secret and one, Jake admitted, that even he hadn't known.

"I'm sorry."

Carl nodded.

They waited for the pizza in the dining room where Sam read

the report faxed to Carl from Interpol.

"This guy has twenty-six aliases? But no one is sure of his real name?" Sam asked.

"We aren't even sure if our guy is responsible for all of these," Frank said as he cluttered the table with photos of Sparrow in various disguises. "This is just a description of their unsolved cases involving someone fitting our guy's M.O., his unique ability at disguises, and his use of torture in some cases."

Jake added, "We know now he used the name Vince Petrenko when he flew into town. He was a no-show on his return flight. So far, we haven't found a Vince Petrenko or any of the other aliases registered at the hotels in town."

Sam continued, "He's suspected of murdering Paco Batiste? And Matt Matteo? His two sons hired Sparrow to kill their father?" Sam read through the pages shaking her head. "Israel hired him to locate three of their soldiers who were being held by Palestinians. He took out twenty-seven of the captors?"

"A modern-day Rambo," Frank said.

Sam skimmed through the remaining pages. "He was hired by the twenty-five-member Hibaki, the underworld organization in Thailand, to kidnap the eight-year-old heir to the throne. The boy was to be returned after the ransom was paid but the Hibaki killed him anyway. So Sparrow went after them and killed every member of the Hibaki."

"Hate to say this," Jake started, "but I'm beginning to like this guy. He only kills the low lives."

"What do you call Reverend Smith?" Frank asked.

"But he didn't kill Reverend Smith," Sam corrected him.

"Almost did."

Carl offered, "Maybe Sparrow didn't know."

"How so?" Frank asked.

Shrugging, Carl explained, "If Menut's bosses were deceitful enough to pay Sparrow in counterfeit money, they might have fabricated a background on Reverend Smith. Sparrow has followed a pattern in the past of conducting intense surveillance of his targets. Seems to kill only those people society can do without. Maybe after following Reverend Smith, he had his doubts about the truthfulness of the report." Carl gazed at Sam, who was reading silently, an intense look in her eyes. "Sam must be at the part where Sparrow has escaped from every prison he's ever been in."

"In each case, he killed and mutilated anywhere from two to five of his captors," Sam whispered. "Good god."

"Doesn't paint a pretty picture," Carl said.

"I can't believe this," Sam breathed. "He's used electric shock, forced people to swallow coins coated with shellfish toxin, used truth drugs...Carl, what is with all this torture?"

Carl shook his head. "I'm not sure."

"What about the CIA files? Did you get any data from them?" Frank asked.

Carl cleared his throat, averted their eyes, ran a hand through his thick hair. Finally, he admitted, "I haven't contacted them."

"Why?" Sam asked as she got up to answer the gate alarm. Jake motioned for her to sit down and he left to answer the security monitor.

"This has got to be good," Jake called out from the front door.

"I'd rather check FBI files first. If I start poking around the CIA and asking questions, John Hastings will dispatch twenty of his agents here to take over the case."

"God forbid they take over jurisdiction," Sam commented as a little side joke since Carl had a habit of doing that himself.

Jake brought in the pizzas and set them on the table. "There's no love lost between you and Hastings."

"That's beside the point," Carl said with a shrug. "The media gets wind of the CIA storm trooping in here, they'll start asking questions, dominating headlines, and this guy is going to bolt." Carl dragged a piece of pizza onto his plate. "No, we'll handle this.

I have my Chicago office for backup, and if the shit hits the fan, then let Hastings scream for my head. I'm retired anyway."

Jake said to Sam, "Tim stopped by earlier. He wants you to give him a call."

"That kid was nervous as hell," Carl added.

Sam picked up the portable phone and sat down on one of the window seats to dial Tim's number. He answered on the first ring and explained how he had obtained a report from Interpol at the same time Carl had received his.

"That's okay, Tim. You tried."

"But you don't know his real name yet, do you? I'm going to find out."

"How?"

"There's something called NID, National Intelligence Daily. It's a news bulletin circulated only to one hundred of the rank and file. There's also something called SCI, Sensitive Compartmented Info."

"Really?" Sam glanced quickly at Jake who was showing a little too much interest in her phone call.

"But that's not the best part," Tim continued.

"I'm afraid to ask."

"I contacted him."

Sam was silent.

"Did you hear me, Sam? He's an E-mail user and he sent me a message back."

She pressed her lips together and glanced over at the curious stares coming from the dining room table.

"What did he say?"

Tim replied, "He challenged me to find out who he is. And he's giving me forty-eight hours."

Sam inhaled, her mind trying to decide what to do, who to tell, if she should tell. Too soon, she decided. No sense getting anyone's hopes up.

"Keep up the good work, Tim. And let me know how things turn out." She hung up the phone, saying, "Tim might have sold one of his programs." It was a lie, a tiny one. Well, maybe a little bit bigger.

36

Sparrow called Davud at nine sharp the next morning. Gholam stood like a palace guard, arms crossed, legs apart. It was amazing there were shirts his size let alone suit coats.

Davud leaned back in his chair while Sparrow's voice blared over the speaker phone. Sunlight streamed through the opened blinds.

"You have the money?" Sparrow asked.

"Yes." Davud looked at the opened briefcase of cash.

"They better be authentic, Mr. Menut."

Davud let out a heavy sigh. "Yes, of course. I went to my bank yesterday. I assure you, these bills are not counterfeit."

"Good. Then we will make the exchange at one o'clock."

"I prefer a public place."

"Of course."

Davud could hear a cocky arrogance in Sparrow's voice. He just wished he could be there when Gholam destroyed him.

"The shopping center," Davud continued. "Do you know where it's at?" Sparrow said he did. "I will be sitting at one of the benches in the center court facing..."

"Not acceptable," Sparrow countered.

Davud shifted in his seat, slammed the lid down on the briefcase, and said, "Now what, Mr. Sparrow. It's my money. It should be my choice."

"Correction, Mr. Menut."

Davud was tiring of Sparrow's soft-spoken, condescending tone.

"It is MY money," Sparrow said. "So I pick the park. I plan on opening the suitcase to make sure the money is there. I will check its authenticity and for your sake, you better be telling me the truth."

"All right. The park."

"There is a bench by the bird sanctuary. I'll be sitting there."

When Sparrow hung up, Gholam said, "Bird sanctuary. How fitting. Maybe I should leave him for the crows to eat."

Menut smiled and fixed his good eye on Gholam. "Keep a safe distance away. After he takes the briefcase, you follow him. Use whatever measures you must to get the plates from him. Then bring the plates back here. The money, my friend, will be yours."

Sparrow sat at his computer after his call to Davud. He suspected that Davud was not alone. He had put him on the speaker phone, obviously had a second agenda. Everyone always has a second agenda. Maybe even his friend, Bond.

Sparrow accessed his E-mail messages and with anticipation read the message from Bond. Aliases, a long string of them. Bond said the information was retrieved from confidential Interpol files.

Sparrow smiled. The kid was good. A computer hack. One of the few talents that escaped Sparrow. Sixteen years old, real name of Tim Miesner, only child, a senior at Chasen Heights Central. Sparrow knew where he lived, what record store he liked to shop at, and that his favorite snack was red licorice. He didn't have a girlfriend, wasn't into sports.

It wasn't hard to obtain a modem phone number of an E-mail user. And once you had a phone number, it wasn't hard to get an address. He had even followed Tim from school, bumped into him at a music store. Of course, Sparrow had looked like a throwback from Woodstock so Tim hadn't given him a second glance.

The printer started spitting out the pages of information. He read them over, a second time, a third time, trying to jog his memory, until a searing pain sliced through his head.

The pages dropped to the floor as Sparrow grabbed his head in his hands and pressed firmly. He focused, inhaled, focused, inhaled, until the pain subsided.

His hands moved to the keyboard as he typed a message to Bond.

Good work so far.

Sparrow

* * *

Carl placed the briefcase on the conference table and opened it.

"Whew," Frank whistled. "So that's what four million bucks looks like."

"That's it. All we have to do now is get it to Yang Chu."

"Damn. That can buy a lot of egg rolls," Frank laughed.

Carl leaned back in the wooden chair and peered at Frank over his horn-rimmed glasses. "Egg rolls is Chinese. I'm sure you mean kim-chi, which is a Korean spiced cabbage."

Frank shrugged, fanning through the stacks of bills. "We're meeting them in a Chinese restaurant so egg rolls fits for me."

Carl unbuttoned his shirtsleeves, and rolled them up his forearm. "His wife will be there with one of her daughters. We will leave the suitcase with her. What about Myla Smith?"

"Stopped by this morning and watched as we destroyed the two tapes of her father. She's taking my suggestion and not bringing attention to the case by engaging in further demonstrations," Frank replied.

Jake cranked open one of the windows, noticing that the mourning doves were gone. He half-listened to Carl. His head was replaying Sam's phone call with Tim.

Carl said, "You're quiet today, Jake. What's rolling around in that head of yours?"

Jake loosened his tie and unbuttoned the top button of his shirt, revealing the silver arrowhead that hung from a black leather cord. The arrowhead had one coral stone in the center, another piece of Alex's artwork. "Just thinking." What he didn't want to tell Carl was that he felt Sam was holding back about her conversation with Tim. The two were cooking up something but he didn't have a clue what it was. "What about the IRS? Did they come back to you yet regarding Menut's filings?"

"They are foaming at the mouth looking into this guy's tax records. I hope we hear from them today."

Frank checked his watch. "It's close to one o'clock, guys. How about lunch?"

The temperature was a crisp fifty-five degrees, the skies overcast. Davud left his overcoat unbuttoned and walked cautiously through the park.

A young couple sat close together on a bench sharing a bag of fries; a mother threw popcorn on the grass for the pigeons as her two-year-old shrieked with glee.

Davud could see the administration building off to his left behind the tennis courts. It was a school day so the park was relatively empty.

He passed a restroom facility and walked toward an area surrounded by trees. He felt swallowed up by the colorful maple and oak trees as he walked along an asphalt path. A jogger in shorts and sleeveless shirt breezed by. A flurry of birds called out from the tree limbs, as if crying for the release of their relatives who were enclosed in the fenced in area.

Davud wrapped his coat around him and searched the trees with his good eye. The briefcase was beginning to feel heavy. The path opened into a fifty-foot circular section with park benches and pots of orange chrysanthemums. At the furthest point was a spacious, caged in area containing trees, a pond, foliage, and bird feeders.

The park benches were empty. No Sparrow. Davud checked his watch, slowly looked around. Clutching the briefcase tighter, he walked up to the cage. Twelve-by-ten-inch signs were mounted every six feet, each one showing a picture and describing a different species. He studied the picture of the quail, tern, heron, then glanced behind him. Still no one. He walked along the path and stopped at another sign. There was a picture and description of a sparrow.

"Interesting bird, don't you think?"

The voice came from directly behind him, so close he could feel the warm breath on his neck. A chill ran up Davud's back. He turned to find a man with gray hair and a beard, rose-tinted glasses, and a black trench coat, leaning on a cane. This is what has been frightening him? Some old codger? The thought sent a slice of fury through Davud's veins.

"I guess it's a good thing they don't have a sparrow hawk. Now there's a bird, part of the falcon family. It preys on small birds and mammals." Sparrow looked Davud over from head to toe and added with a smile, "Man is a mammal, you know."

"Hah. It is nothing but a bully preying on weaker animals," Davud spit out.

Sparrow raised a finger as though in thought and said, "Ah, but other than survival, nothing else matters." He smiled.

Davud noticed straight, even white teeth. Then he noticed

youthful skin behind the beard, youthful hands. Even the voice was young, did not match the graying hair. He suddenly realized Sparrow was wearing a disguise.

When Davud took a cautious step backward, Sparrow said, "Place the suitcase on that bench and open it."

His heart raced as he moved to the closest bench. He knew Gholam was close by should Sparrow try anything. But the man was limping. How could he be a threat if he's limping? Was that part of the disguise?

They sat down a safe distance from each other. Once the suitcase was opened, Sparrow thumbed through several of the stacks and studied a few of the bills. "What about the five million?"

"I'll know tomorrow," Davud stammered. "It takes time."

Sparrow checked the bottom layer of bound bills. Without looking up he said, "You can leave."

Davud looked back several times as he walked away, but Sparrow remained seated, wasn't coming after him, wasn't pulling a gun. But then again, if he did, he wouldn't see his five million. Davud smiled as he hurried to his car. It would be a piece of cake for Gholam to handle Sparrow.

Sparrow brushed a hand against his beard, he was deliberate in his movements. He could feel someone watching, waiting. His cane didn't have a gun in it this time. It had a stunning device that discharged a one-hundred-thousand-volt energy field from up to twenty feet away. Whoever was following him was going to be dropped like a sack of flour.

Sparrow strolled past the cage again, studied the padlocks on the three doors into the caged area, looked up at the various species cawing back and forth, flying between the trees, pattering on the ground.

No one had shown up yet but he could still feel the eyes. He'd know him when he saw him. He had followed Davud to the bank the day before, had seen the massive bodyguard with him. Sometimes even a bullet wouldn't take down a man that size. A tranquilizer gun, maybe. Stun gun, absolutely.

Sparrow reached into the inside pocket of his trench coat, pulled out a small case from which he retrieved a lock pick. Hooking the cane over the crook of his left arm, he quickly set to work on unlocking the doors.

He opened the doors wide, moving on to the remaining two. He took his cane and rapped on the cage, sending the birds scattering to freedom.

That was when the man moved out of the bushes. Sparrow caught him from of the corner of his eye. Calmly, he pulled the cane from the crook of his arm, made a quarter turn, pointed the cane, and fired. Gholam's shriek blended in with the mass exodus of birds.

37

Sam sat on the couch in Tim's computer room surrounded by sheets of paper. "This is basically the same information Carl has."

"Is it?"

"What about the CIA files?"

Tim's fingers flew over the keyboard. "It seems my program can only get so far. It finds this long list of code names for operations. I can get into each of them and have it search but that may take forever."

Sam peered over his shoulder at the list on the screen. "Artichoke, Operation Barber. Where do they come up with these names? How many pages are there?"

Tim scrolled through the list. "About one hundred and eighty."

"Oh, god," Sam groaned. "There's got to be an easier way."

"I'll keep trying."

Sam plopped back on the bed and drew her legs up under her. She brushed cat hair off her leggings and wondered where Attila the Hunter was. Tim's black tabby was bashful but brutal, and was known to walk up behind any non-suspecting visitor and nip him or her on the ankle. Tim's father even had a *Beware of Cat* sign in the front window. She checked her watch. Jackie was meeting her at three o'clock to do some shopping. She also had one other stop to make. She wanted to return to Amid's apartment.

"Print out those pages anyway, Tim. We can go through the listings and put a check mark by anything that looks remotely possible."

Other than the matchbook and glass, Sam had not touched anything else Sparrow had touched. Her initial visit to Amid's apartment had been littered with too many cops and technicians.

She found the landlord on the first floor fixing the washing machine in the small, ten-by-five-foot laundry room. He reluctantly gave her the key to Amid's empty apartment once she showed him a business card Tim had whipped up on his color printer. *Private Investigator has a nice ring to it*, she thought. Now all she needed to do was make it legal.

It hadn't taken Kamel, the landlord, long to haul all of Amid's belongings out of the apartment. It looked like scavengers had picked the place clean. All that was left in the living room was a bare floor, three ashtrays, and the blinds on the windows.

There was a telephone on the floor by the wall jack. Sam ran her hand across the dust on the floor and decided against having a seat. Instead, she pulled the jack out and carried the phone to the kitchen, which also had been stripped of all furniture, so she opted for the bedroom. It seemed no one wanted the bed with the blood-stained mattress.

Whoever Kamel hired to clean up the apartment did a lousy job. The walls and floor were streaked as if someone took a quick swipe with a floor mop.

She sat at the foot of the bed and held the telephone in her hand, closed her eyes. All her mind saw was the tattoo. Against her better judgment, she inched her way up toward the stained headboard, toward where Amid's head had once rested.

The aura running from the bed to the telephone felt like tiny pulses of electricity. Sparrow had been calm, in control. That much of Lloyd's profile was right. Completely fearless of getting caught, of being in danger, of death.

Screams, those terrifying screams she had heard before, echoed in her head. She had to release her grip on the phone and hold her head in her hands until the screams stopped. When she felt a hand touch her shoulder, she jumped up from the bed, dropping the phone to the floor.

"Sorry, miss. I just want to see how you do," Kamel said.

Sam took a deep breath. "I do think you should clean this place a little better if you hope to rent it out."

"You are okay? You look as white as a ghost."

Sam brushed the back of her pants off saying, "I'll be fine once I get some fresh air." Nothing like a little shopping to get her mind off blood and guts.

Parking at Spoil 'em Silly was at a premium. Sam had to leave the Jeep on a side street and fight the brisk wind the half block walk to the store. Upon entering, she assumed a back order of Beanie Babies® must have arrived because the store was wall-to-wall people. A voice in her head kept reminding Sam about the murder investigation and how she had more important things to do. But she mentally told the little voice to call back in an hour.

She made a beeline to a large plastic box on a table and wedged herself between an elderly man and a mother with two kids in tow. The children stood back and waited, leaving the digging to their mother. Gramps was all elbows. He had several Beanie Babies® in the crook of one arm. She wondered why he wasn't home sifting through a stamp collection or at a neighborhood garage sale. A flannel shirt hung on his frail body, and it looked as if a good strong wind could blow him over. His free hand was flinging Beanies™ around as fast as a gopher moves dirt.

Sam immediately spotted a white bear with iridescent wings and a halo. Halo™ was one of those elusive bears, very hard to find and worth more than its selling price. Elated, Sam grabbed Halo™ by one wing only to find that Gramps held onto the other.

"That's mine," Gramps yelled. His thunderous voice didn't match his frail body. He tugged hard.

"I saw it first." Sam pulled harder.

"I GRABBED IT FIRST."

"YOU ALREADY HAVE AN ARM LOAD."

Halo's little arms and legs flopped back and forth, its black, oil-drop eyes staring vacantly. Sam hoped there wasn't anyone in the store she knew, like the wife of a cop, who would go running home to hubby to tell him how the suspended cop who just got out of a nut house was in a drag-out fight with a senior citizen.

"I HAVE EIGHT GRANDKIDS." Gramps pulled even harder.

"I'M PREGNANT," Sam yelled.

A small voice screamed, "You're hurting Halo!" A young girl with a mop of curly hair stood with her tiny fists jammed on her hips.

From the counter by the cash register, a fairly audible "ahem" was emitted. Sam looked over to see Patti, one arm across her waist with the hand propping up her elbow, the other hand pressed under her chin. The room grew quiet. Sam imagined Patti using the same technique at home with her brood. Just one quiet "ahem" probably had her kids lining up like the Von Trapp family.

Reluctantly, Sam let loose of the Beanie™.

"About time," Gramps huffed.

Sam opened her mouth to get the last word but saw Patti press an index finger to her lips. Then she felt the stares from the customers. A headache was building and Sam turned to find refuge in the block room.

"He really doesn't have eight grandkids," Patti said as she appeared behind Sam.

"I'm so sorry. I don't know what's come over me. I find myself doing some of the strangest things."

"I understand. Come." Patti led her to a back office. "I let some of my frequent customers have a choice of the new arrivals. So you can pick five if you'd like."

Sam felt like a kid in a candy store. So many Beanies™, so few picks.

38

Davud checked his watch. Gholam should have returned by now. He walked over to the window and peered through the blinds. Holly buzzed him on the intercom. Davud barked, "Yes."

"Gholam called."

"Where is he?"

"He didn't say. Just said to have you pick him up at the park."

Sweat started to form on Davud's forehead. Why didn't Gholam ask to speak to him? Why didn't he come back here as planned?

"Was it Gholam's voice you heard?" Davud asked.

"Sure. I think so. I mean it sounded like him."

Davud slammed the phone down, opened his desk drawer and pulled out his .357 Magnum.

The drive to the park took fifteen minutes. The sun, which had been dodging clouds most of the day, was tucked behind a ceiling of gray. Davud pulled his coat around him, shoved his hands in his pockets, and held on tight to his Magnum.

He gingerly made his way through the park, checking benches, the stairs at the administration building, the tennis courts. He found himself back at the entrance to the bird sanctuary which had a *Closed* sign in the middle of the path.

Davud stopped and looked around. The chattering of animals

and birds filled the air. Shadows from the trees were growing longer, creating dark pockets, too many for comfort.

He made a complete circle as his eyes searched the park. There were joggers in the distance, people walking dogs. It was close to dinnertime and the park was thinning out.

Davud turned back and looked at the entrance to the bird sanctuary again. He cautiously walked past the sign and entered the circular area. The first thing he noticed were the empty cages. Then he saw Gholam. He breathed a sigh of relief and quickened his pace.

Gholam was sitting at a park bench, his head tilted back, eyes wide. There was something awkward about the way he sat.

"Why didn't you come to..." Davud stopped as he saw the position of Gholam's body. He cautiously walked around to the back of the bench. Gholam's arms were stretched over the back and tied to the wooden slats.

"What?" Davud jerked his head up and looked around quickly. They were alone. Gholam couldn't possibly have made the call to him. "What happened?" Davud asked as he tried unsuccessfully to untie his friend.

A guttural sound came from Gholam. Almost a whimper. Davud saw a tear streaming down Gholam's pudgy cheek. Davud examined Gholam. He didn't have any bruises on him, no gun shot wounds Davud could see. Yet his bulky friend was whimpering like a baby.

"GHOLAM," Davud yelled. "What is wrong with you?"

Gholam's head lobbed side to side, his mouth hung down, drool ran down his chin. Davud's gaze dropped to an object next to Gholam. There was a finger, gray and mottled, lying on the bench.

Something else caught Davud's attention. Right at Gholam's waistline where his shirt seemed to strain at the buttons. Gholam was a big man, but there seemed to be added bulk. It was slight. He had to watch carefully. Now he was sure. The fabric was moving.

39

Sam arrived at the park a few minutes after Jake and his entourage. She and Jackie had just finished two hours of shopping and Sam was ready for a diversion.

As Sam approached, Officer Marty Rizzo, the policeman on foot patrol in the park at the time, was just starting to explain to Jake what had transpired. The area was circled in yellow crime scene tape and thrill-seekers were well beyond the wooden horses that had been set up fifty feet away from the entrance.

Rizzo pulled a pencil from his shirt pocket and read from his notepad. "Witnesses say they saw a man screaming and running from this area at approximately five-thirty. I was immediately alerted, took a walk through the area," he pointed toward the sanctuary, "and saw the victim on the bench."

They walked toward the bench and Sam said, "Oh my god. I know him."

"How?" Carl asked.

"Jackie and I saw him with Menut. I don't know his name."

As the crime lab took pictures of the area, Sam turned her head. A policeman thirty yards away was leaning into the bushes, obviously sick to his stomach. She looked back at Gholam and watched as Carl peeled more of Gholam's shirt away.

"Crissake," Frank breathed. "What the hell is that?"

Gholam's dark pants and shirt camouflaged most of the blood. Carl pressed his fingers to Gholam's neck. "He hasn't been dead long." He straightened up and took a step backwards. "This is a form of torture used in some of the more barbaric countries. An incision is made in the stomach, and a cage, which in this case is a flexible steel mesh bag, is tied to the waist, its opening facing the flesh. Then the rat inside the cage begins to eat his way through."

And eat its way through is what the rat had done. Flesh and entrails were protruding through Gholam's gut. He literally bled to death.

"Obviously, our friend has been here," Jake said, pointing to the finger on the bench.

Sam walked around to the back of the bench, trying to focus instead on any aura Sparrow may have left behind. She had to inhale deeply in order to keep from feeling faint. A voice kept repeating something in her head: *Other than survival, nothing else matters.*

When Benny arrived, she heard Jake say, "Okay, someone get that damn cage off of him."

"Holy shit," Benny gasped under his breath. He made a quick inspection and then had his aides cut the ropes and lay Gholam's body on the ground. "In all my years I have never seen anything like this," Benny said as he watched his aides remove the mesh bag from Gholam's waist.

The rat struggled to stay with its dinner. One officer tossed the rat into a bag. Officers were huddled in small groups. This was probably one for the books. It was bound to be the topic of the break room for some time, at least until the next bizarre murder.

Benny unbuttoned Gholam's shirt and inspected his chest. He studied a burn mark just above the left nipple. "Looks like a stun gun may have been used on him," he said.

"Electric shock?" Carl asked.

"Mega dose, too, to take down a man his size," Benny added.

Sam felt Jake's eyes on her as she sought refuse by the birdcage. Her hands touched the sign that said, Sparrow. Again, she heard the words, *Other than survival, nothing else matters.*

Davud had been here, had been by the birds along with Sparrow. Sam felt fear, unbelievable fear. Probably from Davud and then the victim. She looked back over her shoulder at the body on the ground. The chill in the air made her pull her blanket coat tighter. Leaves, dried and brown, were caught by the wind and circled like errant tornadoes around Gholam's body, eventually to be raked and burned. Dust to dust, ashes to ashes.

He was a big man, at least three hundred and fifty, maybe four hundred pounds. Sparrow had been prepared, which means he had seen Gholam with Davud before. Probably the same day Sam saw him. Probably why she had felt someone watching her.

"You okay?" Jake seemed to appear out of nowhere. He placed his hands on her shoulders and gently kneaded them. She could smell the leather in his brown trench coat, and for a second a black trench coat flashed before her eyes. A black trench coat with a cape collar.

She shook her head. "I don't think I have ever seen anything like this. At least not since Amid."

"His name was Reza Gholam. Has an expired visa on him. No forwarding address. No driver's license." Jake leaned against the railing and looked at the crime scene. Benny's men were struggling to get Gholam's body into the body bag. They gave up and threw a sheet over him.

Sam leaned against him, wishing she could crawl inside his coat, let him hold her. She was overcome with an immense sense of sorrow and she had a feeling it wasn't for Gholam. She wrapped her arms tightly around his arm, as if it were a strong tree in a gale force wind, and leaned her forehead against his shoulder. She didn't expect any response from Jake. One thing she did remember about him was that he showed little affection in public.

His fingertips brushed her hand. "You sure you're okay?" Jake asked. Sam nodded in response. He watched them shove Gholam's body into the back of the ME wagon and then asked, "What kind of man could do that to another human being?"

Sam looked up at the enormous cage, the doors gaping open, the branches void of the species once imprisoned, and said, "The same man who freed the birds."

"Slow down. I can't understand a word you're saying." Sam dragged leftover chicken from the refrigerator as she talked to Jackie on the phone.

"I said," Jackie repeated, "Davud came running in here like Doctor Death himself was on his ass. He threw some clothes and papers together and was just ready to high-tail it out of here when the Revenue boys showed up."

"Who?"

"IRS, Honey, with a capital I."

Sam ate the potato salad right out of the container as she listened. She added salt and pepper, then grabbed a jar of pickles from the refrigerator.

"Good, they can get him on income tax evasion and deport him back to Iran."

"Uh, uh, girlfriend. The jerk claimed some shit about diplomatic immunity."

Sam dropped her fork in the container. "Diplomatic immunity? He's no foreign diplomat."

"According to Davud, he doesn't have to be. He claims he's some kind of diplomatic courier, even had papers."

"Wonderful, just wonderful. Where is he now?"

"Only the lord knows," Jackie replied with exasperation in her voice. "The IRS closed the place down, and Davud hopped on a flight to some embassy in D.C."

Sam put the lid on the empty potato salad container and tossed it in the garbage. She next attacked the chicken breast, peeling off the skin first.

"I'm sorry, Jackie. I guess your career was short and sweet. What happened to Yung?"

"He took her with. Claimed she was his secretary."

"Well, we'll be lucky we don't find his body floating up on the beach somewhere."

Before they hung up, they agreed to meet for lunch one day soon. Next Sam called Tim to get an update on his computer search.

"No word back from him yet?" Sam asked.

"No, but I haven't really had anything new to tell him. It's taking forever to go through all these project files."

"Did you look for an Operation Sparrow or Project Sparrow?" Sam asked.

"Yes," Tim replied.

Again, those words played in Sam's head, *Other than survival, nothing else matters.*

"Tim, try Operation Survival or Project Survival."

Sam could hear him pounding the keyboard.

"There, I've got one. Operation Survival." What excitement he had in his voice was killed with a groan. "It's one of those SCI files, the Sensitive Compartmented Info."

"You can't get into it?"

"It has one of those pyramid codes. You know, like first I would type in planet, next Jupiter, and then maybe Milky Way. So even though we have the file name, we now have to come up with access codes."

Sam tossed the chicken bones in the garbage and put her plate in the dishwasher. "Isn't your program supposed to sidestep all that code stuff?"

"It gets around the *access denied* messages and gets me to the listings but certain files have code padlocks. This file was with the deleted to begin with. But don't worry, Sam. I'll get into it."

"If anyone can, Tim, it's you." When Sam hung up, she saw the message light flashing. She pressed the button and heard Abby's voice.

> *Just called to see how everyone is doing. Alex and I are fine. There are important Council meetings coming up. I think Cora and Louise will be appointed to fill the two empty Council seats. Everyone here says hello. I'm sorry we weren't able to reach you. Maybe next time.*

Sam smiled at the sound of Abby's voice. Sam, too, wished she had been home to receive the call. She needed to ask Abby some questions, needed advice. But Abby had already given her some advice. She had said, "The only way to communicate was not to talk at all." All Sam had to do was figure out what the hell it meant.

40

At least eight hundred residents had crammed into the Council lodge for the hearing and the cake and coffee afterward. Keeping to their word, the Council had appointed Cora and Louise to fill the vacant council seats. They each had given memorable acceptance speeches. Cora stated they could still renegotiate the contract with the managing company for the casino. Instead of a twenty-year contract, they should insist on a five-year contract with the condition that tribal members be trained to take over all aspects of the business by the end of the contract.

Louise had suggested the Council send two people to the National Indian Gaming Association's annual meeting in Phoenix next month. She also suggested the Council compile a list of the various projects on the reservation that could be funded from casino profits. A motion was made to push the election back two weeks to give the residents a chance to understand their options.

"I have never seen Cora look so nice," Abby said pointing toward her friend standing next to Foster Two Bulls. It wasn't often Cora wore a dress, and she had been quick to point out to everyone that she wasn't going to make a habit of it.

Alex nodded in agreement as he looked at Louise. "I think you may have swayed Louise to your side."

"Well, I gave her food for thought. She is bright. One day, she may make a good Tribal Chief. Someone open to suggestion, willing to bend, yet strong in character. Yes, she might make an excellent Chief. I will have to put a bug in Chief Big Crow's ear."

Alex gave her a sideways glance, his eyes narrow slits.

"Don't look at me like that," Abby said.

"Like what?"

"Your eyes are saying, 'a female chief?'".

Cora motioned for them to come over. Alex grabbed another slice of carrot cake en route.

"Abby, I want you to meet Anthony Lone Hawk." Cora had her arm around a handsome youth with straight black hair, a scar above his left eye. "I would like to see the Council appoint a five-member youth group, a group a Council member could meet with on a monthly or semi-monthly basis. Find out what type of youth programs they would like, what problems they or their friends are having. Maybe they need tutors. Maybe they need help getting their lazy fathers off the couch." Cora let out a laugh as Anthony smiled.

"That sounds wonderful," Louise said, overhearing the conversation. "This would work. The possibilities are endless. We could find temporary surrogate families for those whose parents are unable to take care of their children."

"Maybe team up the high-school-age youths with the grade-school-age," Cora added.

"Sort of a big brother/big sister program," Louise finished.

Alex and Abby drifted away from the women.

"Things are really starting to shape up. That was a wonderful suggestion you made," Alex said. "Cora and Louise, I mean."

Cameras clicked as the two new Council members posed for the press. Then they were swarmed by a sea of flannel and Stetsons as all the Council members joined in the picture.

Abby sighed. "I do miss this place sometimes."

Alex settled his own Stetson on his head and grinned. "You can always move back. I think you'd make a great pit boss for the new casino."

Electric shocks, splinters, injections, pots of boiling water, acid, all types of mental and physical tortures crept into Sam's dreams. Screams, piercing screams in the dark, and rats, rats in cages.

She woke with a start, gasping for air as she threw off the quilt and sat up. She could feel the blood throbbing in her neck, her pulse quickening. Her mind kept seeing the rat, Gholam's intestines, and her body began to shake.

Pulling the comforter and pillow off the bed, she moved to the chaise in front of the patio doors in the bedroom. She cocooned herself in the comforter and pulled her knees up, stared at the dark skies. Streaks of lightning lit up the sky as she thought back to the dreams. It wasn't the first time she heard painful screams in her dreams. They had started after seeing Amid's body. No, Sam thought. They had started after touching the matchbook. Her head was playing games with her, jumping from nightmares about her father's death to Chief Connelley's death to the torture dreams. She was getting better at separating them. Now the challenge was deciphering them.

Thunder rumbled in the distance and Sam leaned back, turned on her side to watch the storm build. The thought came as quickly as the flashes of lightning. It wasn't the torture Sparrow subjected his victims to she had been dreaming about. It was the torture someone had inflicted on Sparrow.

41

The next day Tim's parents attended an investment seminar. Tim had tried to sleep late, something he savored on Saturdays, but he had several ideas for passwords for Operation Survival and wanted to try them out. He no sooner stepped out of the shower, then the door bell rang.

"Sam?" he thought. He dressed and hurried to the door. A man, tall, wearing dark sunglasses, flipped open an I.D. All Tim saw was *Special Forces*.

"You know Mr. Underer?" Tim asked, his eyes wide in anticipation.

"Yes. He and Sergeant Casey are at his hotel room. They asked me to pick you up along with whatever information you have."

Tim's heart leaped. "Sure!" He left the door open and ran up the stairs. The man walked in and stared at the great room with its high cathedral ceilings, expensive artwork, white furniture and carpeting that said, "look, don't touch."

Tim came bounding down the stairs, a briefcase in hand containing the one hundred and eighty pages, his notes, and laptop computer.

The man opened the passenger side of the dark sedan and Tim climbed in. He chatted endlessly about Sam, the FBI, James Bond movies. The man just nodded and would glance over at Tim every now and then and smile.

It wasn't until Tim ran out of things to say that he looked over and saw the man's ponytail. Government men don't have ponytails. Then he saw the man's hand on the steering wheel, saw the tattoo. He swallowed hard, stared at the man's face and whispered, "You're not with the FBI. You're him, aren't you?"

Sparrow took off his sunglasses, looked over at Tim and said, "Yes, and I need your help."

"So, what do you think?" Sam stood in front of the mirror holding up a red dress. She looked over at the menagerie of bean-stuffed animals on her bedroom dresser. She had found a grapevine branch out by Alex's house, cleaned it up, and placed it on her dresser. Then she arranged the birds and bears on the branches. Stretch™, her favorite, sat on one of the larger branches, its legs dangling.

Lucky for her, Jake and Carl were at the precinct meeting with IRS agents and Immigration about Menut. She wouldn't want Jake to see how nervous she was about tonight.

She tossed the red dress on the bed and held up a two-piece navy blue outfit. "Or how about this one?" Tossing a quizzical look at Stretch™, she asked, "Don't like the color?" Turning to Halo™, her newest member of her entourage, she asked, "What about you? Is navy too boring?"

The phone interrupted her one-way conversation.

"What are you up to?" Jackie's bubbly voice always seemed to keep Sam in an up mood.

"Getting ready for a date."

"A date?"

Sam explained that she and Jake were going out to dinner.

After Jackie finished her fit of giggles, she said, "Sounds promising. You go, girl. Is tonight the night you're going to break the news?"

Sam sighed. "I'm going to try. Just don't know at what point during the course of the meal to drop the bombshell."

"Tell you what you do." Jackie's enthusiasm oozed through the phone lines. "You just hand him a gift box wrapped all pretty and fuzzy and inside have a pacifier." She laughed again, cackled with amusement.

"You are having way too much fun with this." Sam leaned over, one elbow on the dresser, while she admired her animal-filled creation. She had even positioned a koala bear climbing onto one of the limbs. Jackie babbled on about the perfect perfume to wear for tonight.

"I think I'm in trouble," Sam confessed as she arranged the wing on the cardinal Beanie™.

"Only single women who are pregnant are in trouble."

"For some reason I just can't stop buying these Beanies." She lifted the lid off a small jewelry box she had found on the kitchen window box yesterday. It contained a ring identical to the one Jake wore. Sam slipped it over the first knuckle, then hesitated. It was beautiful but seemed so final, something she wasn't quite ready to do. Slowly, she slid it down the rest of the way and held her hand out, felt a twinge in her stomach. Maybe her stomach was telling her something.

"Everyone's gotta have a passion, Sam. Look at me. I have a closet just for my shoes. I can't go into a store without buying at least three pair."

"But shoes have a use. You wear them. You need them." She tugged on the ring. It wouldn't come off. Maybe her finger was swollen because she just got out of the shower. Licking her finger, she pulled again. Still wouldn't budge. It would be just like Abby, Sam thought, to sabotage her and have the damn thing shrink wrap itself to her finger.

"Well, maybe you just want a pet that don't bite." Jackie

cackled again.

Sam plopped down on the bed. “I’m being serious.”

“So am I, girlfriend. Trust me. The only time you need to really be concerned is when you start talking to the damn things.”

“This is a hell of a time for R and R,” Carl said pacing in front of Jake’s desk.

“Taking my wife to dinner is not exactly like I’m taking a week’s vacation, Carl. We have to eat sometime. So what better place than a restaurant.”

“We’re in the middle of a damn psycho case, Yang Chu hasn’t called, Menut has taken a powder, we have bodies dropping out of the sky.”

Jake had become used to Carl’s demanding attitude. But Carl was retired now. Jake could only assume he was anxious about Lloyd’s findings.

“What about the press release on Reverend Smith?” Carl asked.

Jake fanned through the papers on his desk and handed a print-out to Carl. “Just as you had suggested. It says the Reverend was researching an article he was writing for a local paper. So he was on the boat interviewing people to get their reasons for frequenting the casino, to see firsthand the extent of compulsive gambling. The press release goes on to say he was the victim of a random theft. That the thief double-crossed his own people and was, himself, murdered. It also throws in the lawsuit filed by the widow for neglect on the part of the casino for not having metal detectors.”

“I’m sure she’ll come out with a few million on that one,” Carl said. He checked his watch.

Jake had never seen Carl so edgy. “We can probably handle things from here. Why don’t you go on that fishing trip?”

Carl seemed to mull it over but shook his head.

“What? Can’t go alone?” Jake said, grinning. “Need Lloyd to hold your hand?”

"Nah. Alone is how I've always been." Carl fixed a gaze on his star pupil. "Trust me. Alone is not how you want to spend your life."

42

Serengeti's Steak House was a fairly large, upscale restaurant in the pavilion at the River Queen Casino. It wasn't a fancy French restaurant with overpriced diminutive morsels surrounded by glazes you couldn't pronounce. Jake was strictly a meat and potatoes man and Serengeti's had excellent steak and seafood.

William Borden Jr.'s proposal to Sam had been dinner for two at Serengeti's so Jake had taken him up on the offer.

The waiting area looked like someone's spacious living room, with plush couches and plants that separated the main dining room from the bar. Their table was located next to a large window giving them a good view of the lake. Waitresses and waiters wore tuxedo shirts and bow ties. The room was slowly filling. Tables were draped in white linen and adorned with vases containing red roses and baby's breath. Intimate candles cast a romantic glow to the room.

Sam had finally settled on a jersey knit sheath dress in navy blue with nylons and heels to match. A beaded feather choker hugged her neck. She had been unsuccessful at getting the ring off and noticed it was one of the first things that caught Jake's attention. He had done a slight double-take but didn't comment.

Jake had no idea what Sam would be wearing and surprisingly

selected a navy blue suit and peach shirt. They were already acting like an old married couple who dress alike. The waitress brought him a beer and Sam a glass of white wine. They studied their menus.

"I'm not very good at this," Sam admitted. She was nervous to the point of nausea.

Jake flicked his gaze at her over the top of his menu. "Ordering?" he asked. He folded his menu and tossed it aside.

No smile, no twinkle. She was beginning to recall he had a dry sense of humor. The flutters started to disappear.

The waiter came over and Jake ordered shrimp cocktail for an appetizer and then filet mignon for each of them. He looked at her briefly and proceeded to select her potato and vegetable.

After the waiter left, Sam said, "How do you know how I eat my steak?"

He studied her long enough that she felt he was sucking DNA from her brain. "You like your bacon well done so you probably wouldn't like your steak bloody. You're too impatient to bother dressing up a baked potato so you probably like double-baked, where the cook does all the work." He emptied the contents of his beer bottle into his glass and took a sip, eyeing her inquisitively. "You don't like milk so you probably don't like creamy dressings. So I ordered Italian."

Sam felt at a disadvantage. She obviously wasn't as observant as he was. Although if he were observant, he would have been suspicious at the twenty tons of crackers she had eaten in the past week. She wondered if now was the time to say, "do you like your baby rare or well done?".

"Lemon juice." Her eyes challenged him. His one eyebrow jerked up. "I like lemon juice on my salad," she clarified.

"Noted."

A hint of a smile pierced his eyes and the peach color of his shirt looked damn good on him. She forced her attention to the window, to the charter boats making their way toward the mouth of the Calumet Harbor, to their winter mooring slips or dry dock. Small talk. She wasn't good at it and found herself thinking of words synonymous with small, like infant, baby. Her fingers fumbled with the twist of curls snaking out from her French twist and suddenly felt the hair was all wrong, the dress didn't feel comfortable, and the heels had to go.

The waiter brought their shrimp cocktail, and once he left she said, "How did you get the Chevy running?"

"I wondered when you were going to get around to that. Frank is pretty handy with cars. I'm not too bad. With Alex's help we got it going. It's a shame to keep something like that hidden away."

"Uh huh."

"You're upset because I didn't consult you first?"

"Oh, no. What's mine is yours." Sam said with a slight hint of resignation in her voice.

He eyed her sharply as he squeezed lemon on his shrimp. "And exactly what does that include?" Jake finished his beer and the waiter promptly brought another.

How about a baby? Sam took a polite sip of wine, wishing instead to gulp the whole damn thing and ask for the bottle.

She fingered the stem of her wine glass. "Besides the house and property, there's about ten thousand shares of a variety of stocks, a home in Martinique, about two hundred acres of land in South Dakota, mutual funds, U.S. savings bonds, a number of savings accounts, a two-hundred-and-fifty-thousand-dollar trust fund I haven't touched, a few oil wells in Nebraska, give or take a few..." her voice trailed off as she saw the look on his face.

"Sorry I asked."

"My father meant the land in South Dakota to go to Abby. She can have it annexed to the reservation, maybe get some company to build a plant, maybe UPS. Someone who can bring desperately needed jobs." She looked at his expressionless face. "Unless you have a problem with that."

"No, I just have a problem with, I really didn't know you had..."

"So much?" *Oh, you have no idea what else I have to offer.* "Matter of fact, why don't you ask Carl if he'd like to stay at the house in Martinique. Maybe he can mail us pictures since neither Abby nor I have been there."

"You've never been there?"

Sam shook her head. "Abby doesn't like to fly. There are pictures in the photo albums. Dad and Melinda went there a lot before I was born. But they wanted to wait until I was older before letting me fly. It's modest, maybe fifteen hundred square feet but it has a great view and a large wrap-around porch. I bet Carl could use some relaxation after..." She twirled the stem of her glass and watched other couples in nearby tables. Some holding hands, gazing lovingly through the flame of the candles. She wondered if they would ever get to that point. But Jake wasn't a gaze and fondle-type person. Matter of fact, to the casual observer, she and Jake looked like two business associates having dinner. "Do you resent the fact that Carl didn't tell you about having a son?"

"No, why should I?"

Sam studied him, her eyes glancing at his right hand, imagining how much emotion and grief it would take for him to slam his fist into a wall. Old feelings started surfacing and she could feel her heart slamming in her chest. Maybe now would be a good time to mention that little bundle of joy.

"Did you ever think of having children?" she asked.

He didn't reply. Just looked toward the entrance and said, "Oh, no." A waitress was pointing them out to Carl.

Carl pulled out a chair and sat down. "Sorry to bother you. I just got a frantic call from Menut. Seems he didn't leave town just yet and insists on seeing us now."

"Can't you and Frank handle this one?"

"Frank is making arrangements to have Gholam's body shipped

back to Iran. It will be a quick meeting, Jake. I'll have you back here in less than a half hour."

Jake checked his watch.

"It's all right," Sam said. "I'll wait. Although I can't promise you I won't start eating."

Carl stood. "Come on. The sooner we get out of here, the sooner you'll get back to your dinner."

Jake turned to Sam who said, "It's all right. Honest."

She watched them leave, watched Jake give instructions to the waiter to probably hold his meal. She sliced off a piece of bread and buttered it.

Five minutes later, a man, tall and solid, walked over and said, "Hope you don't mind."

"I'm waiting for someone."

He ignored her and sat down.

Sam was startled and looked quickly toward the doorway to see if Jake and Carl were still around. She studied her uninvited guest. He was handsome with blonde hair pulled back in a pony tail. His accent was thick, Polish or German. Sam wasn't sure.

"They will be a while," the man said.

As he set his glass down, Sam gazed at his left hand and saw the tattoo with the name, *Sparrow*, under the bird. Then she recognized the black leather trench coat with a cape collar. The blood in her veins turned to ice. He was calm, in control. He motioned a waitress over and ordered a Jack Daniel's on the rocks. Turning to Sam, he asked, "Would you like an orange juice, Sweetheart? You really shouldn't be drinking wine in your condition."

Sam nodded numbly.

The waitress smiled, her gaze resting longer than necessary on his handsome features. She kept asking him mundane questions as though just stalling so she could hear his sexy accent.

Sam wanted to reach over and touch his hand, touch the tattoo. But for the first time she was afraid to, afraid of what she might see.

She found herself staring, unable to pull her gaze away from him. How did he know she was pregnant? Had he followed her to the obstetrician's office? Was he eavesdropping on her phone calls?

"I'm not what you had expected?"

She sucked in a deep breath, as if synthetic self-control were being circulated through the air ducts. "No. Far from it, actually." He didn't look sinister enough. Didn't look like a cross between a Mafia hit man and a deranged psycho. He looked like a former star quarterback, all-American guy, maybe a decathlon champion. A guy women had dreams about.

"I take it Menut did not make the phone call."

"Of course not," Sparrow said smiling. The waitress delivered their drinks. Sparrow held his up in a toast, nodding for her to do the same. Their glasses touched, Sparrow took a sip, Sam didn't. "Tell me, Sergeant. Who was the man with your husband?"

He knew her. Knew Jake. Why should that surprise her? "Carl Underer," Sam replied, the hint of even lying to him the furthest thing from her mind. "He's the FBI Security Director."

"Ahh," Sparrow said nodding. The waiter brought Sam's dinner but she suddenly wasn't hungry. The waiter asked Sparrow if he wanted to order. "No," he replied, "and the lady can't stay either. If you could wrap up her meal, and leave it for her husband to pick up, we would appreciate it."

The waiter carried Sam's plate away.

"You know, I could scream," Sam said.

Sparrow studied the last of his drink, then tipped his head back and emptied the glass. He reached out his hand and traced Sam's face. She didn't back away.

"Yes, you could. But you won't. It would complicate matters and I wouldn't be able to take you to Tim."

43

Ten minutes after Sparrow and Sam left, Carl and Jake sped back, aware they were set up.

"She left with a man," the waiter explained.

"How long ago? What did he look like?" Jake fired the questions at him.

Carl ran outside to question the valet. The young man remembered a woman fitting Sam's description. He described the man she had left with.

Carl walked back inside and found Jake seated at the table. He told Jake, "The valet recalls seeing Sam. He said she left willingly."

Jake's eyebrows formed a straight line across his forehead, his jaw was tense. If he had not been in a public place, he may have picked something up and thrown it. He had a napkin in his hand, staring at it. He handed it to Carl.

Written in black ink was a message:

Sergeant Mitchell,

I will have your wife home by midnight.

* * *

Sparrow unlocked the door to his hotel suite at the Ritz Carlton. The drapes were open, the lights on. Rock music played in the background.

"Great, you're back." Tim jumped up from his seat. Then he saw Sam. "Hi, Sam. Wait till you see. I found two of the three code words."

"How can you think with this music so loud?" Sparrow asked, turning down the volume.

Sam looked puzzled. It was either her imagination or Sparrow just changed from a Polish accent to a British accent. And why was Tim so friendly with him?

Sparrow placed his hands on Tim's shoulders. "You should take a break. I promised you dinner." He faced Sam. "And a pregnant woman should eat. I will order room service." He didn't wait for their response. He picked up the phone. "Cheeseburger, Tim?"

Tim smiled. "If you're buying, I want a steak."

Sparrow winked at Sam. "Smart boy."

Sam walked over to Tim as Sparrow ordered room service. "Are you okay?"

Tim beamed. "He's great, Sam. You wouldn't believe some of the places he's been to, some of the things he's done."

"He kills people," Sam whispered. "You sound like he's some kind of hero."

"He's at war. People die in a war." Tim turned away from her and returned to his computer.

Sam looked at Sparrow. He had hung up the phone and was peeling off his trench coat. He wore a black open collar sweater and black linen pants. He slipped Sam's blanket coat from her shoulders.

"Have a seat, please." Now he spoke without an accent.

"You're American."

"Of course." He opened the refrigerator behind the bar and poured Sam a club soda, popped open a beer for himself. Walking over to where Tim was working, Sparrow said, "What have you found?"

"The first code is BIRD. The second is SPARROW. I just have to find the third."

"Good. I have faith in you, Tim." He set Sam's drink on the coffee table and told her, "Please sit." He motioned to a floral love seat. He studied her for a few moments as if she were some unfinished painting that needed tweaking, then started to pick out the pins holding her hair in a French twist. "I don't like your hair up." When all the pins were out, he ran his fingers through her hair as it fell past her shoulders. "That's better."

For some reason Sam wasn't nervous, didn't fear him. She wondered if he had used mind control on Tim. What else could explain Tim's enthusiasm, his genuine affection for this killer?

"Exactly what is it you want?" she asked. She could understand Tim's usefulness with the computer. But why her?

He set his beer down and sat on the sofa across from her. "I need help. I've read a lot about you since I've been in your town. You are on suspension from the police force. That was a messy case, that last one. It is terrible losing your father at age five. And a crooked state representative? Politicians. You and I both have no stomach for them." He took a long swallow of beer.

Sam decided he definitely wasn't bad looking, if you liked Viking gods. He could be very persuasive, he had a certain charisma, that type of *you're-in-good-hands* demeanor. Then again, Ted Bundy was also very persuasive.

Sparrow continued. "Don't feel too bad, Sam. Being suspended might be better for you."

Somehow it didn't surprise her that he had done his homework on her. He explained how he had gone to the library and read past articles about her in the *Chasen Heights Post Tribune*.

"People disregard your gift, Sergeant. They refuse to believe things they can't explain."

His eyes were electrifying, and Sam felt like a specimen under a microscope.

"The mind is capable of a lot of things," Sparrow continued, "things even scientists don't fully understand. So it is good it doesn't bother you when the press or even your superiors don't take you seriously. People like you and me, we function better outside, shall we say, the constraints of a structured work environment. You would be much happier as a private investigator."

Sam studied his gold watch and guessed his sweater to be cashmere. His eyes were a pale blue and only when he smiled did they crinkle at the corners. He had taken extremely good care of himself and Sam guessed him to be somewhere in his forties. "You seemed to have done quite well financially in your line of work."

"Yes. It pays top dollar. Of course, if I had been able to get the contract on a Hussein or Ghadafi, I could have retired."

"You talk as though it is just another day at the office."

Sparrow leaned forward, placed his beer can on the table, rested his elbows on his knees. "That's exactly what it is. A line of work. People make a killing at the stock market every day. I kill people the world would be better off without."

Sam glanced over at Tim. Unfortunately, he didn't seem to be taking any of this in. "So why take the contract on Reverend Smith?"

He shook his head. "I didn't kill him."

"I know. Amid did."

He nodded, impressed. "Thank you. I usually know enough about my targets not to need background information. But I was in town early. I wanted to check out this man of the cloth. He was a good man. There was no reason he should have a contract out on his life."

She stared at her empty glass, saw his eyes drop to her legs.

"You still haven't explained how I can be of help."

He got up, walked over to Tim, and leaned over the teen's shoulder. "I need to know how much the cops know." He straightened up and looked over at her. "You will help me."

Over dinner, she told him all the police and FBI knew about the case thus far. And the important thing—that they had yet to identify Sparrow. But they were sure he was still in town, that he was trying to sell the plates, probably to Yang Chu. The Interpol file on him basically reduced him to a mercenary gone mad, which amused Sparrow.

Sam said, "Reverend Smith had counterfeit money on him. And a representative from the Treasury Department found the discrepancy in the bills."

"Yes. Very good fakes except for that amateur mistake," Sparrow said.

He seemed to be satisfied with all she had told him. Sparrow and Tim monopolized the rest of the conversation during dinner. Sparrow slipped up a couple times and called her Jennifer. She wondered who Jennifer was. More importantly, where was she now?

When they were done eating, Sparrow pushed the cart out into the hallway, Tim returned to the computer, and Sam returned to the love seat.

Sparrow paced back and forth, first slowly as though thinking, but then quickly, until he looked more like a caged animal. He rambled on in different dialects, changing at will. He addressed someone named Otto as if he were in the room. Tim looked over his shoulder at him several times, then over to Sam.

To Sam, Sparrow looked and sounded like a cyborg whose computer board was short circuiting. Then Sparrow started to repeat the same phrase over and over: *Other than survival, nothing else matters.* He kept repeating as if it were some type of mantra.

Suddenly he stopped and calmly said, "I think I'm going to go lie down for a while."

After Sparrow walked out of the room, Sam moved over toward Tim and whispered, "You know, we could just walk out of here."

Tim furrowed his brows. "But, Sam, he needs us." He turned back to the monitor.

Sam glanced over at the phone on the credenza by the couch, slowly walked over, stared at it, even entertained the thought of calling 911. But she caught sight of Sparrow in the bedroom. He was sitting on the bed, head in his hands, slowly rocking. As she cautiously walked into the bedroom, she heard him repeating his mantra. Mesmerized by his unbelievable change in moods, Sam carefully approached him and placed her hands over his.

"Shhh," she heard herself say.

"God, it hurts." His voice sounded normal, vulnerable, in pain. "It's getting harder and harder to stop it."

"I know," Sam whispered. She didn't know why, but her eyes started to fill. He lifted his hands and then placed them over hers, as though her hands could be more effective at releasing the pain. The tears fell quickly and she was overcome with a degree of grief she couldn't explain. There was something gravely wrong here.

Suddenly, he stopped rocking, removed his hands as though the pain had suddenly disappeared. He looked at her strangely, then slowly stood and backed Sam toward a wall, pressed his face in her hair.

"God, I've missed you."

Missed who? Sam wondered.

He kissed her on the neck, ran his lips across her mouth, then kissed her hungrily, passionately. Sam wasn't sure what to do other than respond. It wasn't hard not to. It had been months since she was held, since she was kissed like this. But she also didn't want things to go too far. She wrapped her arms around him, held him.

Suddenly, he pulled back, pressed his forehead to hers, then stepped away and started pacing again. He hadn't responded to her. He wanted to, but somehow he couldn't.

"Mr. Sparrow," Tim called from the living room. "I got in."

Sparrow and Sam stood behind Tim as the monitor flashed a heading, "OPERATION SURVIVAL." It was written by Dr. Otto Heinrich.

"The third code word was PREY," Tim said.

"How many pages?" Sparrow asked.

"It's divided into seven separate reports," Tim said. "Let's see. The first goes to page thirty-five."

Each of the reports had a code name—Panther, Lion, Cobra, Cheetah, Shark, Jackal, and Sparrow. At the bottom of page thirty-five of the Panther report there was a phrase, "Subject Expired."

Tim checked the remaining reports. On the last page of each appeared the same phrase. On the last page of the longest of the reports labeled SPARROW was the phrase, "Whereabouts unknown."

Sam's eyes were glued to the screen.

"Send the pages to print, Tim. All of them. Then I want you to kill the file," Sparrow ordered.

"Kill it?" Tim asked.

"Yes." Sparrow's voice was in control again. He walked to the phone and placed a call, then returned. "I have called a limo for you. It should be here in twenty minutes."

Things started to register and a look of shock crossed Sam's face. "Your message to Tim about, *Who am I*? You weren't giving him a challenge. You were asking a genuine question." She was right. He didn't know who he was.

44

Abby woke with a start. The house was quiet, dark, except for the light above the stove in the kitchen. She stepped into her house slippers, slipped into a robe, and padded off to the kitchen. The clock on the microwave said eleven-thirty. She gathered her robe around her and tied it. Her hair hung loose, parted in the middle.

She made herself a cup of tea and tried to remember what woke her. A noise maybe? Or was it a dream? There was an uneasiness that crept into her calm, an uneasiness she had felt before.

She folded back the plastic wrap on the bowl of fry bread and heated up a piece in the microwave. As she nibbled on the fry bread, she walked over to the picture window and stared out into the front yard.

Cora's house may have been small but it had a large porch that wrapped around one-half of the building. A wishing well, handmade by the high school woodworking class, sat to the left of the sidewalk. The moon, just poking out from behind a cloud, soon flooded the yard in a soft glow. Abby sipped her tea as she surveyed the yard, the houses across the uncurbed street, and the telephone poles which leaned as though not quite anchored to the ground.

As she finished the fry bread and licked the crumbs from her fingers, her eyes were drawn to a cottonwood stump ten feet from the wishing well. Something was on the stump, something big. She saw the head move, turn briefly toward the house. Its amber eyes glowed in the dark. It was an eagle. Abby knew there was a nest on a cliff a few miles away at Snake Mountain. A male and a female. They seemed to always come and visit whenever she was in town. People had told her they were relatives of the two eagles her grandmother had seen when she was born. Hence her name, Abby Two Eagles.

The eagle turned and stared at something on the fence. Abby wasn't sure what it was. She opened the front door and stepped out onto the porch. The night air had bite to it and she wrapped her hands around her cup of hot tea to warm them.

"Don't startle it," a voice whispered from behind her.

Abby turned to see Alex sitting on the redwood swing.

"What are you doing here?" she whispered.

Even though he seemed warm in a flannel shirt and blue jeans jacket, he had wrapped himself in a blanket. "Come," he said holding open the blanket.

Abby sat down next to him and gathered a side of the blanket around her.

"Our friend woke me up," Alex explained as he nodded toward the eagle. "He was making a ruckus outside of my cousin's house. I opened the door and shooed him away but he'd come right back. It seemed as though he wanted me to follow him. This is where he led me."

When Alex had first shown up on Abby's doorstep ten years ago, a part of her doubted his story that the spirits had told him to travel to Chasen Heights to watch over her. She had thought he had chosen a weak attempt at courting her. After all, his wife had left him, he had no children to take care of, and although he still had relatives at Eagle Ridge, she assumed there weren't any available females to his liking.

But little by little, things would happen that convinced her the spirits just might have instructed him on his future. He was a good sounding board, a good friend, and there were times, like now, that the spirits communicated with him on her behalf.

The eagle peered at them through its dark orbs, colored bronze from the reflection of the moon. Then it looked at a bird on the fence and watched as the bird flew from the fence to the wishing well.

"It isn't afraid of the eagle," Alex said. "The smaller bird could be a snack for the eagle and yet he's not afraid." Alex poured himself a cup of coffee from his thermos and together they watched the birds in silence.

"Something is not right at home," Abby said. "I think Sam is in danger."

"You should call."

"Maybe it's my imagination."

Alex turned toward Abby and asked, "Since when do you question your instincts?" Alex slowly started to rock the swing as they continued to watch.

The eagle spread its wings as if ready to take flight or to try to frighten the bird. But the smaller bird didn't move. It pecked at the top of the wishing well, looked over at Abby, and back to the eagle. Then it decided to sit down.

"What kind of bird is that?" Abby asked.

"A sparrow," Alex replied.

The eagle let out another raucous cawing. The sparrow still didn't budge.

"I think I will call home," Abby said as she rose to go inside.

Jake answered the phone on the first ring. "Sam?" His voice sounded frantic.

"Something IS wrong," Abby said.

"No, Abby, everything is fine," but the moment he said it, Jake knew he didn't sound convincing.

"I had a strange feeling that Sam might be in danger."

After a few moments of silence, Jake let out a sigh. "I'm sorry, Mom. I'm expecting her any minute. I'm just not sure who she's with or if she's safe."

Abby relayed the story of the eagle to him. "I don't like the sound of your voice, Jacob. You sound worried."

"How about if I call you back the minute she comes home. Wait up for my call."

"I will, Jacob."

The limo ride felt more like a funeral. Sam was overcome with remorse she still couldn't explain. It didn't help to have Tim asking, "You think we'll ever see him again?" He babbled on about how Sparrow wasn't such a bad guy. Rather nice. And Tim wondered if he had a family, a girlfriend. And exactly who did he work for?

"I wish I could have read the file," Sam said.

Jake and Carl were waiting for them at the front door.

"Tim was with you?" Jake asked as the limo pulled away.

"No lectures," Sam said.

"I didn't mind," Tim added.

"Do your parents know where you are?" Carl asked.

Tim shrugged.

Once Sam told Carl the name of the hotel Sparrow was at, Carl called the hotel, only to find that Sparrow had checked out twenty minutes before.

"Sam," Carl said as he hung up, "you took a chance involving Tim. You put his life in danger."

"We weren't in any danger, Carl." Sam could feel Jake's eyes on her. He was hovering, looming, following her to the dining room where she tossed her purse and coat. Jake hadn't changed out of the suit he had worn to dinner, the dinner that almost happened. "He was really a pretty pleasant guy. Almost reminds me of..." she shook her head. "Forget it."

Jake glared, his gaze moving from Sam to Tim. "Couldn't you call or try to get out?"

"He needed our help," Tim said, shoving his laptop onto the dining room table. "I've been with him since noon."

Jake and Carl looked at the youth. Carl had Tim and Sam repeat their day and evening with Sparrow. Sam told them about the mantra Sparrow repeated and his reference to Otto.

"That's all he wanted? Some report called Operation Survival?" Carl asked. "And I don't suppose you're going to tell me how you got into confidential CIA files?"

Tim's eyes smiled behind his glasses and he gave Sam a conspiratorial glance.

To Sam, Jake said, "This is what you two were talking about on the phone the other night."

She pressed her lips together, returned Tim's gaze.

"I'll drive Tim home and explain things to his parents," Carl offered. "I don't think either Tim or I will go into full details with them. We don't want to alarm them." Carl looked at Sam and asked, "You all right?"

"Of course." She put her arm around Tim and said, "Thanks for your help." The front door closed. Sam tried to avoid Jake but he was standing right there, fists jammed onto his hips, a dark cloud building. "I'm going to get ready for bed." Mentally exhausted, she turned and climbed the stairs.

After calling Abby, Jake hung up and paced the kitchen floor. His mother-in-law hadn't seemed too concerned when he told her about Sam's nightmares. Supposedly, the doctor had been aware of them. How could the nightmares be healthy? He shook out of his suit jacket and draped it over a chair. Jamming a finger behind the knot, he loosened the tie and tossed it on the table.

According to the clock on the stove, it was past midnight. He gazed at a notepad on the counter where Abby had written down the name of Doctor Pelligrini and a phone number. It might be too late to call but he didn't care. Abby had mentioned a Doctor Talbot at Sara Binyon's but perhaps Pelligrini was someone local Sam was supposed to see as an outpatient.

"Doctor Pelligrini's answering service," a raspy voice said.

"Do you have a home phone number for Doctor Pelligrini?" Jake asked.

"Is this an emergency?"

Jake hesitated. It was to him. "No," he finally said. "But it's important I speak with him. My wife is Samantha Casey and I believe she's having serious problems."

"Does she have any bleeding? Cramping?"

"Excuse me?" Jake stopped pacing and stared at the name on the notepad.

"How far along is she?"

Jake blinked quickly, his mind racing. "Is Doctor Pelligrini a referral from Sara Binyon's?"

"No, no. Doctor Pelligrini is an obstetrician."

Jake didn't hear what else she said. He vaguely remembered pushing the POWER button on the phone. His mind sifted through the scenes of Sam's unexplained periods of illness, the endless supply of crackers, her emotional tirades, the damn stuffed animals that were multiplying while he slept. And then her question at dinner about whether he wanted children.

He moved trance-like to the bar cart in the dining room and poured himself a shot of whiskey. It stung going down and did little to clear the haze. He ambled up the stairs and paused at a door Sam and Abby had kept closed. It was one of the bedrooms close to Abby's, right next to the one he slept in every night. He turned the light on and stood in the center of the room. It was bare except for a small dresser against a wall and some stuffed animals on the window seat. He wasn't quite sure what he was looking for. Jerking open the top dresser drawer, he saw several books: *What To Expect When You're Expecting. Be Prepared. Having Your First.*

He stormed out of the room, down the hall and into the master bedroom. The door to the bathroom was closed, the shower running. Sets of beady eyes stared at him and he picked up a bean-stuffed monkey and studied it. A table runner in a Navaho design protected the dresser top from a tree branch Sam had placed on it. Sam was not a stuffed animal person, not even a doll person. Jake had dated a woman once who still owned every doll she was ever given. Even Sam's reading material was more along the lines of *Forensic Science* and *Guns and Ammo*, not Martha Stewart's *Living* or *Better Homes & Gardens.*

"Some damn detective you are," Jake mumbled as he tossed the monkey back on the dresser. He slid open the patio door and stepped out into the cool air. His hands shook as he lit a cigarette, pulled the smoke in, and let it out slowly. Leaning his elbows on the railing, Jake tried digesting the news. There was too much anger from being shut out all these months for him to think of impending...he couldn't even say the word *fatherhood.*

Excitement was not something building up in him. Fear was a more accurate word. He drew a thumbnail across his forehead, took another long drag. His thumb scraped the scar near his hairline. This is what fatherhood had always meant to him when he was growing up. When you live with a drunk for a father and a co-dependent mother, there weren't too many warm and fuzzy memories.

The air was chilly but he was hot, fuming. No wonder Abby had asked him to give it two weeks. What was she waiting for? Sam to get up the courage to tell him? And how long was Sam going to wait? He flicked an ash from his cigarette and stared up at the sky bursting with bright stars. The moon was just peeking over the treetops. He could live the rest of his life here. The house and property were beautiful. Abby was irreplaceable. Alex was challenging.

He had even thought at one time of spending the rest of his life with Sam. That was a large step for him. But then she returned and showed how she felt about him. Now he wasn't so sure. One thing he knew for certain, they couldn't continue the way they were.

Sam climbed out of the shower, her mind still cluttered with thoughts of Sparrow and the CIA file she wished she could have read. The evening was supposed to end differently. Tonight she was supposed to tell Jake about the baby. Now it was back to normal with them not speaking to each other. He was pissed royally.

She slipped into her ratty terrycloth robe. Entering the bedroom, she looked at her reflection in the mirror behind the bed. The steam from the shower was doing crazy things to her hair. The only reason she hadn't washed it was because it would take forever to dry. She thought of Sparrow's fingers raking through her hair and turned her attention to a chair in the corner of the room, to someone else's fingers that had roamed through her hair, over every crevice of her body. The chair used to be in Jake's apartment and he kept to his word when he said it was the only piece of furniture he would take with him.

Sam felt a sudden chill and saw that the patio door was open. Jake stepped into the room and slammed the patio door shut, locked it. He was still working on that dark cloud and Sam didn't want to be around when it burst.

"Why didn't you say something?" he said.

She pulled a hair pick through her thick hair. "I told you. Tim had no idea if he was communicating with the right guy or not." She turned away from him, the robe billowing. The terrycloth hand-me-down was like an old house whose doors and windows no longer fit, drafty in places. She pulled the tie tighter.

"Not Tim." He flung a piece of paper at her and it drifted to the bed.

Sam leaned over and saw Doctor Pelligrini's name. *Oh, god.* She closed her eyes briefly, caught a whiff of whiskey in the air. *Courage in a bottle? Or shock therapy?* His eyes seemed to darken or maybe, Sam thought, it was the subtle lighting. A fire crackled in the fireplace but it wasn't doing much to quell the chill in the room. "I was going to tell you tonight."

"Tonight?" His brows hunkered down even further, adding the finishing touches on his dark cloud. "What the hell happened to all the previous nights?"

"I didn't plan for this to happen, Jake." She tossed the hair pick on the dresser and grabbed a fist full of robe, which only caused it to drape off of one shoulder. "I told Abby I could have this marriage annulled, if that's what you wanted."

He swiped a hand across the back of his neck and glanced away. "You ever try to say no to Abby?"

"These are our customs, not yours," she reminded him. "You can do whatever you want." Her gaze rested on the wing-backed chair in the corner by the window and wondered if he thought much about how it was between them. Wondered if he had been kept awake nights thinking of how nicely their bodies fit together. Then she remembered what Abby had said. She swung her gaze back to Jake. "Before she left, Abby told me the only way to communicate was not to talk at all. I wasn't sure what she meant at first. But..."

He followed her gaze to the corner of the room, then glared back at her with a *you've-got-to-be-kidding* look on his face.

"The feelings are either there or they aren't," Jake said.

Her cheeks felt hot and she looked away, stared at that piece of paper on the bed, wondered if she was wrong again in interpreting Abby's words of wisdom. But what else could it mean? "It's a start," she offered.

The dark cloud was in its final stages as he leveled a stare so cold she had to take a step away from him, as if the chill were seeping from his skin.

"I want your trust and your heart, Sam."

Not your body. Those were the unspoken words she heard loud and clear. She suddenly felt undressed, completely exposed. She grabbed fistfuls of fabric above and below the tie, gathering her robe to conceal whatever flesh was showing. Tears escaped but she didn't have a free hand to wipe them away.

He rushed past her and she turned to watch him leave, humiliation erasing the chill. She had never been a good seducer.

Jake reached the doorway and stopped, straight-armed himself against the door jamb, one fist jabbed at his waist. He stared at the floor, seemed to mull things over, his jaw working, grinding. He blinked, took a deep breath and let it out slowly, the eyes still glued to the floor.

The more Sam tried to make herself presentable, the more skin showed and she caught Jake glancing over, his eyes riveted on the bare skin, the swell of her breasts above the knot of fabric in her hand, the curve of her thighs. His eyes turned a milky brown and his hair appeared damp against his forehead.

Finally, he slowly straightened and turned toward her, saying, "I guess it would be a start."

Her fingers gave up their struggle and the robe slipped to the floor.

Sam stirred, inhaled deeply, stretched, every cell in her body coming alive. Jake was turned away from her and she stared at his back. The bed was bathed in a soft beam from the bridge lights and flames crackled in the gas fireplace. Turning off the lights and fireplace had been the furthest things from their minds. Her eyes traced the scars on his back. She kissed them, pressed her forehead to his skin, felt his heart beating.

Nothing had changed, yet everything had changed. And the last three hours had proved the intensity and love was still there. Abby had been right. The words spilled out. They discussed every painful subject that no longer seemed that important or that painful. Sam was confident they could make this work. But what really made her nervous was motherhood.

"Are you as scared as I am?" she whispered.

Jake rolled over and pulled her toward him, kissing the top of her head. "Multiply it by about three hundred." He untangled his legs from the sheets and looked up at the clock radio. It was four-thirty. "You really know how to exhaust a guy."

Sam smiled, thinking back at how they had gone from the bed to the shower to the chair. "We have to get it all in now because once the baby comes, we'll be changing diapers rather than making love."

"Ummm, hadn't thought of that." He turned and their bodies pressed, skin to skin. His hand reached up at a button on the ledge behind their heads and the bridge light clicked off. "I have to get up in a couple hours," he whispered.

"Uh huh." Her lips seeked his in the dark, hovering, feeling their warm breaths mingle, tongues touch lightly. Their mouths circled as if looking for a place to land. She felt his right thumb brush against the most sensitive part of her breast and a gasp caught in her throat. Gently, Jake began to knead, his fingers working magic, producing soft moans from deep within her.

Smiling, Jake whispered, "Sure beats the hell out of that damn rubber ball."

45

Sparrow stared up at the ceiling, his hands pressed to his head. He didn't mind the nightmares that had kept him up most of the night. After reading the reports Tim printed, his nightmares were interspersed with pleasant memories. Some he didn't quite understand yet, but the memories were like a sandstorm building up in the distance, growing, snowballing, gathering momentum as they became clearer.

Jennifer DeMaurey, a model he met in France when he was between jobs, was blonde and long-legged, with eyes the color of the sky. He thinks he was in love with her but was sure Otto took care of any chances of his ever making love to anyone. He had a vague recollection of her being killed, a bullet that was meant for him possibly.

Slowly he rose from the bed and ripped the pages into shreds. He had read the reports countless times last night. The more he read, the more he remembered. The more he dreamed, the more the pieces of his life fell into place.

He turned on his laptop, accessed AOL, and sent a message to Yang Chu for a final offer for the plates. He knew Davud never planned on getting him the five million. It didn't matter now. This was definitely his last job.

* * *

"Heard from Lloyd?" Jake asked as he pulled the carafe from the coffeemaker.

Carl set his briefcase on the kitchen table. "He doesn't have anything positive to report yet." He warmed his hands on the hot cup of coffee and stood at the patio doors, gazed at the colorful maple leaves as they gathered on the patio, collecting around the potted mums. He slid onto the stool at the island counter and blew at the steam floating at the surface of the cup. He made a cursory examination of Jake's finger-combed hair and pallid skin. "You two must have been arguing til dawn. You look like you haven't slept in days."

Jake grinned behind the rim of his cup. "Not exactly. Little hard to stay mad at the mother of my child."

A smile crept slowly and then spread across Carl's face. "Damn, you two work fast." He stretched a hand across the counter at Jake and the men shook. His smile slowly faded and Carl pulled his glasses off and set on the counter. "I don't need to remind you that you made a few enemies while you were with the Bureau."

"I know."

"Never let your guard down. Especially now."

Jake didn't want to think about the crazies he had put behind bars, the ones who had promised payback. And all this time he was more concerned about strapping a kid with him for a father. "It's a terrible time to raise a kid with all the violence in the world."

"There's never a good time," Carl mused, "from the crucifixion to the eras of Wyatt Earp and Al Capone to present day, there will always be some form of violence."

Jake refilled their cups and watched as a subtle sadness clouded Carl's eyes. He couldn't recall a time he had worked with the Bureau that he had ever seen Carl show any type of personal emotion, no sadness or pain of loved loss, or elation. Only as it related to work.

"It's strange," Carl said. "Here I thought I was protecting the ones I loved and then Judith dies from cancer and my son gets killed in a war we had no damn business being involved in." He shook his head at the irony of it all. Carl retrieved papers from his briefcase and returned to the counter.

"Wouldn't Charlie have been too young for 'Nam?"

"He supposedly was part of the clean-up crew that went in after the war." His fingers sifted through several typed pages. "I think you would have liked him, Jake."

"I'm sure I would have." He glanced at the pages of notes. "Have an early meeting?"

"I ran the name *Otto* past a CIA friend of mine last night. He did a little sleuthing of his own and faxed me some interesting information this morning." Carl assembled the pages of notes and pushed the sleeves up on his sweater. "Ever since the Korean war, intelligence agencies all over the world have been trying to find out what the communists did to our POWs," Carl started. "Our soldiers were shown on television acting like zombies, denouncing the U.S., praising communism. Hell, they even demonstrated in our streets once they returned home. So whatever brainwashing was done seemed permanent.

"So, a Doctor Otto Heinrich, in the mid '70s, with someone's blessing, started experiments on brainwashing and mind control. My friend was unable to get any detailed information on exactly what those experiments involved."

Jake saw a silver sedan pull up toward the garage. Tim emerged, bounded across the patio and knocked on the door.

"Sam here?" Tim asked after stepping inside.

"She's still in bed," Jake replied, eyeing the brown folder clutched in the teen's hands.

Tim's face was ashen, eyes wide behind his glasses. "I forgot that when I send something to print from my laptop that it automatically sends a copy to my printer at home." He swallowed hard as he handed the envelope to Carl. "These are the reports I located for Mr. Sparrow."

He mumbled something about his parents waiting in the car and that they were on their way to church. The two men watched him climb into the car and it backed out of the drive.

Carl pulled the papers from the envelope. "By the look on that kid's face, I'd say he had a peek at this report."

For the next half hour, they read through each of the seven reports on the subjects in Doctor Heinrich's experiments. Carl set his glasses down and rubbed his eyes. Neither said anything and Jake rose to put on another pot of coffee.

"What a sick sonofabitch," Carl breathed. "Should we tell Sam?"

"Tell Sam what?" Sam breezed into the kitchen. She blurted a quick, "Morning, Carl," without even glancing his way, and slipped right into Jake's arms. "Good morning," she whispered. His arms encircled her so tightly she thought for sure her body left an imprint on his skin. She accepted his kiss on the forehead then pulled away and looked into his eyes. This morning his dark cloud seemed to have reappeared but, thankfully, it was directed at someone else.

"What's wrong?" She sat down next to Carl and he explained the information he had received on Doctor Otto Heinrich. Jake set a cup of tea in front of her and she smiled at the plate of crackers he placed next to it.

"Tim dropped these off earlier," Carl said.

She reached for the report but her hand stopped, the fingers unwilling to grasp the pages. Sam suddenly wasn't sure if it was necessary to read them. All they would contain was everything that had been filling her dreams lately.

Sam said, "Could you just tell me what they say?"

So they detailed the experiments, subliminal messages, how the subjects learned different dialects by listening to tapes while they slept.

"That explains how he changed accents so quickly," Sam said.

"Exactly," Carl replied. "Then Heinrich went from non-physical methods, to physical methods. He felt they would be less distracted if they were neutered." Carl reached over and grabbed the carafe and filled his cup before continuing. "He forced them to watch X-rated movies and then subjected them to electric shock treatments to the genitals if they became aroused."

A shudder reverberated through Sam's body. That was why Sparrow couldn't respond to her, she thought.

Carl continued, "The good doctor used hallucinogenic drugs, mescaline and exotic drugs from South American rain forests. Some of them didn't withstand the shock treatments to the brain. Otto had overdone it on a couple, turned them into vegetables."

Sam pressed a hand to her stomach. "You are killing any appetite I might have had."

"Oh, it gets better. It seems that Otto wanted to give his guinea pigs a sample of torture from various countries so if they did survive and were released for intelligence purposes, they would be able to withstand whatever cruelty they were subjected to—hot boiling water, hot oil, sulfuric acid on open wounds."

Jake leaned back against the counter, arms crossed. "That explains the rat," he said, referring to what had been done to Gholam.

"A little method from our Cambodian friends," Carl replied. "Then there's also hanging, upside down. About the only thing Otto didn't try was the Japanese specialty used during World War II. They used to inject prisoners with lethal germs such as bubonic plague."

Jake grimaced as the images playing in his head. "How the hell did he survive all that?" He thought back to Sam's description of Sparrow, the mantra he would repeat, his unexpected bursts but then he would rein in those outbursts and replace them with calm and control.

"Somehow, he was able to withdraw," Carl added. "Was able to use extreme mind control over his own body, withstand everything Otto threw his way. And then, I don't know, one day he just snapped."

"I don't know about that, Carl," Jake said. "I don't think he snapped as much as Otto succeeded. He actually did create something, someone unique. And his star pupil turned on his captors."

"What if they knew?" Sam asked, searching Carl's face, then Jake. "You read the Interpol reports. They didn't try very hard to find him. I bet if you check some of the people who hired him, you might be able to trace them back to our own government."

The men remained silent and Sam's gaze drifted to the seven reports. "I saw it in my dreams." Her eyes filled as she remembered the man she had spent considerable time with last night. "I've had some strange dreams mixed in with my usual flashbacks. But these were different. I could see a room in stark white, hear voices screaming in pain. I could literally smell burning flesh."

"Jezzus, Sam," Carl said.

"I could see a figure running down a dimly lit hallway. Then a door opening to blinding sunlight. It was Sparrow. I saw his escape and I know where he was, Carl. What was done to him was done here in the States. He wasn't a mercenary gone mad. Not even an experiment gone bad. He was an experiment that succeeded and it was sanctioned by our own government."

Carl sank back in his chair and shook his head. "That's stretching it, Sam. And I hope to god you are wrong."

Jake braced his arms against the island counter, stared at the quarry tiled floor. The room remained silent. The coffeemaker hissed and the clock by the stove ticked softly. Finally Jake said, "What are the plans for tomorrow?"

Carl excused himself and went to the study to place a call.

When he returned he said, “We’ll find out at ten in the morning where the exchange will take place.”

“So you’re setting him up,” Sam accused.

“Sam...” Jake started.

“Are you giving your men shoot-to-kill orders?” she asked.

“No,” Carl replied emphatically. “Matter of fact, I have nothing on him. He may be responsible for some of the open cases Interpol has, he may not. We are sure he didn’t kill Reverend Smith.”

“He told me he didn’t,” Sam said.

“And we can only assume Amid had the plates, but there’s still no proof Sparrow killed him, either.” Carl retrieved his coat from the back of the couch and slipped it on. “All I have on him is possession of stolen plates. So, to answer your question, no, I want him alive. I have a lot of questions for him.”

Jake walked Carl to the door and returned to find Sam curled up on the recliner in the Florida room staring out of the jalousie windows. Plants hung from the ceiling and heat emanated from under the tiled floor.

“Hey,” he whispered, settling next to her on the roomy chair. “What’s bothering you?” He kissed her hair and wrapped his arms around her. “Did something else happen in that hotel room I should know about?”

Sam thought back to last night when she had pressed her hands to Sparrow’s head, the unbelievable pain he was in. She hadn’t known then but now understood why she had felt such grief and remorse while she and Tim rode home from the hotel. Maybe she knew that with all Sparrow had been put through, he was not really responsible for his actions. He had been manufactured and brainwashed in a laboratory. Pumped full of drugs, made to endure unspeakable tortures, all in the name of research.

“I touched his soul,” Sam whispered.

Jake felt a chill. He thought he had gotten somewhat used to her sudden bursts of insight but obviously hadn’t.

"What did you see?" he asked.

Sam clung tighter to him, nestled her head under his chin and whispered, "He's dying."

46

Tim woke early the next morning and checked his E-mail for any new messages from Sparrow. His heart quickened as he retrieved his mail.

Bond,

Thank you for all your help.
I'll never forget you.

Sparrow

Tim scrunched up his face in confusion. The message sounded so final. It disturbed him. He quickly tried sending a message back. The screen said:

Invalid E-mail User Code.

Sparrow had either changed or deleted his user code.

* * *

Yang Chu sat with the Wall Street Journal spread open on his desk. Li filled both of their cups with strong tea and looked at his watch.

Without looking up from his paper, Yang said, "It is only ten minutes later than the last time you checked. We have another hour, Li." He looked over the paper at his son. "Patience has escaped your generation."

Yang's cellular phone rang sending Li to his feet. Yang motioned for him to sit.

"Mr. Chu."

"Yes, Mr. Sparrow. You are early."

"Guess I'm tired of waiting around. Listen closely. First, I want your car phone number." Yang gave him the number. "Next, I want you to drive, alone, to the old Nagle Steel Works. Enter through Gate Two and wait for my instructions. I will call you on your car phone."

Yang stopped writing, looked at his son, and hung up the phone. Then he called Carl.

"Would it do any good for me to ask you to stay home?" Jake asked Sam.

She watched Jake check the clip on his gun. "Jake, Carl promised."

"Only precaution," he replied, placing the gun in his belt holster.

"I've been thinking, Jake."

"Dangerous."

She forced a smile. "If he knows Tim can intercept his messages, he must know that Tim might have read his message to Yang Chu about the meeting and told us." She studied his face as it took on that serious, interrogator look. "He must know he's being set up."

"Possibly," he said almost cautiously.

"Why would he go through with it?"

"That's why I checked my gun. He could also be setting us up."

Sparrow peered through his binoculars and spotted Yang's car about a mile away. He called his car phone.

"Yes," Yang said.

"When you drive through the gate, follow the road to Building Twelve. You can pull your car right up to the warehouse." Sparrow hung up the phone. He had tracked Yang's car from the second floor of the warehouse. The empty refinery had been vacant for twelve years. Windows and doors were broken, steel beams left rusting against the chain link fence. A time clock by the far wall held an inch of dust and dirt.

The building smelled moldy, acrid, but he had seen and smelled worse in his time. Compared to some of the prisons he had been in, this was a virtual palace.

No disguises today. Matter of fact, no weapons or even a bullet-proof vest.

He walked over and checked the mound of burning ashes, the remains of the counterfeit money paid to him for the contract on Reverend Smith. It wouldn't do anyone any good now.

He returned to the window and raised the binoculars again. Yang's cream-colored Cadillac was just passing the gate. Sparrow followed the path Yang had taken. Another mile behind him was a dark blue van, one car, and a Jeep. Just as he had expected.

A searing pain knifed through his temple flattening him up against the wall. He took deep breaths and pressed his fingers to his temples. When the pain eased somewhat, he picked up a leather bag containing the plates and tied it around his waist.

He reached the bottom of the stairs and watched through the square of glass in the door as Yang's car came to a stop. The trunk lid of the Cadillac popped open. Sparrow glanced briefly down the road past the gate before joining Yang.

"Remember," Carl said over his walkie-talkie, "no guns. I want this man alive."

In the blue van in front of him were six agents from the FBI's Chicago office. Carl followed behind in Frank's car, with Sam and Jake bringing up the rear in her Jeep. Another ten minutes behind were five squad cars from the Chasen Heights Police Department.

"There's only one way in and out of this place, Jake," Sam said nervously watching the car and van in front of them.

"I don't suppose it would do me any good..." Jake started but saw the look Sam fired at him and decided against finishing his sentence. It would be wasted words.

She peered up at the sky. Overcast. It had been sunny earlier but now the skies were ominous, to match the growing knot in her stomach. She reached over and picked up the walkie-talkie. "Carl, would you let me go in and talk to him?"

"Negative," Carl replied.

"Thank you," Jake said under his breath.

Sam threw down the walkie-talkie in frustration. "I don't like this, Jake."

When the warehouse loomed ahead, the lead van gunned it, spewing gravel and dust. The vehicles soon blocked the entrance. The agents filed out of the van and sought the nearest shelter.

Sam saw Yang and Sparrow standing by the trunk, then Yang backed away. Jake was out of the Jeep first. Sam's hand flew to her medicine bundle as if it could help Sparrow.

"FBI," Carl yelled. "Put down your weapon."

Sparrow turned and looked at Carl. His eyes scanned the area, the agents in position, then the back-up black and whites pulling into the area. He took it all in and didn't seem the least surprised with his reception.

Sam caught up with Jake and held onto his arm. "Oh, god," Sam cried. "He knew this was going to happen. He's committing suicide."

They watched Carl approach, his arms out to show he was unarmed. Yang crouched behind the hood of his car. "I just want to talk," Carl said.

Sparrow watched Carl approach, studied him, cocked his head as if sizing him up. They stood twenty feet apart just staring at each other. Without any warning, Sparrow reached under his coat.

"HOLD YOUR FIRE!" Carl shouted as he turned to the agents behind the van. But it was too late. Sparrow took four shots to the chest. Sparrow's arm continued its motion as he fell to the ground.

"NO!" Sam pulled from Jake's grasp and ran to the fallen man.

One of the agents repeated Carl's directive to "Hold your fire." The air was tense, no one moved. Chasen Heights' finest suddenly arrived with guns drawn. Jake turned and motioned for them to stay back.

Kneeling next to Sparrow, Sam turned on Carl. "You promised, no guns."

Carl lifted Sparrow's head from the oil-stained pavement. "Get an ambulance over here," he yelled. He inspected Sparrow's chest wounds, then gave Sam a worried look. "I told them to hold their fire, Sam." He grabbed Sparrow's hand, squeezed it, his eyes drawn to the crude tattoo.

Sam brushed the hair from Sparrow's face. His eyelids fluttered as he tried to focus. She no longer saw pain in his eyes. He seemed relaxed, a slight smile curving his lips. "You're going to be okay," Sam said.

His lips moved and she had to lean close to hear him.

"You know," he whispered. And then he died.

Frank walked up to Carl with the leather bag in his hand. "He wasn't going for a gun. He was throwing you the printing plates."

* * *

Jake waited until the Meisner family car faded in the distance before closing the door. Walking into the living room, he found Sam sitting on the couch staring at the fireplace.

"Tim didn't take Sparrow's death very well."

"No," Jake replied. "But I think his father is going to heed Carl's advice and take a family vacation somewhere."

"Umm." Sam replied staring at the flames as they licked against the glass fire door.

Jake sat down, stared at his hands. Nothing had gone down as planned because they hadn't been in control. Sparrow had orchestrated it and knew everyone's part. He just neglected to give everyone a script.

Sam didn't stir when the phone rang and Jake picked it up to hear Lloyd's voice. After ten minutes of listening, Jake hung up and wrapped his arms around her. "That was Lloyd. He completed the autopsy on Sparrow." When Sam didn't respond, he said, "He had a massive brain tumor. He was surprised he didn't die six months ago."

"He knew he was dying."

"I know," Jake whispered. "That's probably why he left his bulletproof vest and guns in the car. He was committing suicide, like you said." Jake watched her. Her tears had dried up hours before, replaced by a remorse he couldn't seem to penetrate.

She turned and studied him. "Did Lloyd tell you anything else?"

47

Jake leaned against the door frame in the kitchen and gazed out into the backyard. Sam had been walking through the gardens for the past half hour, something she had done a lot of the past few days since Lloyd's call. It was the first time since Sparrow died that the sun had burned through the ceiling of gray skies, as if nature itself knew Sam's mood.

Jake slid the screen door open and took a deep breath. The air was crisp and the morning sun had burned off the light frost. Sam was dressed in blue jeans, a turtleneck, and Jake's quilted flannel shirt. Her hands were hidden in the sleeves as she pulled the collar up as if inhaling the residue of his aftershave.

Frank had warned Jake that the first things a man loses in a marriage are his shirts. All of a sudden they seemed to become unisex, or the dryer manages to shrink them just enough so it fits the wife. The phone rang and Jake was glad to hear Abby's voice.

"Is everything all right?" Abby had a way of detecting the slightest change in a tone of voice.

Jake explained Sam's despondence about Sparrow and how she didn't seem to be climbing out of her depression. "She still has an appetite, Abby. She sleeps but there are times I get up in the middle of the night to find her standing in front of the patio doors just looking out into the darkness." Call waiting beeped in his ear. He put Abby on hold and heard Jackie's bubbly voice.

"Where is that pregnant girlfriend of mine?"

"In the garden watching the flowers curl up and die," Jake replied.

"Well, you tell her to get her butt out of the house and meet me for lunch. Tell her to meet me at Bev's in half an hour." She hung up before Jake had a chance to call Sam to the phone.

When he returned to Abby's call, Abby filled Jake in on some of the events that had transpired on the reservation. Then she added, "Alex and I have just about wrapped things up here. It's time we came back."

"Thanks, Abby. I think she needs you right now."

Sam positioned the cardinal and snake Beanies™ between the plants in the greenhouse behind the sink. Then she set Stretch™ on the edge and tapped his beak.

"You guys behave yourselves." She gathered her hair back and tied a fabric band halfway down the length of her hair.

"I'm in trouble when you start talking to them," Jake said.

"Where have I heard that before?" She flashed a weak smile. He slipped her medicine bundle over her head and her purse over her shoulder. "Seems like you're trying to get rid of me."

"Never, but if anyone can make you smile, maybe Jackie can."

She wrapped her arms around him and kissed his neck saying, "You make me smile."

He held her tight and after several seconds asked, "Want to go out to dinner tonight? I can call Frank and Claudia..."

"Not really," she replied. "I can defrost something."

He framed her face in his hands, rubbed his thumbs across her cheeks, studied the sadness in her eyes and wished he could make it go away. "I'll make something special."

"Are you sure?"

"Positive."

She gave him another kiss and said, "I could get used to you, Mitchell."

A slow smile spread across his face and he pulled her closer. "Kind of strange coming from a woman who sleeps with a guy on the first date."

"What date?" Sam laughed. "I spent more time with..." Her smile slowly faded as she remembered that night and how Sparrow had interrupted their dinner at Serengeti's. "Well, I guess you still owe me one date, Mitchell." This time the smile was forced and she dropped her head to his shoulder, felt the warmth of his skin through the fabric. His arms held her tightly and she almost wished she wasn't leaving. She whispered into his shirt, "I love you, Jake."

He kissed her, a passionate kiss that practically sucked the air out of her. "You better get out of here before I rip your clothes off."

Smiling, she gave him a light peck on the lower lip and said, "Later."

Sam knew Jake was just finding her a diversion so she wouldn't think about Sparrow. But it was hard, especially when Sparrow had said *you know*. Maybe Sparrow didn't realize her powers were not with the living. The fact was, she didn't know. Not until Sparrow died did she start to have an inkling of what he had meant. Then it only added to her anguish.

Her stomach started growling the moment Bev's was in sight. Maybe lunch wasn't such a bad idea. She hadn't felt like doing much of anything since Sparrow died. She was beginning to doubt her abilities, her powers. Maybe the baby was sucking them out of her. She needed answers and she couldn't find them within. So although a part of her wanted more time alone with Jake, she was glad Abby was coming home.

She pulled into the parking lot behind Beverly Hills and noticed workmen in the front of the building and at the back entrance. They had just taken down the metal canopy that said, *Bev's.* When she stepped out of her Jeep, the workmen were hoisting up a new canopy. This one was burgundy with flesh-colored lettering that read, *Jackie's.*

"Oh my god," Sam gasped. Jackie came running out of the back door. She had never seen Jackie so excited. There was something else different. Jackie was dressed in a very conservative wool pants suit.

"What do you think?" Jackie wrapped an arm around Sam's shoulder and led her through the entrance.

"When and how did this happen? I thought the place had been closed by the IRS?"

"It was but I convinced the bank to let me take over the payments. With the IRS on Menut's ass and no possible way of that boy returning, the bank would lose a ton keeping it closed."

Sam walked into the reception area, which had new burgundy carpeting and mauve leather chairs. "I just don't believe this, Jackie." She ran her eyes down Jackie's frame. "Is this a new business look, too?"

"Well, temporarily. I don't want the workmen getting distracted. Plus, I'm interviewing new girls. And the upstairs living quarters are all being redone, too."

A white-haired woman entered. At least two-hundred-and-fifty pounds were stacked on a frame just over five feet tall. She was draped in a tent dress which rode up a little higher in the front, and her feet sausaged out of the tops of her shoes like excess dough that needed to be trimmed and thrown away.

"Good afternoon, Jackie," the woman bellowed in a truck-driver voice. She disappeared behind the door to the private rooms.

Sam tilted her head, her gaze following the portly woman. Unsightly thoughts were going through her head. Finally, Sam pointed toward the door and said, "Don't tell me she's one of your dancers."

Jackie threw back her head and let out a riotous laugh. "Wouldn't that be a sight." She continued laughing as she pulled Sam toward her office. "I've branched out, diversified, I guess is the buzz word."

Menut's office had been recarpeted and the book shelves emptied out and carted off to god knows where. The walls were freshly wallpapered in a tasteful floral design. Pictures, yet to be hung, leaned up against the desk.

"Listen to this." Jackie pushed the PLAY button on a tape recorder.

A smooth, sexy voice oozed like syrup, describing unthinkable actions and whispering subtle innuendoes. The voice moaned in a sultry gasp. Jackie pressed the STOP button.

"That is the voice of Maddie Lorenzo, the portly grandmother who just walked in."

Sam's eyes widened. "You're kidding!"

"Telephone sex talk is where it's at. That grandmother can make more money in one day here than she did in a full week at her receptionist job. People charge the call on their Visa, Mastercard, or American Express. I pull in two thousand a week from the phone calls alone. The girls get one-half of the take. I have only two girls right now but have a ton of girls applying for jobs."

"No more dancing?"

"Oh, we still have the dancers. But I turned the larger suite into an office with work stations so the girls will have privacy when they are on the phones." Jackie pulled on Sam's arm. "There's one more thing I have to show you."

She led Sam down the hall to another door, the back entrance to Beverly Hills which was now called, Jackie's Boutique. She pulled her around the counter past the sales girls who were unloading boxes, through the aisles to the bras. She took one off the rack.

Sam checked the label and laughed. The two wrapped their arms around each other and giggled incessantly. Jackie had supplied her boutique with nursing bras.

48

Carl had a private burial for Charlie. Only Lloyd and his wife attended, after which Carl requested to be alone. Judith had three plots in the Lady of Peace Cemetery outside Alexandria, Virginia. One had been designated for Charlie, the other one for Carl. Many times he had visited the cemetery and wished he could be with his beloved Judith. The small cemetery was one of the oldest in the state, with weeping willows and ponds bordered by flowers. He was alone in this alcove except for a swan that paddled near the shore.

Carl smoothed down the back of his wool overcoat and sat on the ground. He placed two dozen yellow roses on Judith's grave and one yellow rose on Charlie's. He brought one knee up and rested his chin on it. In his right hand was the last picture taken with Judith and Charlie together.

He hadn't seen the picture in twenty-seven years. After a desperate search, he found the picture tucked in back of the photo of Judith he had kept in his office. He knew there was something about this picture, something he had vaguely remembered.

Charlie had looked so much like Judith. Had a little bit of Carl, too, in the eyes, the nose. Carl had suspected that Charlie knew he was his father. They would go fishing and hiking together. There were times Carl would catch Charlie watching him, mimicking him the way children sometimes do a parent. Nothing had been more important to Carl than Judith's and Charlie's safety. If only he had it to do over again. Carl wiped away tears that had been building up all these years.

The picture had been taken on one of the Caribbean Islands. Palm trees stood tall in the background, exotic flowers in full bloom filled a pot to Judith's right. He remembered buying her the floral dress for the trip, lavender, her favorite color, with a spray of tiny flowers up the bodice. Her blonde hair was long and flowed in the island breeze.

Charlie, hair whitened by the sun, looked handsome in the floral island shirt Judith had forced him to wear. He stood at least a foot taller than his mother and had his left arm wrapped affectionately around her shoulder. Carl guessed Charlie was about sixteen at the time.

A sick feeling had started in the pit of Carl's stomach last week when Lloyd called him from the FBI lab in Virginia. Lloyd had finished the forensic examination of the remaining MIAs, had matched dental records, and identified all of them. One thing Lloyd knew for certain: None of the remains were of Charlie. Carl had asked Lloyd to redo the tests. After all, Charlie's dog tags had been in the grave with the rest of them.

Lloyd double and triple-checked the results and they were the same. Charlie's body was not among the deceased. That's when Carl knew he had to find this picture.

There wasn't a better friend than Lloyd. Carl didn't know what he would have done without his help. At Carl's request, Lloyd had called Jake and Sam and told them the news. Carl hadn't realized the news would have such a traumatic effect on Sam.

Carl stared one last time at Judith and Charlie before holding a lighter at the corner of the picture, a piece of evidence he had to destroy. The flames fed greedily on the chemically treated paper. It curled up around Charlie's swim trunks, up Judith's dress, around Charlie's head. Carl dropped the picture on the ground as flames shot around to the right side of the picture, devouring the pot of flowers.

He watched as the flames met again at the top of the picture and worked their way to the center. The last portion to burn was Judith's shoulder where Charlie rested his left hand—the hand with the tattoo of a sparrow.

END

There is

no death,

only a change

of worlds.

Chief Seattle

RESTLESS SPIRIT

1

Standing deep in the woods surrounded by barren trees and dried underbrush, Sam waited for the dead to speak to her.Usually a cold would slice through her body, the hairs on her arms would bristle, and the voices would lead her to within a few feet of their shallow grave. Her mother, Abby Two Eagles, often said whenever someone died an unnatural death, their spirits were unsettled, cried out to be discovered and released to their spiritual resting place.

Sam believed it was nature that spoke to her, showed her where the bodies were buried. The branches would bend as though pointing their fingers. Animals would scurry then stop, sniff, gaze up at her. Grass and foliage would remain bent where trampled, footprints frozen in place.

But today the voices were silent, probably because the rapists, deviates, and syndicate hitmen were choosing more isolated woods in which to hide their misdeeds. They no longer buried their victims in Briar Woods.

She usually reserved these walks through the woods for early spring when the ground was thawed. But it wasn't spring yet. It was three weeks before Christmas and no one had informed Mother Nature that it wasn't supposed to be fifty-two degrees, not in Chasen Heights, which hugged the southern border of Lake Michigan.

Briar Woods was just a half-mile walk from Sam's house. The air smelled clean and crisp as if cleansed by dew and dried by the sun.

She continued along a walking trail used by mushroom pickers in the fall. Dried leaves crunched under her gym shoes. After the quick snowfall just before Thanksgiving, the weather had been dry, and it hadn't taken long for the dusting of snow to melt.

Sam stepped gingerly away from the trail, knowing from experience gravesites would be tucked further in. Each spring she would try a different direction. Once she had found the remains of a young woman who had been last seen hitchhiking along I-80. After four years, the family and police had all but given up. But Sam found her.

Stopping again, her eyes searched quickly through the bony branches poking out from the underbrush. Looking up at the clear blue ceiling, she tried to get her bearings, listen for traffic noise. All she heard were muffled voices so she followed the sounds.

A clearing lead to a construction site where six brick homes were in various stages of completion. Workers swarmed around the site installing windows, roofing tiles, or pounding wooden decks into shape. Each home was on a half-acre site, a new subdivision she had read about. If she wasn't mistaken, this was the area where Frank Travis and his wife were building a house.

She pulled off her sunglasses and peered through one of the windows of a gray brick bi-level and saw a fireplace in the living room, an island work station in the kitchen. A workman motioned for Sam to enter but she declined with a shake of her head. When she reached the front of the house she gazed up at the shell-shaped elliptical window above the double doors.

"Anything I can help you with?" He was lumberjack-sized wearing a sleeveless flannel shirt with suspenders holding up his dusty jeans.

"Sorry, just being nosey," Sam replied. "I live on the other side of the forest preserve." He nodded, gave an admiring smile. His gaze rested on her eyes that seemed to blend with the sky.

She had taken a quick shower this morning and layered warm clothing over her thermal leggings. Although the oversized sweatshirt wasn't too baggy, it was roomy enough to hide her five-month pregnancy. No make up, but a squeaky clean, just-scrubbed look and a mother-to-be glow.

"No law against admiring." He stuck a large hand out toward her. "Cooper. I'm the foreman." She stared at his dirt-covered hand and then back to his face. He wiped his hand on his shirt but saw that it didn't do much to clean it off. "Sorry. Kinda hard to stay clean on a day like today."

"We have friends who are building a house in this area. I just thought I'd see if I could tell which one."

"Watch your step." Cooper maneuvered her out of the way as a construction bobcat shaped a circular driveway in front of the house.

Lately she was having problems seeing where she stepped. Her stomach was making it difficult to see her feet let alone see where they were going, and the added bulk was throwing her entire equilibrium off kilter.

The sun glistened off of the windows in the widows peak just as a ray of light hit her eyes. She glanced down at an object flickering in the morning light, unearthed by the plow. Kneeling down to examine it, a familiar cold swept over her body. The hairs on her arms stiffened. She gingerly picked up the button and turned it over. It was metal, maybe brass, with the letters *MB* in the center.

Sam slowly wrapped her hand tightly around the button and was suddenly thrown into darkness, the sun replaced by a full moon, the dusty ground replaced by damp grass. She was bathed in moonlight standing in a clearing surrounded by woods. The scent of dewy grass filled her nostrils and dampness sliced through her body.

A young girl, about fifteen or sixteen, appeared before her, stumbling, in a daze, naked. She was pretty with big brown eyes and dark shiny hair cut to chin length.

"Who's there?" the girl called out.

A figure lurched from the shadows as moonlight danced off of a knife blade.

It sliced into the girl, two, three, five, ten times, too numerous to count. Even after the girl fell, the figure knelt beside her plunging the knife, the blood spraying with each motion. Screams cut through the darkness. But the girl was silent. They were Sam's screams.

4

"I don't know if I care to hear anymore, Sam," Frank said. His dark eyes bulged and his body shuddered, like a man trying to shake the willies. With a quick glance to his wife, he said, "Better think about this."

Frank's wife, Claudia, was an attractive woman with flawless, honey-colored skin, and full, sensual lips. She glared at Frank in disbelief, saying, "Frank, I'm surprised you don't check your horoscope every morning before getting out of bed."

"A young girl was murdered on our driveway, Claudia."

Jake shook his head. "Frank, you talk as though it happened yesterday. Get a grip."

They were sitting at a table in Izzy's, a small hometown restaurant with good food and bottomless pitchers. The wooden floors were practical and the old-time jukebox played anything from country western to Buddy Holly.

It was a place to escape with enough distractions in the way of dart boards, pinball machines, and a pool table, to help the cops forget about their day. A small side room held five tables and ten booths keeping the restaurant separate from the rowdy drinkers.

Sam looked up from her plate of chicken to see a man with slicked back gray hair approaching their table. His face sagged and his belly protruded between bright red suspenders.

"Bartender says you're looking for me," the man said.

Jake and Frank stood up and made the introductions. Jake pulled out a chair for Phil. When he saw the retired cop eyeballing the platter of leftover chicken, he told him to help himself.

"Don't mind if I do. They got the best damn chicken in town."

They made small talk while they ate. Phil Cannon retired from the police force two years ago. He now spent his days nurturing his prize orchids in his self-constructed greenhouse.

Phil reached over and grabbed the pitcher of beer, filled his glass. "I hear you want to know if there were any homicides near that new subdivision by Briar Woods. He took a long swallow of beer, waited for the waitress to clear the dishes, then leaned forward, elbows on the table. He whispered like a boy scout leader telling a ghost story around the campfire.

"Seventeen years ago, a warm July night. I remember it like it was yesterday. Catherine DeMarco. She was the same age as my daughter."

Frank moaned, pressing his hands to his shaved head. "So a murder did happen right in front of my house. Oh, god. Now I'm going to have a Cemetery Mary floating across my lawn every Halloween."

"Franklin," Claudia started, "I am not canceling our contract with the builder so quit your whining."

Phil leaned in closer. "It was an empty field at the time with an unfinished street running parallel to the woods. A patrol car came across what he thought was a dog. It was so butchered he couldn't tell at first that it was human. Throat was cut so deep she was almost decapitated."

Claudia winced and took a sip of her coffee. "Glad we didn't talk about this before dinner."

"Bastard raped her, too. You'd a thought he was tenderizing meat. He just kept stabbing and stabbing. Horrible. Many a cop had a sleepless night after that one."

"I take it they caught the killer," Sam said. "Wieczynski."

"Wieczynski?" Phil wrinkled his brow. "Never heard of him. Taggart. Jimmy Taggart's who killed her. He's due to be executed next month."

5

"You seem shocked, Sam," Phil said. "Where did you come up with the name *Wydachinski*?"

"Wieczynski," Sam repeated and then spelled it for him. "The name didn't come up at all in the trial? Was he even a suspect?"

Phil raised his hand toward a smiling, blond-haired woman. Karen, their waitress, quickly brought another pitcher of beer.

"Open and shut case. Taggart was drunk and passed out about fifty yards from the body. The knife and the girl's blood were on him and it was his semen inside her. He pleaded innocent. Didn't remember nothin' from that night other than he had a lot to drink. Vaguely remembers seeing Catherine."

"Who was the detective on the case?" Jake asked.

Phil smiled as though remembering a high school friend. "Pit Goddard."

"Pit?" Frank echoed.

"Yep. Paul 'Pit Bull' Goddard. He was like a dog with a bone the way he attacked his cases. Best damn detective I ever worked with." Phil took another long swallow of beer, then scratched his head. "You know, that case never did set too well with him. As I recall, he had a feeling in his gut that all the pieces of the puzzle just fit too damn well too quick."

"Where is Mr. Goddard now?" Sam asked. She didn't like the look on Phil's face. It would be just her luck that Goddard was dead.

"Pit had a lot of problems. Shot and killed a thirteen-year-old boy by accident. Just in the wrong place at the wrong time. Pit never forgave himself. Started drinking a little too much. Department put him on medical leave for a while then shifted him around from precinct to precinct, job to job. He finally quit five years ago at the age of forty-two. Never really did stop drinking.

"His wife left him three years ago. Took their six-year-old daughter. They were driving out to Phoenix to live with her parents. A semi hit them head on. Pit's life took a spiral. People have seen him late at night shopping at the grocery store. I used to stop by once every couple weeks to see how he was. Got to the point where he just didn't bother answering the door or the phone."

"I take it he still lives in the area," Frank said.

Phil nodded. "The insurance money paid off the house and provides him with enough money to keep his pantry and his bar supplied. But he hasn't really found anything to keep him occupied. Neighbors take care of his yard. They've called the cops a coupla' times. They'd hear a gun shot from his house. Cops arrive. There'd be a bullet hole in the ceiling and a drunken, unbathed, unshaven Pit, sitting on the couch, his .357 Magnum lying in his lap."

Claudia pressed her hand to her chest. "That poor man."

"Where does he live?" Sam asked.

"Ash Street. Five hundred block. Can't miss it. He has a penguin for a mailbox. His wife was into penguins." Phil looked at Sam curiously. "You're not thinking of getting that Taggart bastard out, are you?"

Sam jotted down the information on Pit's location, then looked at Phil and said, "I just want to make sure the right bastard is in."

6

He stood in front of the bookcase and stared at the picture in the brass frame. A pretty brunette smiled back at him, short hair, hazel eyes, deep dimples punctuating her smile. A mirror of her, about six years old, sat in her lap. They wore the same green velvet dresses, patent leather shoes, and sat in a chair next to a Christmas tree. Years worth of dust clung to the bookshelves, except for the clean patch in front of his favorite picture.

The house still held too many remembrances, like Megan's stuffed animals and Colleen's clothes, items he was supposed to ship to them after they arrived in Phoenix. He just hadn't been able to bring himself to discard any of them.

Dragging the picture off of the shelf with his left hand, Pit gripped the Magnum in his right hand tighter. He caught a glimpse of his reflection in the brass frame. A three-day growth of beard, bloodshot eyes (sleep only brought nightmares of a semi plowing headlong into a red station wagon), his face sunken and creased (he ate only when his body protested the lack of food).

He had watched his weight drop from one-hundred-and-eighty pounds to one-hundred-and-fifty. That was thin, even for his five-foot-ten-inch frame. But nothing he did worked. He couldn't starve himself to death, couldn't drink himself to death. Hell, he hadn't even been able to keep the barrel of the gun in his mouth. Always pulled it out at the last minute. But not this time.

He carried the picture over to the blue plaid couch and sat down. This was how he wanted to remember them. Youthful, innocent, beautiful. He raised the Magnum, pulled back the hammer. His hand shook as he slid the barrel into his mouth. Tears welled up as he looked at his wife and daughter for the last time.

Sam studied the penguin that stood vigil by the curb. The house was a split-level, vinyl siding, country blue trim. The lawn had been carefully edged and fertilized for the winter. Evergreens were shaped, flower beds weeded. Phil was right...Pit had exceptional neighbors.

She pressed her finger to the doorbell and heard its response echoing back. She pressed the buzzer a second time, a third, each time a few seconds longer than the previous.

"Shit," she muttered under her breath. Her blanket coat was a little too warm. Nine o'clock in the morning and the sun was already beginning to burn through the morning chill. Her hair was still damp but it was the only way she could get her long, natural curly hair to go into a French braid.

Opening the storm door, she pounded continuously with her forearm. The door suddenly jerked open. She had seen worse figures on State Street waiting for the soup kitchens to open. Well, maybe not worse.

He wore a sweat-soaked tee shirt and blue jeans. His face was haggard and had enough stubble to sand a hardwood floor. Damp, stringy hair hung past his collar and clung to his moist forehead.

Sam gazed down at the .357 Magnum clenched in his right hand. Pushing past him, she said, "Can you put your plans on hold? We have work to do."